I Lived
on
Butterfly
Hill

I Lived on Butterfly Hill

Marjorie Agosín

**Translated from the Spanish
by E. M. O'Connor**

Illustrated by Lee White

A **Atheneum Books for Young Readers**
atheneum
New York London Toronto Sydney New Delhi

*To the memory of my father, Moisés Agosín,
who taught me about courage, imagination,
and beauty.
And to the countless children who traveled
beyond their homelands in search of freedom
and possibility and found themselves in the
kindness of others who welcomed them with
generosity and understanding.*
—M. A.

ATHENEUM BOOKS FOR YOUNG READERS • An imprint of Simon & Schuster Children's Publishing Division • 1230 Avenue of the Americas, New York, New York 10020 • This book is a work of fiction. Any references to historical events, real people, or real places are used fictitiously. Other names, characters, places, and events are products of the author's imagination, and any resemblance to actual events or places or persons, living or dead, is entirely coincidental. • Text copyright © 2014 by Marjorie Agosín • Illustrations copyright © 2014 by Lee White • All rights reserved, including the right of reproduction in whole or in part in any form. • ATHENEUM BOOKS FOR YOUNG READERS is a registered trademark of Simon & Schuster, Inc. • Atheneum logo is a trademark of Simon & Schuster, Inc. • For information about special discounts for bulk purchases, please contact Simon & Schuster Special Sales at 1-866-506-1949 or business@simonandschuster.com. • The Simon & Schuster Speakers Bureau can bring authors to your live event. For more information or to book an event, contact the Simon & Schuster Speakers Bureau at 1-866-248-3049 or visit our website at www.simonspeakers.com. • Book design by Sonia Chaghatzbanian and Irene Metaxatos. • The text for this book is set in ITC Souvenir. • The illustrations for this book are rendered in in watercolor, ink, digital. • Manufactured in the United States of America • 0114 FFG • First Edition • 10 9 8 7 6 5 4 3 2 1 • CIP data for this book is available from the Library of Congress. • ISBN 978-1-4169-5344-9 • ISBN 978-1-4424-9476-3 (eBook)

Acknowledgments

I am grateful for growing up in a family whose love of art and beauty inhabited our lives. For the constant presence of my father, who raised us with his love of music and poetry, and for my mother, a true storyteller of our family's past. For my husband, John Wiggins, who is my lighthouse and my harbor, and for our children, Joseph and Sonia, for their laughter and their presence in my life.

Like for many other works of art, the support of a loving community of artists, editors, and readers was more essential for the creation of this book. I thank my friend Lori Marie Carlson, who told me that I could write a novel for young adults. I thank her for discovering this possibility in me and for her support during the process of writing *I Lived on Butterfly Hill*.

Jennifer Lyons, my extraordinary agent, also sustained me with an incredible kindness and faith and allowed me to write with confidence and inspiration. I want to thank Caitlyn Dlouhy for being an outstanding editor whose vision has deeply influenced this book. I also thank her for her patience and belief that literature transforms all our lives.

Many friends have accompanied me on the journey as I wrote this novel. I am unable to name them all but want to express my gratitude to Elena Gascón

Vera, Carlos Vega, Vivianne Schnitzer, Monica Flores Correa, Teresa Agosín, Michal Held, Ilan Perrot, Fanny Rosenberg, Marcelo Perrot, Mauricio Agosín, Jennifer Rowell, and Laura Nakazawa.

Finally I want to express my deep gratitude for the translator of this novel, E. M. O'Connor. She has created a true work of beauty in the English language and understood and executed the complexities of translation with grace and honesty.

To the city of Valparaíso, which offered refuge to many members of my family during World War II and continues to offer refuge to me in my many returns to Chile. Much of this writing was inspired by the beauty and poetry of this city.

PART 1
I Lived on Butterfly Hill

Celeste
Like the Sky

The blue cloud finally opens—just when the bell rings to let the Juana Ross School out for the weekend. I'd been watching the sky from the classroom windows all day, wondering just when the rain would pour down. I run down the hall and through the front doors with Lucila, Marisol, and Gloria at my heels. "Quick, girls, get under my umbrella!" Marisol shouts, and her cousin Lucila and I huddle close, one on each side of her.

"Valparaíso will be a swamp for the third weekend in a row." Gloria groans as she opens her own umbrella. Cristóbal Williams catches up to us, grinning hello, but his smile quickly turns into a yawn. "Here, Señor Sleepyhead. I'll share if you hold it." Gloria shoves her pink umbrella into Cristóbal's hand—the one not holding the magic pendulum he almost always carries with him.

"I'm starving," he says. "Let's go eat something." That's Cristóbal. Always sleepy and always hungry.

"Café Iris? Sopaipillas?" I suggest.

"Where else?" exclaims Lucila, who loves Café Iris

just as much as I do. The others nod their agreement and start walking up the narrow sidewalk crowded with people rushing to escape the rain, all trying not to fall into the gutter. A crowd of people swarms the cable car stop at the bottom of Barón Hill. From the weary expressions on their faces, I can tell this cable car is probably running slow—or not at all. On days when the rain is heavy, the mud flowing down the hills leaves all sorts of obstacles—tires, trash barrels, tricycles, and many lost umbrellas—on the wooden tracks.

We look at one another and roll our eyes. "Not again," Gloria groans. Cristóbal yawns and throws his hands up like a question mark. We are all used to waiting for, and wondering about, the cable cars. Valparaíso is a city of hills—forty-two of them—that rise in the shape of a crescent moon overlooking the harbor. The cable cars are painted in beautiful crimsons, sapphires, greens, and golds that from a distance conceal their age—some were built a hundred years ago. And they still manage—on most days, that is—to carry people to and from their homes on the steep hills. No matter how many times I have ridden the Barón Hill cable car, it's always exciting. The track is so steep and the car so shaky that sometimes I fear it will topple down into the harbor far, far below. So that's when I look out the other window, up toward the hills. They look like they're on a canvas where a painter has made one brushstroke with each of the colors on his palette, side by side in rows and columns atop one another. Such are the houses on the hills of my city, all knit tightly together like a quilt my Nana Delfina hangs out on the clothesline to dry, blowing in the wind—up, up, up—into the sky.

"Wait. I hear one coming," Marisol says. We all look up toward the low humming noise that reminds me of Abuela Frida's voice when she has a scratchy throat.

"There, I see one coming," I say.

"But the line is so long," Lucila reminds us. "We'll be waiting here for at least two more to come before it's our turn."

"Let's walk!" Gloria calls to us over the din. Marisol, who can be a bit lazy sometimes, groans under her breath.

"Come on. It's good for you," urges Lucila.

"Easy for you to say, Lucila Long Legs," Marisol retorts.

By the time we reach Café Iris at the top of Cerro Barón, one of the highest and most famous of Valparaíso's hills—the one sailors look for to spot our city from their boats at sea—we are breathless, soaked, and shivering. It always feels like I can see the entire Pacific Ocean stretch out beneath me from this spot. I look out today on the harbor, covered with a gray mist. Then I blink my eyes a few times. I've been looking down at the harbor all my life, but today something seems different. Wrong, almost.

"Does the harbor look strange to you?" I ask my friends. They look at me as if to say, *Not another one of your stories. We're too big to play pretend anymore.* "No, really, look!" I protest. "This isn't my imagination. Just look and tell me what you see."

"Water?" suggests Lucila. "Fog, boats . . ."

"Boats! That's it!" I exclaim.

"What's it?" Gloria asks.

"The boats," I say. "They're bigger than usual, really more like ships than boats. And there are a lot of them. I just think it's strange, that's all."

"That's not the only thing that's strange," Marisol teases me, and turns me in the direction of Café Iris.

"Don't be mean, Marisol!" Lucila scolds her.

We go inside and shake off the rain. Cristóbal finds us a toasty booth in the corner, and we order a plate of steaming sopaipillas to share. With my mouth full of delicious fried pumpkin bread, I mumble, "I think we're lucky the winds are always bringing in rain this time of year."

"Not me," proclaims Marisol.

"Me neither," says Gloria.

"Why's that, Celeste?" Lucila asks.

"Sopaipillas!" I say, my mouth full now with my second bite. "Just when I almost forget their taste, another storm blows in and I get to try them all over again." In Chile it is a tradition to eat sopaipillas—round and warm like smiles—only on rainy days.

Gloria rolls her eyes, and the other girls giggle. But Cristóbal says, "Me too. I agree with Celeste."

"Ahh! A wise choice, young man, to agree with the lovely Señorita Marconi. For I have known Celeste since she was just a little bean—more wee, if you can imagine, than she is now—and she is a wise old girl, wise beyond her years." I laugh at the Café Iris magician. He's always teasing me but also always encouraging me to trust what he calls my intuition. El mago winks, reaches for my hand, and gives it a kiss. Like always, he wears a green silk shirt and bright orange suspenders, his frame as tall and narrow as if someone had pasted patent leather shoes to the bottom of the map of Chile.

Cristóbal loves visiting el mago, probably because Cristóbal does a kind of magic too. He uses his pendulum to draw maps in the sand—to find lost items and predict the future. Last week the pendulum showed him just where the sun would come out and paint a rainbow over Butterfly Hill.

Cristóbal's mother made his pendulum when he was four years old, after his father died. The only thing that made him smile was to visit el mago and watch him read the crystal ball and pull doves from his cape. One day el mago told Cristóbal's mother to give her son a pendulum—that it would become an inner compass that would stay with him all his life, a firm hand to guide him the way his father might have. His mother, not having much money, made the pendulum herself. She polished a piece of crystal-blue sea glass until it was smooth and round like an egg. Then she hung it from the silver chain that had once carried her husband's pocket watch. And because el mago told her the pendulum must end in a point, Cristóbal's mother melted a hairpin and fastened it to the bottom of the sea glass. Ever since, whenever we've had a question, serious or silly, we've begged Cristóbal to ask his pendulum for the answer.

Today, over our second steaming plate of sopaipillas, Marisol asks with a wicked smile, "So, just who at this table is in love with Juan Carlos, the new boy in eighth grade?"

We all know the answer, but wait with bated breath for the pendulum to prove us right.

Cristóbal dangles the pendulum in the air so that its hairpin point just grazes the flat surface of the table. Then he closes his eyes. Quick as a flash the pendulum moves in Gloria's direction. We burst out laughing. Everyone, that is, but Gloria.

"I knew it! I could have told you that a week ago!" Marisol gloats triumphantly.

Gloria tosses her blond curls and rolls her eyes. "Of

course I'm not *in love* with him! I just think he's hand-some, that's all." But the pendulum, with a life of its own, stretches the chain farther across the table, straining to reach Gloria. Lucila, Marisol, and I squeal and giggle some more!

Cristóbal, seeing how flustered Gloria has become, pulls the pendulum from the table and tucks it into his pocket. But Marisol isn't done teasing. "We can always get a second opinion and ask el mago about your love life, Gloria. What do you think he'll say?"

Gloria blushes as pink as her umbrella. "No! Never mind! Don't call el mago over here. . . . Fine, I admit it, I like him. I said *like*, not love. Are you satisfied?"

"¡Sí!" the rest of us shout in unison.

We all laugh, Gloria included, until we clutch our full bellies. Then I start to hiccup, and the laughter starts again, until all our cheeks turn as rosy and warm as Gloria's.

When we leave Café Iris, we step into torrents of muddy water pouring down the steep street. The wind blows hard from the west, over the harbor and up the hills, making the raindrops fly sideways, stinging my cheeks. When it rains in Valparaíso, not only the skies open. My eyes, the sea, the streets, even the ships—everything fills with water and overflows. *Ships.* Suddenly remembering them, I shield my eyes and peer toward the harbor. But it's hard to see anything except blankets of gray.

Winds from the south, then the north, meet and swirl around us like a windmill—blowing newspapers and flowerpots and lost umbrellas all over the place—making it hard to see one another. "Celeste, stay close to us!" I hear Cristóbal shout.

"Ah!" Something strikes me in the head. I look down to see a doll—a body without a head—rolling at my feet. I shiver, the hair on my arms standing straight up.

"Lucila! Where are you? Grab my hand!" I hear Marisol call to her cousin. I look in the direction of her voice, mesmerized by what I see. Swiftly, silently, slyly the fog swallows Lucila's head, then her hands, her feet, most of her torso. The only thing I can make out is the place where her heart is. My own heart starts beating fast.

"Lucila!" I cry out, panicked. "Are you all right?"

"Celeste, I'm here. I'm fine."

I let out my breath when I hear her voice. Then Marisol's—"Don't worry. I got her." I breathe even easier when the fog begins to lift like a veil from their faces. Why did that scare me so much? I'm used to the tricks the weather plays. Why am I so nervous today?

"Celeste, earth to Celeste." Gloria tugs at my sleeve. "It's late. You better get moving or your nana is going to be cross and waiting for you at the door."

"Gracias, Gloria. I'll hurry." I give my friends each a kiss on the cheek. "Bye, everyone! See you Monday!"

"¡Adiós, Celeste!"

"¡Adiós!"

As I climb the winding paths up Butterfly Hill to where my house sits—rather slanted—at the very top, I pause every so often to look around. I look at my feet, remembering the doll, and then out toward the harbor, remembering the ships. And I shudder when I recall how eerie it was to see Lucila disappear bit by bit.

I feel better when I pass our neighbor Señora Atkinson's tall pink house. On days like this she always stands in the window with a china teacup in one hand, tilting her head like a swan. She says the rains remind her of her youth in London, and there is never a more perfect time than a wet Valparaíso afternoon to drink tea and look out the window.

I wave to her, and she opens the window. "Cheers, Celeste!" She calls to me in English that sounds like the trilling of the yellow canary she keeps in her parlor.

I wonder if she's noticed anything different about the ships today.

Delfina has been waiting, as Gloria predicted. She opens the door and wraps a warm towel around my shoulders. "At night everyone returns to their proper place, including mischievous girls who always lose track of the time." She puts on her sternest face. "Now go upstairs and change, and then come down to the kitchen. I want you to help me chop herbs for dinner."

"Sí, Delfina." I climb the drafty, winding stairs to my blue bedroom that's so high, at night I imagine I am sleeping on a cloud in the sky. Which makes sense to me, since that is what my name, Celeste, means—like the sky. Like any sky, I suppose, sometimes I am bright and clear, and other times I can be quite a raincloud. I like to think more often than not that I'm a sunny day, with just a few easy clouds that blow in and out with the breeze.

Humitas
Are Like Heaven

"Celeste! ¡Niña mía! Where did you go?

"Come chop the herbs!

"Celeste, are you on the roof?

"Not on the roof in this rain, señorita! And after just drying off!

"The cilantro is asking for you! Get down from the roof this instant!"

Delfina knows I've climbed up to the roof, just like she knew when to come to the door with a towel, because she almost always knows everything that goes on in our house on Butterfly Hill.

The roof is where I go every day to look at the sky, rain or shine. I swallow a pang of guilt. I *should* go right down to the kitchen to help Delfina, but I want to get a better look at the harbor. The fog has only grown thicker, though, making it impossible to see the ships.

"Celeste, this instant!" This time Delfina's voice wakes me from my daydream.

I scramble into the kitchen and take my place beside

Delfina, who is already chopping parsley. I love to watch how quickly she moves her brown, wrinkled hands that look like eucalyptus bark as she chop chop chops. "Here, you do the cilantro. I'm making chimichurri sauce," she says. "But be careful with the knife, Querida!" Delfina frowns and her voice is stern, but she has still given me the chore I like to do best. She has known me since the day I was born, so of course she knows how much I love the sweet-sharp smell of cilantro, and how that scent stays on my hands like a perfume long after I have sprinkled the leaves into her pot. Delfina calls cilantro and parsley "little trees for the palate" and adds them to every dish, even desserts.

"Well, young lady," Delfina tries to scold me, but she can't hide the gap-toothed smile blooming on her lips. She dabs at my damp hair with her apron that smells like cinnamon, and asks, "How is that handsome Cristóbal Williams?" in a voice slippery with mischief.

Cristóbal is my oldest friend—we've known each other since before we can even remember. Delfina would carry me as a baby in her fruit basket to his mother's vegetable stand in the market, where Cristóbal would swat me with corncobs.

Delfina thinks I have a crush on Cristóbal. Which I don't. At least, not much. So I make my voice as casual as possible and say, "Oh, you know, sleepy as usual."

With my hand I brush Cristóbal Williams away like a flimsy cloud, to float with the dish-soap bubbles through the open window.

Delfina chuckles. "Delfina will pack some humitas for you to take to him in school. When Cristóbal visits, he gobbles five and takes five home for later, yet he is tall and thin like a string bean. But that is what happens to boys at his age. . . . He will grow to be muy guapo, a very handsome young man, with his black hair and his freckles."

I ignore Delfina, pretending to be absorbed in the cilantro, but from the corner of my eye I see her grin in my direction as she continues to tease me in a singsong voice, "Just you wait and see, Querida . . ."

"¡Ay, Nana!" I stop chopping, exasperated. "I certainly don't plan to marry a sleepyhead! I've sworn to myself that I will find a husband who can stay awake!"

"Who's looking for a husband?" I hear my father's voice in the hallway as he and my mother come through the front door. "Celeste, you're too young. And, Delfina, you're too picky."

Papá pulls my long reddish-brown braid as my mother takes from around his neck the stethoscope he always forgets is there.

"This smells delicious, Delfina." My mother's voice sounds tired, but she pulls me into a strong hug. Then she turns me in the direction of the parlor and says, "Go tell your Abuela Frida that supper will be ready soon!"

"Sí, Mamá." Then I remember what I wanted to ask my parents. "Mamá, Papá, have you noticed more ships in the harbor lately?"

They glance at each other.

"Not really. But we aren't always watching from our perch on the roof like someone we know." Mamá's voice sounds a bit high and strange. "Maybe the ships—"

But Papá interrupts her. "Do what your mother told you and get your grandmother, Celeste. The humitas are getting cold."

Why is his voice so stern? It was just a question. "Sí, Papá." I can't help giving him an annoyed look as I head toward the parlor.

Abuela Frida is still asleep in her chair, but she wakes with a sigh as I kiss the top of her head. I've always loved my grandmother's hair, as fine and white and soft as a cirrus cloud. "Celeste of my soul!" she says with a smile, taking the hand I hold out for her. "Hmmmm . . . is it true what my nose tells me?"

"Delfina's made your favorite tonight, Frida," my father answers as I lead Abuela Frida to the kitchen table. "Lucky for Celeste, humitas are her favorite too!"

"¡Ay, que rico! They smell delicious, Delfina," my mother says, inhaling. There is a special magic, like opening a present, when you eat a humita. It's best to lick

your fingers first, so the hot corn husks don't burn them.
Then you peel back the layers and find a steamy, sweet
cake made of ground corn.

"Eat up, mi joya." Delfina looks lovingly at my
mother. "All that work is making you thin!" My mother
was named Esmeralda because she has green eyes, but
Delfina still calls her "my jewel," like she did when my
mother was a little girl and Delfina was her nanny.

My parents are doctors. They work in a hospital for
the poor on the outskirts of Valparaíso, and also run a
small clinic where they see patients free of charge. That
is why at home we always have an endless supply of fruit
jams, fresh eggs, and corn on the cob: this is the currency
that poor people use when money is short.

"Humitas are like heaven," Abuela Frida pipes up,
grinning at the corncake on her plate. "I am just glad
you let us share with you, Celeste!" My grandmother is
teasing me because, like her, I love humitas—love, love
them. Abuela's Viennese accent is thick as she peels half
a lemon and begins to chew on it. She loves to chew on
lemons. Besides knitting long blue scarves, it's the thing
she loves to do best all day. We call her the Empress of
the Lemon Tree.

The Empress of the Lemon Tree places another
humita on my plate, but I pause before picking it up. My
parents care for people who don't have homes to keep

them warm or sometimes don't even have enough teeth to chew the little food they have. "So many toothless people in this country!" my mother always says, and sighs. So no matter how much my mouth waters, I always bow my head and whisper a little "Thank you" before I take the first bite.

The **Rain**
Gives

After dinner I go up to my bedroom. My blue room is one of my favorite places. It has a great window as tall as my father and as wide as his outstretched arms. I always leave the window open, even when it's raining, because Valparaíso is full of life. It's a mysterious city where fairies and lost sailors live, and ghosts stroll through the port. They are usually happy ghosts and a little bit tipsy. That's why at night things seemingly float through the air and land somewhere else in the morning. In my window I have found blue scarves, anti-wrinkle creams, a bottle of rum, and—what I loved most—a dozen pink balloons.

Below my window lies one of the several gardens that surround our house. Some are diurnal gardens that dance in the sunshine, and others are full of shy, nocturnal flowers that wait until Valparaíso is sleeping to bloom. There is a garden of lilacs and honeysuckle vines that wrap their spidery arms around the corner of our house where Abuela Frida sits by her window and knits. By our front door is a garden that touches the sky. And below my window is a plot with nocturnal flowers that reach out to touch the ocean. My mother planted this garden below my room when I was a baby so that I could be lulled to sleep by the fragrance of moonflowers with heart-shaped leaves, angel's trumpets, and fairy lilies, all blossoming in the moonlight.

Delfina once told me that the fairies dance to the music of the angels under my window while I sleep, so I thought that next to the moon garden would be a good place to put my own garden for my dolls. This is an invisible garden, and the plants have names like Malula Gomez or Cactus Face. The flowers are named Rainbow and Hope of the Hills, and my favorite flower is called Butterfly Hill because it spreads its petals from the insides of tiny stones.

My reverie is interrupted by a knock on my bedroom door. "Come in!" I say without turning my head.

My father opens the door and finds me seated on the cushions below my window.

"Just watching the rain, Papá."

"It's *still* raining?"

He sits beside me and lets out a low sigh. My father doesn't like the rain. "It's another one of life's mysteries, Celeste," he says in that serious way of his. "The rain gives us water to drink and cleanse ourselves, food to eat, flowers to admire, puddles for my daughter to splash in.

But"—my father peers over my shoulder toward the hills on the outskirts of the city—"the rain also takes away. In the poor neighborhoods where the houses are nothing but cardboard and aluminum, the hard rain and mud sliding down the hills will leave people homeless."

I lean against his arm and wait for him to continue—I can tell he has something more to tell me.

"Your mother and I are going out to visit some places where our patients live to make sure they are all right, since it's been raining for over a week now. We'll go to other neighborhoods tomorrow morning too. Would you like to come then, hija?"

Ever since I was little, I have gone with my parents to see their patients on the outskirts of the city, but only on routine visits. Come to think of it, the sun has *always* been shining—they've never invited me to come with them during rain like this. The storm must have left things really bad out there.

"Can I go with you tonight?" I plead. I'm eager to help, and I like going out at night.

"No, you know your mother doesn't like it when you are out too late. But tomorrow is Saturday, and we can head out early. Tonight you can help Delfina and your abuela prepare baskets of food and clothing."

"All right, Papá. Buenas noches."

"Good night, Celeste."

He's getting up to leave, when suddenly I remember something. "Papá, wait—I want to ask you something. Why didn't you want to talk about the ships in the harbor?"

"Oh, Celeste, I'm sorry. I was just tired after work, that's all. I'll take a look at them tomorrow. Now get some rest."

"All right, Papá."

Tonight the rain strums its long fingers up and down the roof. I can barely make out the familiar sounds of my grandmother snoring like the letter Z and Delfina talking to her saints. I sit by my window and wish Valparaíso good night. The lights on the hill are hazy, their usual brightness washed away by the water pouring from the sky. Mamá and Papá aren't home yet—they must be soaked and shivering, wherever they are. I've never liked going to sleep when they're not here. I hope they come home soon.

. . . And the Rain Takes Away

I wake to gusts of salty air and a creaking noise through my open window. At last the rains have cleared. Two swings move back and forth—*creak, creak, creeeeak*—in the morning fog. The swings are wooden, and one is painted pink and the other purple. My Abuelo José made them for his daughters. The knots he tied to secure the thick ropes to the long branches that extend from either side of the old eucalyptus tree never unraveled. "That's because your Abuelo José was as dependable as the tides rolling in and out, and he is here holding this whole house up so we never fall in an earthquake," Abuela Frida says. My mother swung on the pink swing, and her big sister, my Tía Graciela, on the purple, which goes a bit higher, I think.

I love hearing the swings creak in the morning. But what I love most about our house in the mornings are the pelicans that always fly over it. I really could say the pelicans are my next-door neighbors. They are the kind of neighbors who stick to the same routine day after day.

I see them when I leave for school, and when I return home, they are coasting lazily in the purply blue of the evening sky. Pelicans are strange. They look as if they are dressed in tailcoats, and their mouths are huge—no, humongous!

Since before I can remember, I have always called out to the pelicans:

"It's Celeste Marconi! Good morning, pelicans!"

They eye me and move their long beaks up and down as if they're responding to my greeting. Sometimes I wonder if I am only pretending that I hear the pelicans say hello. But my grandmother always says that people are what they imagine. So maybe I really do hear them call out:

"Good morning, Celeste Marconi!"

"Good morning, Celeste's garden!"

"Good morning, Valparaíso!"

There are always eight of them. The first seven fly by in one very straight line. And then a few feet behind them is this one old, lazy pelican, with his wings dipping up and down in the sky, always lagging a bit behind.

The sky reminds me of a highway. I imagine the clouds are traffic signs, but this makes me wonder what the pelicans would do when the signal says STOP. They'd have to stop flapping their wings, and would need a sturdy place to rest their big webbed feet and not fall from the sky. Someday I will ask them.

My mother pokes her head into my room. "Celeste, Querida, put on your rain boots. Your father is anxious to get an early start. He's already pacing at the front door with his stethoscope. We'll need a lot of help from you today."

Our taxi driver, Don Alejandro, helps us load bags full of food, medical supplies, and Abuela Frida's scarves into the car. Then he takes us as far as the rising waters will allow toward the outskirts of Valparaíso. "I will pick you up here at eight tonight. May God save them and protect you, Señor and Señora Marconi. And Niña Celeste." Don Alejandro speaks to us, but his eyes are fixed on our surroundings. It is an awful sight. What is left of the houses floats like driftwood. The little children play on them while the older ones rush to help their parents collect the remnants of their possessions, floating every which way and sinking down into the mud.

I don't know if it is the stench of rotting homes and putrefied food, or the sight of the vestiges of entire lives floating down a murky street, but suddenly a great wave of nausea passes over me. I clutch my stomach and bend over, keeping my face turned toward the ground, praying I don't call attention to myself. *Calm yourself, Celeste. Please, don't get sick!* I feel so embarrassed—I want to be strong and capable like my parents. Haven't I seen them cleaning wounds and setting bones all my life? I am here to help. I have to be able to handle this. But this isn't one patient or one ailment—this is so many people, all suffering from loss and hunger, shivering in the damp morning cold. My head spins as fast as my stomach. It's almost too much to bear. . . .

I feel Mamá's hand on my shoulder. "Celeste, what's wrong? Are you all right?"

I stand up straight and manage to nod. "Sí, Mamá. I'm fine."

Mamá understands without me telling her. "Here."

She unties the kerchief holding her hair back from her face and hands it to me. "Tie this around your neck. When the stench is bad, put it over your nose."

"Gracias, Mamá." She gives me a look that says, *I know you can do this.*

We wade through streets that are now black rivers. It is difficult for me to walk; my feet sink and stick, and the water splashes far past my knees. My father takes my hand. "This is poverty, Celeste. A deep puddle that you can't step out of."

I turn my eyes upward to see his face. My father doesn't speak much. He says he is most comfortable in the quiet next to the people he loves. But when Papá does speak, especially in his low voice with a furrow in his brow, I know his words come from such a deep place of thought that I never forget them.

That long, cold day we walk up and down two hills whose names don't match the neighborhoods built on them: Cerro Campana and Cerro Delicia. Bell and Delight. All sorts of people—men, women, old people, children, sometimes their dogs—shiver with pinched faces around fires. My mother approaches huddled group after huddled group and gives them food from the large basket she carries and a pint of milk from the backpack on her shoulders. She always tries to give extra to the families with babies and young children. My father cleans the wounds of those who have been hurt, and I reach into my backpack stuffed to the brim and pull out Abuela Frida's blue scarves. My mother takes three and wraps one around a shivering woman with hair like a black waterfall, and two small, silent babies tied in a blanket to her back. Then she offers the remaining scarves to two passersby and presses a packet into the woman's hand.

"Put this powder in the milk I gave you, Minerva. Just a bit each day will help your twins gain weight and grow strong." Minerva bows her head in gratitude, but my mother turns to me quickly and says. "Come, Celeste. Your father is determined to get to one more neighborhood before night falls."

"Sí, Mamá." But I take one look back at Minerva. She is walking in the opposite direction with her back hunched. Four bare baby feet stick out of the blanket. I gasp. Even from this distance I can see . . . *they are blue.*

Frozen, I stand knee-deep in the murky street, watching those little feet grow smaller and smaller as Minerva makes her way to . . . where? Where will she go? Her home is destroyed. Oh, those poor babies, those poor little feet . . . Maybe if I wrap them in scarves . . . ?

"Wait!" I call out to my parents and run to catch up with them. "Can I just go back and give Minerva—"

"No, Celeste." Papá's eyes are sympathetic, but the rest of his face is stern. "We have to keep moving—there are so many people to help and so many problems to solve. We'll never get to them all—"

"But her babies!" I interject.

"Celeste." Papá's voice is even firmer now. "There are so many babies. We just have to accept our limitations and do the best we can."

I can't accept that! I look to my mother. Surely *she* will understand. But she just nods and puts her arm around my shoulders, gently guiding me forward.

I plod ahead, defeated. We pass a wiry old man seated on what looks like the remains of an aluminum roof. His head rests upon his knees. His legs are shaking. I take the longest scarf from my backpack and silently approach him, averting my eyes like I am witnessing something I shouldn't. I feel bad for him—maybe he is embarrassed to have a young girl's pity? I drape the scarf over his shoulders. He looks up quickly with red-rimmed eyes, and then just as quickly looks down again. I hurry to catch up with my parents.

Maybe Papá is right—there is always another person who needs help. An endless number, it seems, on the outskirts of Valparaíso today. And we are only three people!

"Mamá?"

"¿Sí, Celeste?"

"Why are you and Papá the only ones here helping?

How come everyone doesn't come up the hills to help? At least other doctors should, shouldn't they?" My mother glances at my father, who is walking fast with a fierce look and a set jaw.

"People like us, lucky to have more than we could ever need . . ." Her voice trails off, and her eyebrows scrunch into tiny knots. "Well, it's our duty to share with those who have so little. But many people are so quick to forget this."

"But we have new hope," my father adds, "now that Presidente Alarcón took office last month. He promised to help the poor, not just by giving them food and shelter but by making all Chileans responsible for looking out for one another. There will be all sorts of new programs."

"Like what, Papá?"

"Well, for one, there is the Smile for Chile campaign your mother is helping with, which will help set up dental clinics in poor neighborhoods. And the president will pay young college students to teach adults who are illiterate."

"Is that a new one for your notebook, Celeste?" my mother asks, and repeats the sad-sounding word: "'Illiterate'?"

"No, I already know it." I shake my head, thinking of Nana Delfina, who doesn't like people to know she cannot read or write.

I look back at the ramshackle neighborhood and

think about Minerva. Can she read? Even if she can, how could she keep any books in a house that floats away? She must have to make up stories from her head to put her children to bed. What must she imagine at night, after seeing what she sees each and every day?

The Smell of
Sundays

Butterfly Hill is filled with many smells. Most of them are delicious, like the scent of buganvillias in full bloom or of dulce de leche—caramel—cooking in kitchens. And there are some that make my nose curdle. Like today, when the rains have made the marsh behind Marga Marga Street overflow, everyone in the house gets a bit dizzy.

But that murky smell will be overcome by my favorite smell in the world, the one I call the smell of Sundays. Today our house will smell of empanadas, delicious meat pies shaped like half-moons.

I stand barefoot on the balcony in my pajamas, watching my parents walk up the path that leads to our house—home at last from our favorite bakery, Panaderia Estrella, with a big package of empanadas and other goodies. Delfina doesn't cook on Sundays. It's her day off and time to just enjoy being part of the Marconi family too. I rush to the table and set down plates. Papá begins making café con leche. Abuela Frida tiptoes in with blue yarn trailing from her skirt. Her small, wrinkly feet are bare like mine, and her hair hangs down her back in long white braids. She grins mischievously, grabs the empanada I just placed on my father's plate, and takes a bite while his back is turned toward the stove. I stifle my giggles. Sometimes Abuela Frida reminds me of a girl my own age.

Papá pours everyone a cup of coffee. Even me, although mine has more leche—milk—than café. He frowns when he sees his empty plate with a few stray crumbs on it, but Abuela Frida quickly puts another empanada on his plate, telling him, "Andrés, you must be losing your memory in your old age! I warned Esmeralda about marrying an older man!" We laugh, and then there is a rare silence. We always start with the empanadas. We chew and smile at one another, devouring them one by one while they are still warm, and capturing on our sticky fingers any crumbs that have escaped to our plates.

But a pang of sadness interrupts my enjoyment. I think of Minerva's babies and the children on Cerro Campana and Cerro Delicia. I'm sure they don't get empanadas today, even though it's Sunday.

I think about how before yesterday I had visited the poor neighborhoods of Valparaíso only in the sunshine. The colors of the flags strung between the houses, the music played by old men on the corners strumming guitars with one string and tapping rhythms on empty paint buckets—that's what I always remembered when I thought about the outskirts of town. And the children— they were running around, playing in the streets. When I think back, they *did* wear ragged clothes, and most of them were barefoot—but I hardly noticed since they were laughing like all little kids do. Somehow the sun's sparkle seemed to land on everything on the hills, making them beautiful. Or maybe it was the people themselves.

And now a strange idea is forming in my mind,

one I will try to make sense of by writing it down in my notebook: I think there may be two kinds of rain in my country. It falls from the same sky, but then the rain changes depending on who it falls on. There is the rain of people like me. As it falls, I watch from the windows of Café Iris while eating sopaipillas with my friends, or listen to its pitter-patter while reading on the sofa next to Abuela Frida knitting blue scarves, enjoying the feeling of everyone safe and snug under our strong roof in our sturdy house on Butterfly Hill.

The rain of the poor is rain that knocks houses over, makes roofs cave in, and spoils food. It is rain that makes mud and illness rise up from the ground. It is rain that shows the Minervas of Valparaíso all they lack, by taking away the little they had. Sun and rain, city center and city outskirts—I used to think all was beautiful and good. But now I am not so sure.

Abuela
Frida

On Sundays it is my job to wash the dishes after our big
afternoon meal. It was Abuela Frida who insisted on giving
me this chore, because Mamá and Papá have always been
happy as long as I focus on my studies. "I raised you and
Graciela to value hard work, Esmeralda!" Abuela told my
mother one day as I sat beneath the kitchen table. "And I
don't want my granddaughter to grow up like all the lazy
upper-class children at her school!"

But I don't mind washing dishes . . . at least, not
much since discovering I can make up stories in my
head and scrub Delfina's stew pot at the same time. My
grandmother has given herself one endless chore—she
knits, knits, knits—huge scarves that move and stretch
like rippling waves from the invincible ocean called the
Pacific. Abuela Frida falls asleep when she knits, and
I often hear her speak in a low voice, as if something
troubling were happening. I wonder if she is dreaming
of the long journey she took to Valparaíso Harbor on
the Ship Called Hope. Papá says Abuela suffers from

an illness called nostalgia, which often is cured with a sprinkle of love, some lemon, a few raisins, and many slices of avocado.

When I was younger, my grandmother would say things like "Celeste, take your zzzzzzshoes off the zzzzzzsofa," and I'd wonder why she always sounded like a bumblebee when she spoke.

I place the last plate in the dish rack and wipe my hands on a dish towel. The window over the kitchen sink looks out at the eucalyptus tree with the pink and purple swings, and by the shadows they make on the grass I can tell there are a few hours of daylight left. I wonder if Abuela Frida will take a walk with me. I want to talk to her, just the two of us, and ask her what she thinks about the ships in the harbor, and tell her about Minerva and her twins shivering with cold, and all the other troubling things I saw on Cerro Campana and Cerro Delicia yesterday.

I poke my head into the parlor. She is sitting in her rocking chair as always, knitting a blue scarf. "Abuela Frida, I'm done with the dishes. Will you take a walk with me, maybe to get some ice cream?"

"It's a bit late, Querida." Abuela Frida looks up at the cuckoo clock on the wall.

"But"—I clasp my hands together—"is it ever really too late for dulce de leche?"

My grandmother's eyes light up at the mention of her favorite flavor. "Mmmmm . . . Okay, okay!" She laughs. "You know my weakness is caramel—besides you, that is. It will be good to get some fresh air after so much rain. Check with your parents first while I touch up my hair. I'm sure I look a sight."

I run down the hall to the study, where my parents are reading. Before I say a word, Mamá asks me, "Are the dishes done? And your homework?"

"Sí, Mamá."

"Then you two girls have fun," she says, laughing. "And bring me back some chocolate chip!" Sometimes Mamá is like that—she somehow just knows exactly what's on my mind.

Papá glances up from his medical journal. "Strawberry for me, hija."

Abuela and I take a cable car down to the bottom of Barón Hill, and walk the rest of the way to the marketplace near the harbor. We visit our favorite ice cream shop, Luigi's, the very same spot where Abuela Frida went with my Abuelo José on their first date. We find a bench to sit on and watch the people—old women selling carnations; men with their hands in their pockets, talking to one another with cigarettes hanging from their lips; families heading home from a Sunday in the park, their little children trailing kites behind them. I wait until we've both licked the last drops of ice cream from our fingers to tell her about the strange fears I've been feeling in my bones.

I look at Abuela Frida and open my mouth, but no sound comes out. I look down, flustered. I'm always collecting words and writing them down in my notebook, and I can be a real chatterbox, too, especially with my grandmother. But somehow talking about these fears feels different—almost dangerous—though I don't know why. I just don't know how to explain how I'm feeling.

Abuela Frida takes my hand and clears her throat: "Mmmmmmm rrrrrrrr zzzzzzz." Her sounds swirl around my hair, all tangly in the salty breeze. "Celeste of my soul," she urges me gently. "Don't worry about finding the words to speak your mind—simply tell me what's in your heart."

"Abuela, I've been feeling uneasy lately. Mostly because of what I see in the harbor. The ships are different—they're so much bigger, and there are so many of them. It feels dangerous. Is it just my imagination or is something going on?"

Then Abuela Frida speaks to me in German, which she does when she has something very serious on her mind. "Celeste, I will speak to you honestly. I have noticed the harbor is more crowded too. I don't know of anything amiss, but when you speak of big ships gathering together, it makes me afraid . . . but maybe that's just because I have seen war. When the Nazis arrived in Vienna in 1938, it was not by ship—they arrived on foot. So, I'm not sure . . ." Her voice trails off.

Maybe I've worried Abuela needlessly? Reminded her of all the horrible things she went through when she was young, just because she was Jewish? I search for something to lighten her mood. "But ships can be wonderful, too," I say. "Remember how you used to love to tell me stories about the Ship Called Hope?"

"Yes, how you loved those stories. And how I loved telling them."

I take her hand. "Tell me again, Abuela."

She smiles and her voice hums. "The couple who helped me escape the Nazis drove me all the way from Austria to the city of Hamburg, in Germany. When we got to the port, they gave me a ticket for a third-class passage on the most enormous ship in the Hamburg harbor, bound for Chile. For another port—called Valparaíso. The name sounded so strange but beautiful, too. I went aboard, all alone, a young girl only a few years older than you are now. But that night, in steerage—the belly of the ship, where the poorest passengers slept—I met your grandfather José. We became friends, and stayed friends when we arrived in our new city. And a few years later I married him." My grandmother's eyes fill with a soft light. "He brought me peace. He helped me make a new life in the new world."

I love hearing about the Ship Called Hope, and imagining how white it shone in the moonlight, crossing the dark Atlantic. I decide to leave my other questions for another time. "Thank you for telling me again, Abuela."

"De nada, child." Abuela Frida squeezes my hand. "But now I'm tired. Let's go home, Celeste."

We go back inside to buy ice cream for my parents, then we walk through the streets of Valparaíso hand in hand. As we climb the winding path that leads to our house, Abuela Frida turns to me. Her face is beaming, lit from within by a memory. "Vienna was a beautiful city before the war. It had many lilacs in springtime, and that is why José planted them outside my window on Butterfly Hill."

Mornings with
Delfina

My parents wake with the sun and leave for the hospital while I am still in bed. But sometimes my mother's good-bye kiss on my forehead wakes me up. If not, Delfina barges in and bangs on the bedposts with her purple broom.

"¡Buenos días, señorita!"

She always worries I'll be late for school, but it doesn't take long to get dressed. I wear the same navy-blue uniform every day. Girls can wear either skirts or pants—I almost always choose pants, although Abuela Frida says I should wear a skirt because it looks more ladylike—and over them we tie white smocks with our names embroidered in red letters.

"Good morning, pelicans! Good morning, Valparaíso!" I call out the window before turning to my backpack, overflowing with papers from the night before.

It's hard to get all my school books and homework to fit. Now that I am in sixth grade, I have so many subjects. But the one thing I always seem to be learning is poetry. "To know Chilean poetry is to know your history," our teacher Marta Alvarado reminds us over a chorus of groans every time she assigns poems to memorize and recite. I am one of the few students who never complain. Another is Gloria, because she is a perfect student. And Cristóbal, because he has usually fallen asleep. But me? I just love, love poetry. My favorites are the Odes of Pablo Neruda. Poems about ordinary, everyday things that anyone sees, like sprinkles of salt or a chestnut on the ground or a fish in the market. Today is my turn to recite a poem, and I've chosen Neruda's "Ode to the Watermelon." My mouth waters every time I repeat the words: "the coolest of all the planets . . . the green whale of the summer."

"¡Niña, ya! All right, already! You'll be late for school!"

Delfina wakes me from my daydream. My fingers fly through my long, unruly hair as I twist it into tight braids. "I'm coming, Delfina!" I call as I scramble down the twisty staircase, then scramble back up again. "I forgot the watermelon!"

"What on earth . . . ?"

I wave the poem at Delfina as she gives me a gentle nudge out the door.

Earthquakes of
the Soul

Since I don't have a pair of pelican wings, there are only two ways for me to get down Butterfly Hill to school. When I am late, I take the cable cars. It makes me feel grown-up to ride them alone.

On days when I have a few extra minutes, I walk along a steep, winding path, a series of small ups and downs that remind me of the beating of butterfly wings. And at night these ups and downs, illuminated by the lights of the cable cars, seem to cast the shadows of a thousand dancing fireflies all around me.

At the bottom is Café Iris, where el mago waves to me as he sets up his little table with tarot cards and crystals on the patio. And then I come to the busy streets of Valparaíso, where there are fruit stands, squares with statues, the harbor full of flags, and women carrying white baskets, selling red carnations and caramels for just one peso.

My school looks beautiful from a distance—its white dome topped with red that hides a brass bell, which

seems to laugh instead of ring—but inside, the building is full of cracks and crevices. The school has stood at the bottom of the hill for more than a hundred years, ever since a woman named Juana Ross decided to use her fortune to build hospitals and schools all over Chile, and it has survived many earthquakes.

Every day the brave building sways a little in the wind, as if the earth were dancing a very slow waltz with it. But some days the ground moves too fast, like a Brazilian samba, and our desks shake and dust fills the air. But we are all accustomed to tremors like this, and to our ramshackle school, where the desks are nailed to the floors.

Everyone in Chile has an explanation for earthquakes. I say that the earth has the right to yawn and stretch just as I do in my bed when I don't want to wake early for school, and also has the right to sneeze as we all do when covered in dust. "Maybe she is shaking off the sands from the Atacama Desert!" I tell my mother that evening as I recite "Ode to the Watermelon" for her, and a tremor breaks a few teacups in the kitchen.

Mamá puts my handwritten copy of the poem down and smoothes the crinkled paper with her hand.

"Celeste, I am not worried about earthquakes that come from the ground as much as those that are born in the soul."

I'm not sure what she means, and she can tell,

because she goes on. "When the earth trembles and you don't have anything to hold on to, you can't steady yourself. It seems like even your house, which you thought was so safe, is nothing but a flimsy raft being knocked about by waves."

"So—are you saying that our souls can be knocked down like houses?"

"Yes, my wise girl," she says. "Our souls can crumble when we don't care about our neighbors, or when we say hateful things about others, or exclude people for being different." She begins to pick the shattered pieces of porcelain from the teacups off the floor.

I bend down to help her, and she continues, "But remember, Celeste, that there are always so many more ways to heal and help a soul than to break one. Human beings are just like the earth. We want to be whole. Remember that. Promise?"

My mother's voice sounds urgent, so I nod gravely. Something is wrong, I can tell. So I ask her straight out. "What is it, Mamá?"

My mother sweeps the last bits of porcelain dust off the floor with her hands before answering me. I feel she is not only gathering the broken bits but her words as well. For then she says, "Celeste, your father will be cross with me if he knows I told you this. But I feel you are old enough to know what is happening around you.

I've heard you asking about the ships in the harbor, and truthfully I'm not sure what is going on. Hopefully, what I share with you are my fears and nothing more: I feel that Chile soon will suffer many earthquakes of the soul. I've heard rumors, in the hospital, that the military wants to end health care for those who cannot pay for it. And some even say that the military would try to take over Alarcón's government if it ever were strong enough . . . perhaps if it had aid from afar . . ." Her voice trails off, and she throws the sharp pieces of broken porcelain into the trash. Then she turns to me and shakes her head. "But—likely my imagination is carrying me away. Surely nothing can happen as long as Presidente Alarcón has the people on his side!"

"It's all right, Mamá," I tell her. But a shiver runs down my spine as I watch Mamá fill the kettle with water.

"More tea, Querida?" She smiles at me, maybe a little too brightly.

"No, Mamá," I say. "I'm going to the roof to think."

Rose Petals
on the
Pavement

The next day in school I can't stop thinking about what Mamá said about earthquakes of the soul. I think also about all the real earthquakes I have known. I still have nightmares sometimes about the big one, the biggest to hit Valparaíso in decades. I was seven years old, and right here at the Juana Ross School, when the earth exploded beneath our feet. We all started screaming and running, and our teacher almost fainted. I squeezed into a tiny ball beneath my desk, and Lucila crawled across the aisle to hide with me. We clutched each other, too scared to cry, to even breathe. All I wanted was to run home to Butterfly Hill.

The earthquake lasted only a few minutes, but it felt like forever. Soon after, Nana Delfina came to look for me on foot, and as we made our way home, it looked like someone had clutched the world in his hands and shaken it upside down. Churches, houses, trees, telephone poles had fallen. Bathtubs and beds had crashed through windows, and people in the streets below had hidden under them. And the worst of all was when Delfina told me to hide my face on her shoulder. I knew why, although I didn't tell her. We were passing by bodies. People also had fallen.

I look over at Lucila at her desk, remembering how we held on to each other for dear life that day. How small we were, and yet Lucila somehow knew we should cover our heads with our hands. Picturing us huddled under that desk gives me shivers. I look over at Lucila once more, just to make sure . . . I'm so anxious all of a sudden, just like when I look at the ships in the harbor. Lucila feels my gaze and smiles at me. I smile back, relieved. I am so glad that we are big girls now, and Valparaíso hasn't had an earthquake so awful in a long, long time.

I put my elbow on the desk and prop my chin in my hand, daydreaming some more. I hear Señorita Alvarado talking about Chilean independence. My head starts to dip and nod . . .

"Señorita Marconi, there will be nothing on next week's history exam about napping."

I jerk my head up with a start. "Perdone. I'm sorry, Señorita Alvarado."

Marisol giggles, and Señorita Alvarado's attention is diverted away from me.

"Señorita López, will you please read the next paragraph about Chile's war for independence?"

Marisol tries to make her face serious. "Sí, Señorita Alvarado."

Our teacher is strict but never unfair. And I like that she always answers our questions, even if all she can say is "I don't know."

The heater in the classroom is broken again, and Señorita Alvarado holds a cup of steaming jasmine tea in her hands to stay warm. She drinks it, sip by sip by sip, and puts it down only to pull one of her many maps from the belt of her skirt, to show us the site of a battle with the Spanish.

Like me, Señorita Alvarado is very small, and no matter the weather, she always wears a red leather coat that's a bit threadbare at the collar and the elbows, and so long that it drags behind her like a train when she walks. She paints her lips the exact same red as her coat.

Marisol, Gloria, Lucila, and I like to watch and see if Señorita Alvarado's boyfriend will pick her up after school. He has curly hair and dark sunglasses, and drives a motorbike. Señorita Alvarado looks a bit funny as she tries to climb on back with her long leather coat and satchel full of books. Today we catch a glimpse of her boyfriend kissing her on the lips before he puts a helmet on her head. As they speed away, a trail of red rose petals appears on the pavement. "Now that," Marisol says, clutching her heart dramatically, "is romance."

"Don't you think so, Celeste?" Gloria asks.

But I barely hear her as I rummage through my backpack for my blue notebook. I pull it out and write: *Someday I will wear red lipstick and ride a motorbike up and down the hills of Valparaíso. I'll be sure to wear my hair loose so it can blow behind me in the wind.*

Beneath
a Black
Umbrella

Essays for Señorita Alvarado are due next Friday. Every evening this week I have rushed through dinner and climbed to the roof to work on it. This is what I have written so far:

My Nana Delfina Nahuenhual Marquén arrived in Valparaíso holding a black umbrella and wearing a yellow rose in her hair. I like to imagine that she floated to my house in a downpour of rain. But Abuela Frida tells me that the long-ago day when Delfina knocked on the door, it was during a heat spell in summer. My surprised grandmother asked Delfina about that umbrella, more appropriate for funerals and sad times. Delfina said she needed protection from spirits, the sun, and the wind, and often the umbrella served as her home since she had lost so many houses in earthquakes. Then, after making a very deep bow, she smiled at newborn

Graciela, my aunt, in Abuela Frida's arms and asked if she was looking for a nanny.

Just like that, Delfina became a part of the house on Butterfly Hill like the stars are part of the Valparaíso night sky. Back then, Abuela Frida said, we all trusted one another. So without any letters of recommendation Delfina moved in. Her only belongings were her black umbrella and a box of bark from a cinnamon tree. My Abuela Frida loves people with courage, and right then and there she and Delfina became lifelong companions.

Delfina cures our colds by putting potato peels on our foreheads. She cooks our meals and protects us from earthquakes of the earth and of the soul. She keeps our house clean and filled with magic. At night I peek into her room. She quietly watches the trees among the shadows. She always knows I am there, and without turning her head, she pats the place beside her on the bed. She braids my hair as together we watch the orange sunsets. I watch her face fill with amazement when confronted with so much beauty.

Delfina talks about herself in the third person. She says, "Here is Delfina." She always wears a green woolen shawl and covers her mouth when she laughs because she is embarrassed by her missing teeth. She was the one who taught me not to be afraid of ghosts but to approach them and ask questions. She is always reminding me, "Ask heaven for a sign, Querida Celeste."

Delfina is continually asking for signs. She asks her Mapuche ancestors, and she asks the Catholic saints. She marks an old calendar with her favorite saints' birthdays, like Saint Peter, the patron saint of the sea. On this year's feast day we walked to the harbor, where a large crowd had gathered. In the sand we made starfish and mermaids, wrote the names of the fishermen we know, and prayed for an abundance of fish and for safe returns during storms. I know I am Jewish, but I love to be around saints. I love the eyes on the Virgin Mary statues in the tiny wooden ships, which we parade on the ocean on holidays. I learn to pray Delfina's prayers because prayer, Papá says, "is a beautiful poem."

"That Marta Alvarado is excellent." My father nods approvingly when he comes to the roof and sees me writing pages and pages of cursive in my notebook, which I promptly snap shut. "She pushes you to be your best."

"Yes, but sometimes she is tougher on me than the other kids," I complain.

"That is because she sees your potential. And Mamá and I do too."

I listen to my father's heavy feet descend the rickety stairs and don't open my notebook until I hear his low voice speaking to Abuela Frida. I don't want Delfina to find out I am writing about her—it would make her feel embarrassed. First, because she is so modest. "What is there to say about Delfina?" she might protest. And second, because she will only recognize her name and won't be able to read the rest herself. Maybe someday I will teach her to sound out the letters of every word.

A Dark Cloud
Opens

"Cristóbal, did you notice how quiet Señora Espindola has been all this week?" I whisper to my drowsy friend in the school cafeteria. Cristóbal nods. Señora Espindola is the roly-poly lunch lady who all the kids say swallowed an electric radio—that's how much she prattles on and on between ladles of chicken stew. I suddenly notice how old she looks when she isn't jabbering on and waving serving spoons around like an orchestra conductor.

Marisol, in line behind us, hears me. She sticks her head between our shoulders and whispers, "Her son lives three houses down from me, and our next-door neighbor says he heard a lot of noise in the middle of the night last week." Marisol pauses and looks this way and that to be sure no one is listening. "The next morning the doors to the house were open—and he and his pregnant wife were gone! No one knows if they ran away or if someone . . . something . . . happened . . ."

Marisol's story jerks Cristóbal awake. "But—why?

Why would they leave?" he asks, his face going pale. Then he gasps.

"What? Cristóbal, what?" I press him.

"It's just . . . that my pendulum's been acting funny. Something's not right . . . and I've heard Mamá's customers in the market whispering about the military. . . ."

Just then Gloria brushes right past us in line. "Hey, Gloria!" I wave to her to join us, but she quickly turns her head away. "Didn't she see us?" I ask the others.

"Oh, she saw us, all right!" Marisol tosses her head, clearly annoyed. "What's wrong with her? She's acting so snobby!"

When I get home from school, I go right up to the roof without even eating a snack. It's been drizzly all day, and suddenly a dark cloud opens up above Butterfly Hill and hard rain begins to fall. I know I should come down from the roof and begin my homework, but I stand there and turn my face to the sky. I want sharp droplets of water to wash away my confusion—about Gloria, about families vanishing in the night, about everything.

"¡Niña Celeste!" Delfina's voice wafts up to me with the scent of sopaipillas. "Cristóbal Williams is here!"

I go downstairs to the kitchen, where Nana is already heaping piles of warm pumpkin bread onto Cristóbal's plate. He tries to smile at me with his mouth full, but his mouth looks sad and misshapen. Nana Delfina hands me a sopaipilla, then begins to dry my braids with her apron.

"Cristóbal, what are you doing here?" I ask tentatively, almost afraid of his answer. "You're not here to walk to Café Iris in the rain . . . are you?"

Cristóbal shakes his head vehemently. "No, amiga. I feel deep down in my bones that these dark clouds aren't for playing under, and that they won't be lifted for a long time."

Even though I never used to mind, it frightens me now to hear Cristóbal speaking in riddles. "What do you mean?" I ask, frustrated. "Just say what you came to say."

"I've had dreams about soldiers, too many to count, marching on the map of Chile until we are nothing but a long line of darkness teetering toward the Pacific Ocean."

My heart starts beating fast. Nana Delfina nods at Cristóbal to continue. "And have you noticed the buganvillias that fill the plazas? I've walked all over Valparaíso because I couldn't believe it." Cristóbal takes a deep breath. "They've suddenly started to shrivel!"

"Does your pendulum show anything?" I press Cristóbal.

"That's the worst of it: my pendulum just spins in circles, like it is lost, or going insane."

* * *

That night I toss and turn in my bed. It's as if my skin is on fire. I lick beads of salt from my lips, and even when I kick off the covers, I don't stop sweating. Finally my eyes close and don't open again. I dream that I'm walking up to the roof to look at the stars. But instead of stars, the sky is full of fire. I jump all the way down to Valparaíso Bay to escape the flames, and land without a sound in the dark water. But it's so hot! "Help! Please! Get me out of here!" The water burns. I fear I am boiling alive! I swim toward a nearby fishing boat and pull myself in. I try to put out the flames that have appeared on my skin.

"Ahhhhh!" I sit up in my bed, trembling and cold. "The ships!" I yell as Delfina rushes in to wake me up from my nightmare. "They are full of dead fish!"

The **Time**
of Fear

On Friday, Señorita Alvarado looks paler than paper. And she acts so strange! She hardly says anything and instead passes out a worksheet of facts and dates for us to fill out and sits at her desk with her hands folded, face turned down. I creep up to the big desk covered with maps and empty teacups. The map on top, a faded map of South America, is covered with tears. "What do you need, Celeste?" asks Señorita Alvarado without turning her face to me. Her voice is a tiny echo.

"Señorita Alvarado, what is wrong today?" I whisper.

She is quiet for a long, long time. Then finally she sighs. "You will find out soon enough. Now please go sit down."

This isn't like Señorita Alvarado at all. What's wrong with her? Taken aback, I hold in tears and do what she says. Then Marta Alvarado turns her pale, wet face toward the entire class. She tries to smile, but the look in her red-rimmed eyes makes my heart drop to my stomach.

The day seems so long. I can't wait to go home. "I just know something really awful is happening," I confide in Lucila as we pound erasers against the outside wall of the building to clean them.

Lucila's eyes are wide through the cloud of chalk dust. "Has Cristóbal predicted something?"

I nod, and Lucila bites her lip until it's so red, it reminds me of Señorita Alvarado.

When the old brass bell finally rings to tell us the day is done, I race down the hall and out the front door. The wind seems to chase me as I run all the way home. Panting and trembling, I shut the door behind me and run up to my bedroom without saying hello to Abuela Frida or Nana Delfina. I just want to be alone to think. I grab my notebook and climb the rickety old stairs to the roof. But just when my heart quiets and I finally regain my breath, I hear someone on the stairs. Mamá! Why is she home so early? I rush back inside and down the stairs to meet her.

"Something feels just like it does before an earthquake, Mamá. What is happening?"

"Remember how I told you how earthquakes remind us of what really matters?" she says. "Well, there have been some tremors felt in Alarcón's government. Some opposition. But we believe the people are what give Alarcón his strength. So we have some friends coming over to talk about how we can help maintain peace and order."

Mamá's voice sounds too casual. She's trying not

to worry me. But knowing something is wrong, and not knowing exactly what, is so much worse! Suddenly I remember what she told me a few weeks ago about her fears for Alarcón's government. Does she remember that? Doesn't she know I am not the little girl who used to eavesdrop beneath tables just for fun . . . doesn't she realize I listen so I can *know* things?! I decide to stay close by to hear what my parents and their friends say during "onces."

"Onces" are an important time of day in Chile. And even though "onces" means "elevens," they happen at five o'clock. Señora Atkinson says in Britain they call it "teatime." Since I was very small, I have been sitting under the table during onces, listening to my parents' colleagues from the hospital, professors at the university, painters, and all sorts of people talk about all sorts of things: the Beatles, space exploration, but mostly, lately, more and more—politics.

Today politics is the only thing they talk about, and in voices that sound like rubber bands about to snap. I listen to words hurriedly flying back and forth about "the situation in this country." Solidarity. Justice. Criminal. Consensus. Those words repeat so often. Mamá's friend Clara keeps insisting, "I admire Alarcón for taking such a big risk—trying to change our society into a place where everyone is equal. He had to know that would make the people with money and power angry." I know what Clara is talking about. My parents, Señorita Alvarado, Lucila's father in his newspaper column—many people have talked about Alarcón's plans for Chile since he became president. Health care for all, education for all, everyone having enough to eat and somewhere to sleep at night. But I don't understand how equality can be dangerous. How could it make someone . . . anyone . . . angry?

I sneak back upstairs to my blue room and think of what I have overheard. I write the word "riesgo"—"risk." I used to think it was a beautiful word, but now it makes my hands shake. My cursive "riesgo" looks like it's trembling with fear.

Teatime
Aflame

I'm still writing when I realize that I smell smoke.

I drop my notebook. "Mamá!" I scream. All is quiet in the house, but I hear a commotion outside—shouting and a sharp crackling. The smoke smell grows stronger as I climb to the roof. Strange light and shadows flicker on the street below. "Ma—" I clasp my hands over my mouth to stop myself from screaming. A stern voice from deep inside me is telling me, *Celeste, hush!*

My heart pounds. My eyes fill. I want to run and find my parents, but I can't move or look away. There, in the tiny plaza at the center of Butterfly Hill, is a tall pile of books.

They are burning.

"Celeste! Celeste!"

I nearly lose my balance—my mind is reeling in shock and confusion. There, on my roof, crawling toward me, is Cristóbal Williams!

"Cristóbal! How did you get up here? What are you doing? What is going on?"

He arrives by my side, panting, and presses his hand on top of mine. "Stay low," he whispers. "I don't want them to see us!"

"Who? Don't want *who* to see us? What is going on?!"

"Soldiers. But, Celeste, it's not only here. They are burning books everywhere! All over the city! In Plaza Aníbal Pinto there is a giant bonfire! Piles and piles of books! Soldiers—hundreds of them, with metal helmets and boots—are marching around it and throwing the books in! And people are watching from the alleyways and roofs, but no one is saying anything, or stopping them. . . . It's like the people are ghosts."

"What?! Cristóbal, are you sure?" My head spins even more. I remember what Abuela Frida told me about the Nazis burning books in Vienna. But that was so long ago—it seemed more like a nightmare to me than something real. . . . Could something like *that* happen *here*? In Valparaíso? Oh, what what *what* is going on?

"Sí. I am sure. My pendulum told me. And then I went and saw it for myself. I started to head home, but all of a sudden I thought of you—and I had to find you and tell you that I wanted to be with you. I don't know why . . ." His voice drifts off, and I see the fear in his eyes. I shiver at the violent flashes—of flame, then shadow, then flame again—from the ground below.

"Cristóbal, don't go home. It could be dangerous. Stay here at my house tonight."

Cristóbal pauses. "No, I don't want my mother to be alone. I left without telling her . . ."

"She must be worried sick! We'll call her, and then you can stay . . ."

"No!" He shakes his head adamantly. "Just call her, and let her know I am on my way."

"All right." I give in. Cristóbal can be as stubborn as he is sleepy, but when did he become so brave?

"¡Adiós, Celeste!"

"¡Ten cuidado! Please, be careful!"

I hold my breath and watch Cristóbal climb down the trellis that leads to my dolls' garden. I clasp my hands together and pray the way I have seen Abuela Frida do. Please, please, let no one see him! Please let him make it home safely!

I climb inside and run downstairs, wanting my mother's arms around me more than I ever have. I wish Mamá could rub my forehead like she used to when I had a nightmare, and erase this night from my mind forever.

My father meets me on the stairs and catches me in his arms. "Papá! Papá! What is it?! What is happening?! Why are they burning books?! Why are there soldiers?!"

"Shhhh. Shhhhhh." Papá holds me against his chest for a long, long time. Finally I stop crying and look at his face, gray like ashes from the fire.

"Papá?" I whisper, afraid of his answer.

He opens his mouth, but no words come out. He shakes his head and holds me tighter. "Papá?" Every second of his silence takes me closer to screaming in terror. But then I see my mother climbing the stairs. She puts her arms around us both. Her eyes are full of tears.

"Mamá? Mamá, what is happening?!" My voice pleads with her. Oh, please, please tell me this is all a bad dream! Tell me you can erase it and make everything good again!

Tears trickle down her face. "Celeste, do you remember when we talked about earthquakes?"

"¿Sí, Mamá?" My voice is tentative, a trembling question mark.

"Well, tonight we felt an earthquake of the soul."

I don't remember what happens next.

I awake in my bed with my mother lying next to me, still dressed in her hospital clothes from the day before. There are tear stains on my pillow, and the air smells like smoke.

The Subversives

The rest of the weekend is like a bad dream. Everyone knows about the book burning, but no one says anything about it.

"Papá told me not to talk about it to anyone, even to you, Celeste!" Lucila whispers to me when I run to her Monday morning with the words "fire" and "soldiers" already falling from my lips. "Marisol, too. Don't ask her about it, okay? Don't say anything to anyone. Promise? It's dangerous!"

"But why? Why is it dangerous?!" I protest. Doesn't anyone want to know what is happening?! How can we figure things out if we all stay silent?!

Lucila shakes her head and puts her finger to her lips.

If Lucila's father says it's dangerous, then it must be. He always knows what is going on. He's a journalism professor and writes a weekly column for Chile's biggest newspaper. My parents like his articles about how jobs pay little and food is so scarce, how maids are forced to eat leftovers in back rooms instead of sitting at the table with their bosses, how there should be equal rights for women, and education and health care for the poor . . . And suddenly I feel dizzy. Lucila's father—the words he writes—are they like the books the soldiers burned?

And every day there are fewer of us in school. Today there are only fifteen—out of thirty-one in our class! One of the absent students is Ana, who is so quiet that I wonder how many days she has actually been gone.

"Where's Ana?" I whisper to Gloria, who sits next to me in class. They both live on Cerro Alegre, so I figure she must know—I figure she must care. But Gloria shrugs and turns her face down to *Don Quijote*. I stare at her. Her curly blond hair, usually loose in ringlets we all envied, is pulled tight back from her face. Since we were little girls, she has been our leader, the one we all look up to. Now I feel like a door has been shut in my face. Gloria has never acted so cold toward me.

When school lets out for the day, I grab Lucila's and Marisol's hands and hold the girls back until the classroom is empty. Señorita Alvarado looks sharply at us, pauses for a moment with her forehead scrunched up, and then finally speaks in a stern tone I've never heard her use: "Just talk softly and close the door behind you, chicas, por favor!" She pokes her head out and looks back and forth down the hallway before she leaves, closing the door behind her.

"What's going on, Celeste? What is it?" Lucila taps her foot impatiently. "My mother wants me to go home right after school. She said she'll ground me if I'm late!"

"We need to talk to Gloria! Something's going on with her. And Ana, too—she hasn't been at school. I'm worried. I just don't know how we can sit in class and pretend everything is okay when everyone around us is either changing or suddenly leaving without saying good-bye! There were only fifteen of us in class today! It must have something to do with the soldiers who were burning the books! And the ships in the harbor! Don't you notice there are more every day? And they keep getting bigger and bigger!"

I burst into hysterical tears, and Marisol hugs me close while Lucila whispers, "Celeste, everything will be okay. That's what Mamá keeps telling me over and over." She casts a nervous glance over at Marisol. "But please, please, *please* be careful what you say in public, and who you say it to . . ."

Marisol picks up where her cousin's voice trails off. "Our parents told us to show how we really feel only at home . . . behind closed doors."

Marisol pulls a tissue from her pocket and wipes my face. "Now let's go find Gloria! Things with her can't be as bad as you think, Celeste."

I thought it would be hard to find Gloria, but as we walk into the courtyard, we see her seated on our bench with Cristóbal. She's watching him swing his magic pendulum back and forth with an annoyed look on her face. Gloria calls out as she sees us approach. "Come over here! I want Cristóbal to predict the future for me, but he says he can't anymore! Help me convince him!"

"Is that true, Cristóbal?" I ask.

"Yes! Leave it alone, Celeste."

It's the first time I have ever seen Cristóbal agitated. Then he adds, his face stormy, "My mother forbade it."

"Then why do you still have the pendulum?" Gloria prods.

He shrugs his shoulders. "Don't know. What's it to you?"

"What is it you want to know, Gloria?" Marisol asks.

Gloria gets that cold, unreadable look in her eyes again. Then she says, tilting her chin upward, "I want to know if Señorita Alvarado is a subversive."

At that word, "subversive," Marisol shifts on her feet uncomfortably, and Lucila turns pale.

Gloria looks right at Lucila. "Don't you want to know?"

Lucila shakes her head, and I interrupt, "Gloria, what's all this talk about subversives?"

"Oh, please! You don't know what subversives are, Celeste? You? The princess of words?!" I just stare at her like she's insane. "The poets and writers you love so much are subversives! Neruda is!" she says.

We gasp.

"But Pablo Neruda is a national hero!" I protest.

"Of course!" Gloria shrugs matter-of-factly. Her voice sounds old and bitter, like it belongs to a person who carries an umbrella everywhere, always expecting a storm. That eerie voice now inhabiting our friend continues: "My father says that poets, writers, and journalists are subversives. And some singers and artists, and those people who work with the poor and think they can change things themselves." She casts a glare like a knife in my direction. "*Those people* are weakening Chile. My father says they are enemies of the fatherland and very dangerous."

But why? I feel like I've forgotten how to think. Then I realize that, of course, my parents and almost all of our friends and neighbors fall into this group! And my parents— they know Gloria's father. I wonder if he remembers how my parents will accept a bag of limes or sweet breads or a dozen eggs in exchange for their medical services. Would he consider them enemies of the fatherland?!

A long stifling silence passes. Then Marisol pulls Lucila's arm. "We should be getting home," she says quietly, and the two walk rapidly toward the front gate.

"We should be getting home too, Celeste," Cristóbal says, and tucks his pendulum inside his backpack. "You too, Gloria?" he asks.

"No, I am waiting for my father," she says coolly. "He's having a meeting with Principal Castellanos."

"About what? It can't be your grades; you get all As!" I say, forcing a smile, trying to reach the friend inside Gloria. But she gives me a cold stare that makes my blood feel icy.

"You know what about. But Cristóbal's right—you should get home, Celeste. Don't you need to help your grandmother make scarves, or practice some witchcraft with your crazy nana?"

I back away from her—Gloria's words land in my heart like a dagger. My whole body fills with hurt and fear.

"Come on, Celeste." Cristóbal grabs my hand and leads me out into the street. We walk quickly, in silence, for a long, long while. Then finally I realize that Cristóbal is walking me up Butterfly Hill.

"You need to get home too, Cristóbal! I can make it alone from here."

Cristóbal shakes his head. He looks more wide-awake than ever. "No, Celeste. I want to take you all the way home today." All I can do is squeeze his hand. I will never find another friend like Cristóbal.

And I have to ask, "Is it true your mother told you not to use your pendulum?"

He nods. "She thinks it is dangerous. But I don't care, Celeste. People are nervous and wanting answers.

So I am using it but only to help them. Not for people who ask questions like Gloria's."

"Cristóbal, please, please, please only predict for people you trust. And do it somewhere safe and secret!"

Blot Out
the Horizon

I can't stop looking down at the harbor. More ships—more than ever before—have been arriving all week. Now instead of six, eight, ten, the harbor is full of them, too many to count. And they grow more immense by the day—two, no, three—times the size of my house, maybe even the size of my school. Have those monster ships swallowed all the other boats? The fishing trawlers, the tugboats, the sailboats? I can't see them anymore. These dark ships with flags that barely wave nearly blot out the horizon.

I feel a tightness in my stomach and a jumpiness in my throat. Delfina's word for this feeling in Mapudungún is "julepe."

"Celeste, come and eat your empanadas!"

"Coming, Nana!" I call down. But I don't move from the window. I am trying to remember the last time I've seen the pelicans fly by, and I can't. I shake my head in disbelief. The julepe must be getting to my head!

I run downstairs, where everyone is around the

table, talking in low voices and not eating the cooling stack of empanadas. My father is on the phone. "What are those huge ships in the harbor?" I blurt out.

My parents exchange glances, and Abuela Frida murmurs anxiously under her breath in German, "Tell her, Esmeralda."

My mother speaks slowly. "They are navy warships, Celeste."

Warships? No, they can't be. I've studied enough history with Señorita Alvarado to know that navies don't work that way. They only use their warships when there are wars, and to have a war, there has to be an enemy. "But, Mamá," I protest, "Chile isn't at war with our Valparaíso. That's like my hand fighting with my thumb. How can we be at war with ourselves?"

Mamá's face is pale, and her eyes look lost. But she tells me calmly, "I know it's hard to believe, Celeste, but it's true. Cristóbal's mother called earlier today to tell us that military marches have started in the center of town."

I stare at her, both aghast and disbelieving. Then I look to Abuela Frida, whose eyes look as lost as my mother's. *Why hasn't anyone told me anything about this? What, oh what, is going on?*

Papá has been talking tensely into the telephone, his face strained. He sets the phone down and stares at us. "That was Bernardo. The military has Presidente Alarcón trapped in the Presidential Palace in Santiago. The capital is under siege. Bernardo says . . . He says that people . . ." My father's voice falters. "Teachers, students, doctors . . . anyone they suspect would support Alarcón . . ." He grasps my mother's hand. "They are being taken from their homes! Cars without license plates are driving around Santiago, forcing people on the street into the backseats and speeding away!"

"Andrés! That's enough!" Abuela Frida interjects sharply. I look to Nana Delfina, who is peeling potatoes at the kitchen sink. I wish she would come and put a potato skin, so cool and soothing, on my forehead. But she keeps her head lowered. It's like I don't know any of them! My legs buckle beneath me, and I sink to the floor. Mamá and Papá rush to my side, and each takes an arm and pulls me to my feet.

"Are we—are we—at war?" I stammer, wanting so much to understand. "I mean, are they . . . at war with us? And who are they, these people who are telling soldiers to march in the streets and sending ships to swallow up our sky?"

Mamá gently guides me toward a chair next to Abuela Frida. "Do you remember what I told you, Celeste, about earthquakes of the soul—"

"Sí." I hear my own voice, as sharp as my

grandmother's a few moments ago, interrupt my mother. I pull away from her. "I'm so tired of hearing about your earthquakes of the soul," I snap. "I'm fine now, Mamá. Just let me go to my room. Tomorrow's Monday and I have homework."

I run up the stairs and hear Nana tell them, "Let her go. She needs to be alone to understand in her own time, in her own way."

I climb to the roof and stare down at the harbor again. All the sounds of Butterfly Hill have stopped. The buganvillias smell of rotting things.

Waiting
for You

On Friday, Lucila doesn't come to school. As soon as classes are done, I run to where the older kids hang out to ask her older brother where she is. "Where's Javier?" I ask them. They all shrug and look at their scuffed shoes. Then a tall boy with long brown hair and a bruise on his cheek hisses, "Javier and Lucila aren't here anymore, Celeste. Get yourself home quick, and be careful who you ask questions, okay?"

I run to find Cristóbal. He is in a shady corner of the school yard. As I approach, I see that he is tracing what looks like a map with his finger in the dirt. When he looks up and sees me, he runs his hand over the dirt and erases whatever was there. "Cristóbal! What are you doing?!" I ask, surprised. Cristóbal never hides anything from me!

"Waiting for you." He pauses. "Do you want me to walk you home?"

I exhale, fear subsiding for a second. "That's exactly what I came here to ask you, Cristóbal! Thank you. Will you stay for dinner?"

I can tell Cristóbal is worried about making it home on time, so I blurt everything out in a rush: "I'm so worried. Not only is Lucila not in school, but neither is Javier. And all these warships in the harbor and military marches—they must all be connected. Everyone's whispering, talking about people being taken away by soldiers in Santiago. I'm so scared, Cristóbal. I keep imagining the most horrible things. Do you . . . do you think your pendulum might tell us what's going on?" I clutch his arm and struggle to catch my breath.

"It won't!" Cristóbal sounds frustrated. "Don't you think I would have told Marisol—and you!—if I had even a little clue? I've asked my pendulum to draw a map in the sand a hundred times. It just goes around in circles like it's crazy!" His face looks stricken, his blue eyes dark. "It only keeps trying to say one thing—a thing too terrible . . ." Cristóbal's voice cracks. "Let's go to Butterfly Hill. . . ."

"What does it tell you? You have to tell me more!" I shake his arm forcefully.

"Never mind, Celeste! It can't be true. It's just a dumb piece of glass!" Cristóbal cries.

"I don't believe you! Tell me, please!"

Cristóbal stares at the dirt he's just kicked, then back at me. He takes a deep breath. "The navy. They are here to block the harbor. Celeste, soldiers will be going to Santiago to kill the president!"

"Liar!" I cry, and knock Cristóbal's pendulum right out of his hands. I run with all my might toward Butterfly Hill.

Before It's Too
Late

I have wanted to go find Cristóbal all weekend, to apologize. But my parents won't let me go any farther than Butterfly Hill. They are afraid that the upheaval in Santiago might spread to Valparaíso.

"Why don't you call him? Just say your fear made you hurtful," Delfina suggests when she finds me brooding in my room. How does Nana always know everything without me saying a word?

"I will, Nana," I promise. "Soon."

"Don't wait too long, Niña Celeste," she tells me sternly. "Something that is hard to do just becomes harder when you wait. Don't hope it will go away on its own—because it won't."

In the evening we eat spaghetti with pesto sauce, and nobody speaks much. Abuela Frida just sucks lemons. The noodles look sad all drooped over my plate. Maybe I should call Cristóbal now? But instead I follow my parents into their study. Papá turns on the radio. A Beatles song about a place called Strawberry Fields is playing, and I start to wonder if I'd ever get sick of eating strawberries forever, when the song is interrupted by a solemn voice:

"Buenas tardes. Good afternoon." The voice coughs, then continues. "Ahem, countrymen and countrywomen. Your attention, please. It has been confirmed that at approximately two o'clock this afternoon, Presidente Alarcón was killed. The Presidential Palace was set on fire by an explosion of unknown origin. That is all the information we have right now."

We sit in shocked silence, frozen for what feels like a very long time.

The song comes back on the radio. I hear the lyrics in English—"Living is easy with eyes closed, misunderstanding all you see"—echo through my reeling mind. But I don't understand them.

Terror moves up and down my body in shivers. Terror like a poisonous snake . . . Suddenly I jump out of my skin! Something's touching my arm! But then I exhale in relief—it's just my father's arms around me.

"Celeste, shhhh!" he murmurs. "Let me hold you." I look and see tears falling down his face. I have never seen Papá cry!

There's a loud pounding on the front door. Now we all jump and exchange nervous glances. Except for Abuela Frida, who remains as still as a statue in her chair. Papá, his face gone gray, walks quickly to the door. It's our elderly neighbors, Señor and Señora Vergara, whose twin sons live in Santiago. As they drink the coffee Delfina prepares for them, they tell us that a general with a long mustache and enormous dark glasses has taken power.

"In the capital they are saying Alarcón was killed by a rifle, but they can't say for certain who fired the shot . . ."

I don't want to hear anymore. I slip away to the roof, and nobody stops me. I don't want to, but I can't stop picturing the president with a bullet in his forehead. And then I see his heart, on fire and bleeding all over the Presidential Palace. The heart bleeds until it stops beating, until it has no more blood to lose, until Presidente Alarcón is nothing but ash.

Lines Tied or
Cut

The next morning I try to greet Valparaíso like I always do. "Buenos días, Valparaíso."

I hear nothing but silence. The silence feels heavy. It presses on my head like a helmet that's too small. I wait and hope for the pelicans to appear.

"It's Celeste Marconi! Are you there?"

But the sky is covered by a gray fog.

The pelicans don't fly by.

I go downstairs to finally call Cristóbal and apologize for calling him a liar. I wince when I think of how right he was, and how unfair I was to him.

I dial his number, but the telephone line is busy. I try again and again. "Mamá? Why can't I get through to Cristóbal?" I ask, frustrated.

Mamá, who looks like a sleepwalker, doesn't answer me at first. Then she says, "What? What was that, Celeste? Oh, the phones . . . So many people trying to call their loved ones, trying to figure out what is going on . . . The lines must be tied up, or they've been cut."

I know Mamá is talking about the phone lines, but her words terrify me. *Tied up or cut. The same thing could happen to people!*

It's not just my mother. All day everyone in the house is preoccupied: talking in whispers, listening to the radio, speaking furtively to neighbors who come to the door. Abuela Frida keeps putting her head in her hands and crying out—"José and I met Alarcón when we were just married! He was a law student then, and a fine and respectable man!"—over and over in disbelief.

I find refuge on the roof as much as possible, sitting on my hands to stop them from shaking. It is spring, but I feel so cold!!! My limbs tremble and tremble—this is the earthquake of the soul Mamá spoke about. How could someone kill the president? A good man who wanted to help people? How could someone kill *anyone*? What is the General going to do to Chile? I heard on the radio that he wanted to "clean the country." Clean it of what? He says strange things like "bleaching the streets of dirt" and talks about making the whole country pure and white! I think of all the colors of Valparaíso—the flowers, the kites, the paint on the houses and stores . . . and what will happen to all the murals that line the streets going up and down the hills?! And all the colorful people . . .

Suddenly, I don't know exactly why, at the heart of all my confusion, I feel afraid for my parents. Very afraid.

Before,
I Only Feared
Earthquakes

I wake early the next morning and creep, barefoot, to the kitchen. But I stop when I hear the voices of my parents and grandmother, for what my father says makes me sit on the stairs and wrap my arms around my stomach. He is telling them how he snuck down to the harbor last night, and how the biggest warship has a belly full of prisoners. "I could hear the cries of the men and women trapped in the storerooms." He pauses, then adds, "The rumor is that they're being beaten and thrown into the ocean."

Before, I only feared earthquakes. So I thought I knew fear. But now I realize I didn't. Not at all. Because this new fear is entirely different and strange. I put one icy foot in front of the other. It takes me forever to get down the stairs. I walk into the kitchen, and everyone stops talking. I sit down and hear my own voice sounding like a stranger's: "Buenos días, Mamá, Papá, Abuela Frida, Nana Delfina."

I shiver as I try to eat the sweet bread Delfina places

before me, and pretend that I haven't heard anything.

"Are you cold, Celeste?" Abuela Frida asks, and wraps a blue scarf around my shoulders. I nod my head up and down.

At school a man with a uniform covered with medals stands at the front door. He nods at each one of us as we enter the building. I keep my head down—everyone does. And everyone is absolutely quiet. No one laughs or runs or shouts in the halls. The man looks like he is counting each student. Is he looking for something or someone in particular?

And Lucila still hasn't returned to school! I look over at Marisol. She smiles at me weakly. Ana is not back either, and it looks like a few more classmates have left too. Once, doce, trece . . . I count nineteen missing! Is the man with the medals looking for *them*?

I crane my neck to see Cristóbal's desk, and breathe a sigh of relief. He is still here. I manage to catch his eye and mouth the words "I'm sorry." He looks down at his desk for a moment. When he looks up again, he looks much older. His eyes, especially, are so serious and alert. Then he flashes a quick grin in my direction. I grin back, for a single moment forgetting everything except how lucky I am to have him.

Marta Alvarado sits quiet and still at her desk. The enormous black shadows under her eyes make her look like a raccoon. But she still wears her red lipstick. Finally our teacher—who always flew joyfully this way and that about the classroom with maps and teacups in her hands—speaks.

"Students." Her voice is hoarse. "It is my duty to inform you that Principal Castellanos's time in the Juana Ross School has ended. Beginning today the military authorities are in charge of your education."

Principal Castellanos! But he's been at Juana Ross for twenty years! *Gone?* Just like that?! Where did he go?!

Marisol raises her hand, but Señorita Alvarado just shakes her head and puts her finger to her lips.

She glances toward the classroom door, which is open to the hallway, where another man in uniform stands at attention. Even from the back of the room, I see the fear in her eyes. Then, as if she has made a big decision, she says, "I promise you children we will keep learning as best we can. And without fear."

A single tear slides down to her chin. She quickly wipes it away, with another glance at the open door.

"Today our first task is to paint over the murals we painted on the walls. The authorities have ordered that all school walls must be white. And, girls, beginning tomorrow, you can only wear skirts to class, no pants. And you must wear your hair tied back in a bun. Nice and tidy, no loose strands flying in the wind. Boys, you must all cut your hair short, to above your ears. If you do not do it, the authorities will do it for you."

What?! Erase the paintings we all worked so hard on at the beginning of the school year? The children doing cartwheels, the hills and harbor of our city, a white dove that Marisol and I painted with the word "paz," peace, emerging from its mouth on an olive branch? So we can be surrounded by blank walls, by nothing? Why?!

And what does it matter how we dress, or if our hair is long or short, up or down? Can they actually tell us what we have to look like?!

My head starts to ache. I rub my eyes, suddenly feeling so, so tired. Nothing makes sense anymore.

That night the voice on the radio calls what is happening to Chile "the restoration of order to the country." I write the words down in my notebook and wonder—what was out of order before?

A Horrible
Trick

Another day at school and no sign of Lucila. Where is she? Where is Ana? Every day there are one, two, three more empty chairs in the classroom. How can it be that so many people are leaving without a trace, telling no one?! It's horrible, like an evil magic trick. And there's even a word for it—"disappearing."

Disappear. I hear that word on the cable cars when I go to school in the mornings and come straight home in the afternoons. No more eating ice cream in the market or exploring the harbor with my friends. Our parents all want us safe at home. Disappear. I hear that word when I sit under the table late at night, when my parents think I am asleep. Disappear. Marisol whispers that word to me in the school yard before the first bell rings. "I heard Papá tell Mamá that my uncle was made to disappear."

"But *how*? By *who*?"

"The soldiers!" she hisses back into my ear, glancing around to make sure we don't see the soldier who tramples his big black boots all over the school all day—"in order," the new principal tells us, "to maintain discipline worthy of the fatherland."

"But," I protest, "Lucila's father has to be somewhere! People don't just vanish! And"—I gulp—"what about Lucila and her mother?"

Marisol begins to sob. "Mamá tells me there is a chance that they escaped and went into hiding. But then I heard Papá tell Mamá not to get my hopes up, that she knows that is nearly impossible, that there were witnesses the night my uncle was taken away who say they left a guard at the door and that a car with no license plate came back soon for the rest of the family. It would have been impossible to escape!"

I hardly know what to say. I think of what my father said, about the cries from the bellies of the warships. I shake my head, trying to erase the image from my mind—Lucila *cannot* be there! And I say the only thing I *can* say. "We can't lose hope, Marisol! I heard my parents talking about how many of their friends are escaping by climbing over the Andes by night and hiding in caves during the day!"

Marisol draws a raggedy breath. "Yes, you're right. There's a chance." She gives me a wry look. "Even though Lucila hates the cold . . ." I think of my friend shivering in a snowstorm. Is she freezing? Is she hungry? Where is she?!

The bell rings and I jump. "Ay! Hurry so we aren't late!" I hand my handkerchief to Marisol. "Dry your eyes so nobody asks you why you're crying!" I urge her.

Marisol wipes her face and blows her nose. "Gracias, amiga." Then she looks at me urgently. "Celeste, can I tell you a secret?"

"You know you can!"

Marisol takes another raggedy breath. "I feel selfish saying this—I do!—especially since Lucila is the one I should be worried about—but I have nightmares every night that I will be taken away!"

"Me too."

"Celeste, I don't want to disappear!"

"Me neither." We file into the building, and I try to imagine that one day I woke up and just didn't exist, was swallowed up by a black cloud without saying good-bye to anyone. A strange thought comes into my head. I think tomorrow I will bring photos of myself to school, just in case I disappear. I don't want people to forget I existed.

I pass Gloria on the way to my desk. She meets my gaze and quickly turns her head down to her math book. Her brown shoes tap quickly against the floor— tap tap tap—the way they always did before a test that made her nervous, or sometimes when she talked about how strict her father could be. But she doesn't talk about her father anymore. In fact, I realize, she doesn't say much to anyone at all.

She Is So Like
You

Today my parents do something they've never ever done: go to work late. They want to ride the trolley cars with me to school before heading to the hospital.

"I can walk from here by myself," I tell them when we get out at the bottom of Barón Hill, but my mother shakes her head and takes my hand. Papá follows a few steps behind us, fiddling with his stethoscope. Last night after supper he announced he didn't want to let me go to school anymore. But I told him I wanted to keep going, no matter what.

"I won't leave Juana Ross!" I yelled at him. "What does the president getting shot two hours away in Santiago have to do with *me* leaving school?! It won't change anything!" I crossed my arms over my chest and glared at Papá defiantly, all the while knowing what I'd said was childish. I know my parents are worried about all the families disappearing around us. About the soldiers at my school and in the street and what they could do to me. But that childish part of me hopes that if I pretend my own life is still normal, everything around me will somehow magically go back to normal too. The warships in the bay will go away, and Lucila and Ana and everyone else will come back.

Then Papá looked very cross. He had met Presidente Alarcón and helped in his campaigns for health care for the poor. I guess I supported our president too, but right now he just seems to be part of this big argument in our country that has messed everything up! Maybe he shouldn't have tried to help the poor so much . . . though I don't understand why that made the soldiers so angry . . . but I don't care, because then Lucila and Ana and Señor Castellanos wouldn't be gone . . . and then Gloria wouldn't have become so nasty. . . .

"Andrés, we must let Celeste see her friends, keep her life as normal as possible!" my mother spoke up for me.

"It's dangerous, Esmeralda! Those people know where our sympathies lie!" my father snapped in a tone I had never heard him use with my mother before.

I opened my mouth to ask him what he meant by "sympathies," but my mother had already started waving her hands like she does whenever they disagree. "Andrés, listen to what you are saying! Chile will never be free if we don't let our children *be* children! Mi amor, we had our child so she could follow her heart! She wants to stay in school!"

"She is so like you, Esmeralda," my father said with a sigh, and reached across the table for her hand.

Before we left the house this morning, my mother put a letter "to Señorita Marta Alvarado" in my backpack. "For your teacher's eyes only," she said sternly. I stared at the envelope's whiteness. It was exactly the same color as our new school walls.

"Can't I know what it says, Mamá?"

Mamá's voice was oddly nonchalant. "Oh, just that we want her to keep you safe. . . . Now finish your bread, Celeste."

As we approach Juana Ross, I spot Cristóbal walking through the gate. He waves to my parents. "Hola, Señora Marconi, Señor Marconi!"

"Hola, Cristóbal!" they call out in unison.

"Adiós, Mamá! Adiós, Papá! See you later!" I run ahead of them to join Cristóbal before my father changes his mind.

"Celeste, come see! My pendulum has been acting stranger than ever today!" Cristóbal's eyes dart this way and that as he leads me over to an empty corner of the courtyard. We sit with our backs against the broad trunk of a eucalyptus tree so no one can see us. Cristóbal pulls the pendulum from his pocket and holds it between his index finger and his thumb. "Wake up!" he commands it loudly. The pendulum doesn't move to and fro like it usually does. Cristóbal pushes it with his other hand, and the pendulum doesn't budge!

A chill comes over me. "That's weird," I say, then add hopefully, "Is this a new trick?"

"Really, Celeste! Feel for yourself!" Cristóbal reaches for my hand and places it against the pendulum. It is stiff and holds firm as if it is rooted in the air!

"Ow!" I draw back my hand. "It's cold!"

"What's going on here?!" A voice like a thundercloud booms from behind us. Cristóbal and I jump and turn in unison. The guard who patrols the school is glaring at us from the other side of the tree. "What—I mean—Buenos días, sir," Cristóbal stammers. I clutch his arm in fear. I feel him trembling.

"Let me see that." The guard's voice is low and cruel, but as I look at his face, I see he is young. He looks like one of the senior boys—he can't be even twenty years old. His leather-gloved hand grabs the pendulum from Cristóbal's.

"What are you up to back here? I've been told to watch out for this voodoo of yours!"

"Please, sir!" I stand up to face the guard. "It's only a game! A toy! He wasn't doing anything wrong."

The guard's face reddens. "You, niña! Sit down! Or

I'll report you for conduct unbecoming of a lady, sitting behind a tree with a boy!" He laughs to himself.

"Leave her alone!" Cristóbal stands up and moves between me and the guard.

In a flash the guard pulls out the club he carries at his hip and smashes it down toward Cristóbal's head! Cristóbal darts out of the way, but the club still lands hard on his shoulder.

"Please! Stop!" I move close to Cristóbal's side just as the bell rings.

The soldier smirks again. "One more thing before you go to class . . ." And he picks up his heavy black boot and stomps with all his might on the pendulum! Amazingly, all the sea glass stays intact! He stomps again and again, and it doesn't break. And every time he steps on it, it glows more and more red. I can feel the heat from it on my face—it's turned hot as fire. . . .

Finally the guard backs away. "Let me never see that again!" His scowl has turned to a look of terror.

"Cristóbal!" I cry. "Are you hurt?!" I touch his shoulder lightly, and he winces and pulls away.

"No, it's just a little sore." He tries to make his voice brave.

"Let me see if anything's broken." I start to press my fingers lightly up his arm like I've seen my parents do. I watch myself go through the motions as if trapped in a nightmare from which I can't wake up. *How could this be anything else but a bad dream? It just doesn't make sense—Cristóbal bludgeoned by a guard at the Juana Ross School? The school we have both known since we were five years old?!*

I must be pressing Cristóbal's flesh too hard, because suddenly his hand covers my own and gently takes it off his arm. "Celeste, I'm fine!" he protests. "If we don't get to class, things will get a lot worse for both of us. Come on!"

He's right. I nod and take Cristóbal by one hand and his pendulum by the other. And we run, all the way into the building and down the hall to Marta Alvarado's classroom, without saying a word.

Marisol looks sorrowfully at me when I enter the classroom and sit down without even taking off my coat.

"That was a test!" Gloria whips her head around and whispers to me viciously. "And you failed, Celeste!"

My mind reels in confusion. Test of what? Did Gloria tell on us? Is that why the guard came over?! She gives me a little smirk. She did tell! How could she be *so . . . so . . . cruel?!* I am stunned and scared and hurt but angry, too—angry enough to meet her cold gaze without wavering until she turns back around. Then I put my head down on my desk and close my eyes, trying to still my racing heart.

I hear Señorita Alvarado asking questions and students answering her, but she doesn't call on me. I don't realize how much time has passed until Marisol taps me on the shoulder. "Celeste, it's time for lunch." I raise my head and shake it—saying, "I'm not hungry"—and put my head down again.

Marisol gently tugs one of my braids, and I hear her say, "I will bring you a sandwich in case you get hungry later." I want to tell her thank you, but I can't. I am trapped even deeper in the nightmare, terrified that if I lift my head or speak or even move an inch, another horrible thing—something *even more* terrible—will happen to me or one of my friends. I stay frozen like that until the final bell rings. Then I spring to my feet like a hunted rabbit, and without looking left, right, or anywhere but straight ahead, I run all the way home to Butterfly Hill.

I don't want to talk about what happened to Cristóbal, so I tell Delfina I want to take a nap, and run upstairs before she can ask me about my day. That night when my father comes home, he knocks on my bedroom door.

"How was school?" he asks, opening his arms wide like the sea. I fall into them, and he hugs me tight.

"It was fine, Papá." I can feel his relief.

If I told him about Cristóbal, he would be more

worried about me than ever, but instead Papá tells me, "You can keep going if that's what you want."

Is that what I want?

"Gracias, Papá."

Never before have I been untruthful with my father.

Even the
Sea Has
Stopped

Delfina no longer sweeps the path that leads to our house with rose water. She constantly tells me, "Celeste, child, don't look out the window!" I stop myself from looking, but when I turn on the radio, the music is gone, replaced by the harsh blaring of military marches. I quickly turn the radio off.

I stop adding new words to my notebook. Because the one word that repeats and repeats in my ear terrifies me too much to write it down. If I imagine it, it might come true! Was it only a few months ago that the word "disappear" made me think of the magician at Café Iris, always trying to pull a rabbit out of his hat and losing doves all over the café instead? "Disappear" is no longer a magic trick. The more I listen to the radio, the more I sit under the table late at night, the more I look at the grim faces on the cable cars and watch my teacher's trembling hands, I realize that "disappear" can now mean death.

The man in the uniform who stands at the front door

of the school every morning, we are supposed to call Admiral Retamales. He never smiles, and walks around with a toothpick in his mouth, constantly inspecting everything. Today he tore down a poster of Chile's great poets that hung over the blackboard in our classroom. In its place is a giant portrait with a gilded frame. And staring down at us from inside that frame is the General—the General who has taken over Chile—with his enormous black cape and enormous black sunglasses. Nobody has ever seen the General without those sunglasses.

"Mamá says the eyes are the window to the soul," Marisol whispers to me as we file outside in two lines— there is now one for the girls and one for the boys. We are going out for physical education, which is now taught by another scowling man with a mustache like the General's. As we walk past the other classrooms, we see the framed sunglassed general over every blackboard!

"Abuela Frida does too," I whisper back.

"So maybe the General doesn't have eyes?"

Our own eyes meet.

"Maybe he doesn't have a soul?" I say.

Cristóbal, at the end of the boys' line, passes close to us. "Chicas! Listen!" His voice is panicked. I put my finger over my mouth too late. "The sea has stopped speaking!" he says too loudly.

The instructor, by his side in a flash, hits Cristóbal

twice across the back with a long sharp pointer. Marisol and I wince and clutch each other's hands. "Keep walking!" the instructor barks at us.

My burning eyes turn to the ground and watch my feet move one in front of the other, as if I were a robot. But I *have* to know if Cristóbal is all right, so I peek back for a quick second. Cristóbal's eyes, wide, alert, and angry, meet mine. His shorn head nods defiantly. "Sí. Even the sea has stopped."

Curfew

That night the sirens begin to wail. "What is it? What is it?" I cry out and run downstairs, race into the parlor. Abuela Frida puts her arms, which smell of lemons, around me.

"That sound announces the curfew," she says. Her voice is calm but very sad as she explains what that means. That night I am determined to add the new word "curfew" in my notebook. It means that nobody can leave their homes. And if they do, the police take them prisoner. I know what happens then, what word follows, but I am *not* going to write that one down.

Every evening I can hardly draw a breath until my parents return from the medical clinic. Every minute past seven o'clock feels like another stone placed upon my chest. They always arrive just as the sun begins to set, minutes before the call for curfew blasts needles up and down my spine. And then, with the door latched behind them, the stones fall to the ground, and I finally am able to catch my breath.

Tonight I sit outside my parents' room. It sounds like they're arguing.

"Mi amor, we should all stay together! We can go north to my sister's!"

"No, Esmeralda! There is no way the military can stay in power! We must be here to help when this is all over. It won't be long!"

"But what about Celeste?!"

"It's better for her to be with Frida and Delfina. . . . Our friends will let us know if it becomes dangerous." I lean in closer to try to hear better, and my head bumps against the door!

"Ow!" Afraid they heard me, I run to my bedroom and put my head under the covers. I am half hoping they come to check on me and tell me I was just having a nightmare, but they never do. All night I try to forget what I heard, but I don't think I sleep one minute.

The next day at school I keep replaying my parents' conversation in my throbbing head. What were they talking about? Going north? To that faraway place called Maine my Tía Graciela moved to when I was little? Staying close? Me being with Abuela and Nana? So . . . *where* would *they* be?

For once, my parents are home when I get home from school. "What are you doing here?" I snap at my father when I walk in the door.

"Well, hello to you, too! Don't be too happy to see us!" he jokes, and I feel my shoulders drop and my lungs exhale as I drop my backpack onto the floor.

"It's just that everyone and everything is so tense lately. . . . I feel I am always expecting bad news."

"I know, hija." He rubs the top of my head until the static makes my hair stand on end. I used to love for him to do that when I was little. Now I don't. *At all!* But I stay quiet, wishing I could be, pretending that I am, that little Celeste again. "Delfina told us she would prepare her famous chicken stew tonight," my father continues, "so we decided to get home early so we could all enjoy it together. That's all."

Papá lets go of my hair and walks toward his study, suddenly preoccupied. "Why don't you see if Delfina needs any help . . . or maybe do your homework . . . ?" His voice fades as he closes the door to his study, but not before I get a glimpse of a box of books and a pile of maps on his desk.

Love Is That Powerful

I climb to the roof and stare out at the dark fog that covers the houses, covers the harbor, even covers my hand when I reach it out far enough. I look toward Señora Atkinson's house. She never strolls out to her balcony like she used to. I sit like that for what feels like a long, long time, until finally I hear Mamá calling me.

"Celeste, I'm afraid that fog will swallow you up! Come downstairs!"

Everyone is gathering around the kitchen table. I notice that Abuela Frida has brought out the candles she reserves for religious holidays. What used to make me happy now makes me feel uneasy. "Abuela, what's going on?" I whisper, but she just bows her head and begins to pray in Hebrew. When she finishes, she keeps her head lowered and starts to eat Delfina's chicken stew in silence.

My parents do the same. I have never heard such quiet around our kitchen table. Finally Mamá says, "This is delicious, Delfina!" But her voice sounds so sad, like a broken necklace.

Papá coughs, clears his throat, and says, "Celeste, we need to talk to you about something very painful." I freeze as he begins, "We don't need to tell you these are difficult times." My heart begins to pound so loudly, I can hardly hear my father. A fear like ghostly fingers wraps around my throat.

"Celeste, your mother and I worked very hard here in Valparaíso to support Presidente Alarcón in his campaign to make health care a right for everyone. Everyone in the city knows about our free clinic and our visits to treat people in the poorest neighborhoods. They know how your mother was on the board of the Smile for Chile campaign."

"Yes, but what does that matter, Papá? Now that Presidente Alarcón has been killed?"

Mamá reaches across the table for my hand. "Celeste, it was not enough for the General to kill the president. For him the only way to control the country is to rule by fear. So anyone he perceives as having been in support of Alarcón is being threatened."

"What do you mean, 'threatened'?" The fear tightens its grip around my throat.

Papá's face pales to a strange shade of gray. "Your mother and I have received letters at the hospital. And . . . the clinic has been vandalized. It isn't safe for us to be here in Valparaíso right now. And it isn't safe for you, and Frida, and Delfina, either. Your mother and I . . ." He clears his throat and tries to begin again. "Your mother and I . . ." He coughs and looks to Mamá for help.

"Celeste." Her voice is so firm, she almost sounds like a robot. "Papá and I must leave you for a little while. We are going into hiding."

What?! My mind screams, but no sound emerges from my open mouth.

I turn my face down. I can't bear to look at them right now. Leave me?! Hiding?! What are they saying?

My mother continues. "Celeste, how can I explain to you something I myself can barely comprehend? But I have to trust in that wise old woman who lives inside our little girl. That somehow you will find a way to understand what we must do, and to forgive us."

Suddenly the kitchen begins to spin. I feel nauseous. "Oh!" I clutch my stomach and run to the bathroom. Mamá follows me in, and in that soothing way that only Mamá has, holds back my hair and rubs my back.

"Come." She leads me to the sink. "Let's wash your face and your mouth. There!" Then she gathers me into her arms. "Nana is brewing you some ginger tea to calm your stomach. Celeste, I am so sorry! My poor girl!" Mamá begins to weep, and teardrops like frail little pearls roll from her chin to the top of my head. "Please believe me, it hurts us so much to leave you, but it would hurt us even worse to lose our lives and not be there for you anymore. We must take precautions. My brave girl, we must all endure this sacrifice so that when finally peace is restored in Chile, we can all be together again."

"But when will that be? How long will it take, Mamá?" I press as she leads me back out to the kitchen, where Abuela Frida, and then Papá, hold out their arms to hug me. Then Delfina sets a steaming mug before me. "Ginger tea now, Niña Celeste, and questions later. You must settle your stomach."

And Mamá finally answers my question. "I don't know how long we will be apart."

"But . . . but . . . where will you go? When will you leave?" I blurt out, choking back tears.

"Celeste of my soul," Abuela Frida speaks up. "Your life will go on as normally as it possibly can, given the circumstances. You will stay here with me and Delfina. And the three of us will take good care of each other."

Papá nods. "Celeste, I don't like to hide things from you, but it is better that you don't know any of the details about where and when your mother and I will go. That way, in case anyone ever asks, you can answer truthfully that you don't know."

Tears roll down my cheeks. "You mean, we can't even say good-bye?"

"No good-byes, Celeste," Papá says sorrowfully.

"But we will carry you with us in our hearts." Mamá smiles through her tears. "And in that way we will never be far from you. Love is *that powerful*, Celeste. Even though you won't see me, I will tuck you into bed each night in my heart."

I Can't Bear to
Say the **Word**

I leave early for school because I can't stand to be in the house anymore, knowing that our family might not be together tonight. I walk to school in a daze, as if all the strength has been sucked from my bones. Somehow I find myself at the gate to Juana Ross. My heart beats faster. I don't want to see anyone. I am afraid to tell my friends about Mamá and Papá. Partly because Abuela Frida told me not to mention it to anyone, but mostly because I can't bear to say the word "gone" out loud. But Cristóbal and Marisol run over to me as soon as they see me enter the school yard.

"We've been waiting for you, Celeste!" Marisol hugs me. "Our parents told us about your par—"

"Marisol, hush!" Cristóbal cuts her off midsentence.

Marisol quickly changes the subject, keeping her voice low. "I might not be coming to school anymore."

"Why?!" Fear makes its familiar flip-flops in my stomach. "Are you in danger? Are you going into hiding too?"

"Papá says that all I am learning now is lies. I hope I don't have to go anymore. I have nightmares every night about the guard who hurt Cristóbal."

"What about you, Cristóbal? Are you afraid to come to school?"

Cristóbal scratches his head. "It's strange, but I was more afraid *before* the guard and the gym teacher hit me. Now I know what to be afraid of, which is better than just being afraid of the things I imagine." He looks down at his feet and shifts back and forth. "I think . . . I will stay. That's what my pendulum tells me I should do." Cristóbal's jaw sets with determination. "It says I need to stay and see all this."

The rest of the day is a blur. I walk home from school with my eyes turned toward the ground. One scuffed black shoe in front of the other. I don't feel like seeing anyone and having to stop and say hello. Especially Señora Atkinson! She never fails to ask me if my parents are still working themselves to death at the hospital and clinic. But as I near the top of Butterfly Hill, I hear a creaking noise and look up. The front door of the Vergaras' house is swinging open. That's odd. Chills run up and down my spine. I approach cautiously. "¿Hola? Anybody home?"

I enter the house on tiptoe. There, in the hallway, is their poodle. "Princesa! Come here, girl! Are you sleeping?" I take a few steps closer. The stench overwhelms me, and I cover my mouth in horror.

She is dead.

Señor and Señora Vergara are gone.

How could they just leave and forget to take Princesa?! Or did someone come and take them away?! Could that someone have killed their dog?

I run home with a cry caught in my throat.

"Celeste! Is that you?" I hear Nana Delfina's voice from the kitchen, but I don't stop to say hello. I just keep climbing until I reach the roof. I sit there and wish I could cry until the sirens ring for curfew.

"Celeste!" Nana appears on the roof. "That's enough of being alone, Querida. It's time to come in and eat your supper."

It's hard to swallow the saffron rice Nana has set before me. I keep looking at the door expectantly. But they don't come home. What I knew in my heart all day is true. Papá and Mamá are gone.

Abuela Frida keeps her head down. I watch as a tear slides down onto her plate. Our house that used to hum with voices has gone mute.

I go up to my room after supper. I could go back up to the roof. But I don't want to look at the sky, so gray. I don't want to see what is happening to my city. Instead I try to sleep. That way, I won't have to think. But instead

I have nightmares that the soldiers are coming to take us away. I creep downstairs and look at the clock in the hallway. It is midnight, but I tiptoe into Abuela Frida's room anyway.

She is awake, sitting up in bed. The moonlight shines through the window on her nightgown and sheets, on her skin and hair—all are ghostly white.

"Come here, Celeste of my soul." Abuela Frida holds her arms open and makes room for me in her bed. I gratefully snuggle down beside her.

"Your pillow smells like lilacs . . . ," I say, and then I take a deep breath. I don't want to say a word about Mamá and Papá. But something else is also bothering me. "Abuela, I don't want to go to school anymore. Marisol's not going anymore, and my only real friend left is Cristóbal, and he . . . he . . . well, he's much braver than I am!"

"We can all be brave in our own way, Celeste," Abuela Frida murmurs into my hair.

"I'm not, Abuela. I'm afraid of so much. Of the cable cars—that I'll be trapped on them with a soldier! Of the soldier who marches around our school! I'm afraid of never seeing Mamá and Papá again! I am afraid something awful is happening to Lucila!"

Fear. So much! Fear that slithers up and down my body and walks beside me like a shadow.

"Abuela Frida, please don't make me go to school! Papá didn't want me to! He was right!" And I can't stop myself—I start to sob.

"Shhhh, Celeste, shhhh! That's enough, child! There, there, my brave girl." She begins to stroke my forehead the way Mamá does. "Celeste, you have so much courage—always know that. But something I have learned in life is that we must not waste our courage, but rather save it for the right battles. I learned early when I left Vienna that sometimes it is best to walk away. . . . I believe this has helped me survive. . . ."

I lift my head and look into her big blue eyes. They are not as sad as they are determined. "You don't have to go, Celeste, if you don't want to. I wanted to respect my daughter's wishes and let you choose, but she also left me in charge of your well-being, and, well, I also feel safer having you home on Butterfly Hill."

The Empty
Calendar

Days go by. Days I spend mostly on the roof. I watch
and wait, but Mamá and Papá don't return. Another day
passes, and another. A week passes, then another. I decide
to stop counting. Still, they don't come home.

My jaw feels so tight, I am afraid my teeth could
shatter into a million pieces. "Too young, too young."
Delfina's voice has the cadence of prayer. "Do you have
a headache, Celeste?" I nod. She reaches out and rubs
my temples with her fingers. They are still wet with olive
oil, the softness of cilantro from the soup she's just made.
My head aches all the time since my parents disappeared.
And none of their medicines or Delfina's herbal remedies
can lift the weight of this constant fear from my shoulders.

"Sit down and eat while Delfina feeds Doña Frida.
You both are getting the look of air. Then once you are
fed, ask for a sign."

It feels good to sit. I feel so very tired, though I hardly
do anything but lie on my bed and wonder all day. I take a
few bites of the chicken and vegetable soup that I know is

so delicious. I have slurped it up a million times and licked the dribbles from my chin with a smile. But now everything is less than what it was before. I loved eating so much, and now it is work, and I wouldn't bother if Nana Delfina weren't here taking care of me. My throat is constricted too, so that I nearly choke on each swallow. And with each swallow I can't help but wonder if my parents have anything to eat.

Nana Delfina returns quickly from Abuela Frida's room. "She is asleep," Delfina says with a sigh. "But Delfina left the soup on her night table, with her rosemary bread soaking in the bowl." My Nana Delfina's wise eyes miss nothing. She sees I am struggling to eat. She quickly fills her own bowl and sits beside me. She rubs my back gently. And almost by magic my chest opens up bit by bit. It is easier to breathe, and the taste returns to the food. Delfina stays like that until I have eaten every bite of soup. Patient and quiet, she lets her own soup cool until I put my spoon down in my empty bowl and say, "Eat, Nana Delfina. You take care of all of us! Who takes care of you?"

"God and her ancestors take care of Delfina, Querida." She smiles. "You never have to worry for your nana." I lean my head against her shoulder as she eats her soup. I can hear her heart beat and the strange gurgling sound of her belly, like when two little tides collide and swirl together in a hollow stretch of sand. I think about Nana

Delfina's faith. It's so strong, like her straight back and wrinkled brown arms.

"What are you thinking, my Celeste?" she asks as she pushes her bowl away. I am thinking about my parents, but instead I say, "Where were you born, Nana?"

"Delfina was born in Cautín, the place where the forests and the desert and the sea merge into one."

"That's where you learned your magic, verdad, Nana Delfina?"

"Yes, that is true, niña. Delfina's ancestors taught Delfina to heal. They passed on knowledge with their voices. You know some words of Nana's language from the songs she sings to you. But you can't write the words down in your notebook. Mapudungún is an oral language. It is sacred and can only be kept safe on your tongue."

She looks deep into my eyes. "When you are older," she says, "Delfina will pass many secrets on to you. She will teach you to dry peppers and grind them with cumin, coriander seeds, and salt to make merquén to season foods." Delfina pauses to glance at me mischievously, because she knows I am always more eager for mysteries than for housework! "And she will teach you to visit with your guardian spirits in your dreams." I smile for the first time in weeks.

"¡Sí, sí! I would love that, Nana!" My arms tighten around her, and a laugh bursts from her lips like a pink balloon.

The **Sign**

Although Abuela Frida does not let me open the windows, that night I crack my bedroom window up a few inches. Nana told me to ask for a sign, and so I pray for something to arrive from heaven. I imagine that a piece of candy, having escaped a sad birthday party, might arrive. But all throughout the night I feel nothing, not even the wind.

It is hard to fall asleep surrounded by so much nothingness, so much silence that it seems I am in another city, a strange city inhabited by the dead. At dawn, when I finally have fallen asleep, I am startled awake by the sound of a loud cry. It's the old pelican! He came back!

"Good morning," I whisper, fearing my voice will be heard by the scowling, uniformed men who patrol the streets enforcing the curfew. The pelican flies closer to my window. Suddenly he taps his giant beak against the glass. That's when my eyes fall upon an envelope tucked into the windowpane. It must have been left there overnight! I snatch the damp paper, my mouth open wider than the pelican's beak with shock. When I look up, the old pelican is flying toward the harbor. I clutch the letter to my chest. My heart beats a song of wonder and gratitude.

I sit cross-legged on my bed open the letter, and see a familiar handwriting. Mamá! I hold my breath and read:

My beloved Celeste,

How are you, little star? What have you written in your blue notebook? How is your dolls' garden and your grandmother? How is the house? Has the roof blown away yet?

Your father and I are safe. We are staying by the ocean, kept safe by the good will of brave friends.

Keep faith that liberty will return to Chile soon. Each day I dream of seeing you.

Papá and I send our love.
Your mother, Esmeralda

I run into my grandmother's room. She is still in her bed, half-asleep and half-dressed. Abuela Frida said that if anyone came to look for us, it was always better to have clean underwear on.

"Abuela Frida, look what arrived!" She blinks again and again as she recognizes her daughter's handwriting. Abuela's eyes widen into oceans.

She presses the place where my mother signed "Esmeralda" to her lips.

Uncertainty **Crackles** in Each Corner

I wake up early to a blue room filled with shadows. I curl up on my side and try to count how long it has been since I received Mamá's letter. Time has passed so slowly. Each day is like one immensely long spaghetti that we choke on here, prisoners in our own house.

I sit up and look out the window. Valparaíso is still enveloped in a heavy fog. I lie back down. I have no energy, no desire to be awake. I feel so tired of having to stay near my house at all times. At least I can go to my roof! I feel as if every time I ask Abuela Frida or Delfina a question about what's happening in the world outside, all I hear are confused words that are worse than their silence. Uncertainty crackles in each corner of the house.

At breakfast the three of us are so quiet that every time I chew my toast, the sound echoes through my skull and makes it throb. Abuela Frida, who lives half her days in another world and the other half in fear, breaks the silence when she reaches across the table and grips my arm tight. Her hand is wrinkled and bony but strong. She presses my flesh as if she is afraid of losing it. "Celeste, I have to ask you to not climb on the roof anymore. I know how much you love to, Querida, but since there is a curfew, now any crazy person could see you up there and shoot you!"

I glance pleadingly at Delfina, but she nods emphatically. Abuela Frida continues, "And, Celeste, don't wear those jeans anymore, even when you are in the house. We never know who might knock on the door, and the military demands that girls dress only in skirts and do up their hair in proper buns. And your hair, Celeste, is wilder than even your mother's when she was your age."

I scowl and pull my arm away. "Abuela Frida, am I still allowed to laugh?"

The anger in my voice takes us all by surprise. Delfina looks down at her brown palms. But Abuela Frida's bumblebee voice is gentle. I am the one who sometimes speaks with a stinger. "Of course you can laugh. But now it is better to laugh softly, in whispers."

I look at my grandmother's blue eyes in her frail face. They still sparkle like stars in the sky, like a map of her inner world. I get up from the table and sit at her feet. I feel her hands play with my tangled strands of hair as she says, her voice low but strong, "Celeste, the country is enduring what your mamá calls earthquakes of the soul. Never in Chile have I seen neighbor turn against neighbor. I would never have imagined that in this country someone could knock on your door and pull you from your bed, tell you they are taking you for only a few short hours, and then interrogate you with violence. That you could never be heard from again, and from then on they call you 'disappeared.' Celeste, I wish I could protect you from knowing anything of evil, but it would be wrong to hide the truth from you. People, more and more people, are disappearing."

I look up at Abuela Frida. Her jaw is set with a strength that gives me the courage to ask what I most dread. "Like my classmates disappeared? And some teachers suddenly returned to the places they came from? Is that, is that . . ."—my voice falters—"why Mamá and Papá had to go into hiding?"

"Sí. This earthquake we are living in is called dictatorship. It is called intolerance. Never forget these words. They are the words I escaped on the Ship Called Hope so many years ago."

Cuchuflí
and Abuelo
José

That night I knock on Abuela Frida's bedroom door to wish her good night. She is lying in bed, the sheets tucked up to her chin, gazing at the picture of my grandfather on her bedside table.

"¿Abuela Frida?"

"¿Sí?"

"Abuela Frida, tomorrow is Sunday. I want to go down to the city like we used to. We can still go out as long as we are home before curfew, right? I promise to do my hair up and wear my blue pleated skirt."

My grandmother looks at me for a long, long time. "Well then, tomorrow we will call Alejandro and ask him to drive us."

I sit up with a bounce and clap my hands, and tiny Abuela Frida bobs up and down on the mattress like a fishing boat in the bay. "¡Gracias, Abuela! I am so excited!"

Abuela Frida wears a mischievous smile. "To tell you the truth, I am too! You aren't the only one who is sick of being stuck in the house. We'll have such fun! I wish I could take you to buy cuchuflí wafers! Would you believe your grandfather and I used to buy a pack of four for a single peso?"

"Oh, I haven't tasted cuchuflí in such a long time, Abuela! I love how they are shaped like flutes, but instead of music they are filled with sweetness."

Abuela Frida gasps. "Celeste, that's exactly what your Abuelo José would say when he'd bite into one!" I rest my chin on my knees and watch my grandmother travel back to the days when she was a beautiful young girl from Vienna. "It's a shame you never met your Abuelo José. He had such green eyes! I would tell him he must have an immense, verdant forest in his soul. He was the most generous person I ever met. You remember that I met him on the ship that brought me to Chile?"

"Sí, Abuela Frida. On the Ship Called Hope."

She suddenly pulls me into a tight hug. "Oh, what I wouldn't give to see those white sails and feel his arms around me once more!"

Dreaming
Runs in the Family

Alejandro arrives the next day to take us down to the harbor. He used to just beep the horn of his taxi when he came to pick us up, but today he gets out and quietly raps on the door.

Usually the silver-haired taxi driver was always laughing. When I was little, I thought that God had given him extra teeth, his smile was so big. But today his face is grim—he doesn't even smile when Abuela Frida comes to the front door with a flourish. As always she is dressed elegantly in an orchid dress and pearl necklace and earrings.

As Alejandro begins to drive down the hill, I stick my head out the window and wave to Nana Delfina, who is standing at the front door whispering prayers of protection for us. "Celeste"—Abuela Frida tugs on my blouse—"please stay in the car. You know we have to take more care now." I roll up the window, and Abuela Frida smoothes the pieces of flyaway hairs back into my braids.

"I'm sorry. Can you believe I actually forgot for a minute, Abuela?"

"Well, that's nothing to be sorry about, Querida. But we must keep our wits about us and not get lost in dreamland. You know how dreaming runs in the family! Don't you agree, Don Alejandro?"

I actually see a wide grin in the rearview mirror.

"After forty years serving you, Doña Frida, I do know something about dreams."

"See, that's why I only ever call Don Alejandro, Celeste! We know that wherever we travel, we always make it back home to Butterfly Hill."

We fall into silence as we gaze out the window. All the shops and cafés are closed. I can't even smell empanadas baking. I look to Abuela Frida in dismay. She reads my thoughts and tells me, "The Dictator has forbidden businesses opening on Sundays."

We turn onto the Paseo 21 de Mayo. The wide avenue, usually filled with couples walking arm in arm and street vendors selling everything from lemonades to rainbow-colored kites, looks so empty. But the air is still thick with the lush scent of honeysuckles. Abuela Frida has grown very quiet, her brow furrowed in thought.

"What's wrong, Abuela Frida? Do you feel well?"

"Sí, sí, Querida." She pats my hand. "But I think some fresh sea air will do me good! Alejandro, can you take us down to the beach?"

With **Abuela**
on the Shore

We remain quiet for a while, enjoying the feel of the soft white sand on our bare legs. The tides seem to creep in and retreat on tiptoes. Maybe the sea is afraid to make too much noise. Even the air has changed. The wind smells less of salt and more of ashes. But I don't share any of this with Abuela Frida. I glance at her sitting with her legs crossed like a proper lady, even in the sand. Her blue eyes are fixed on the blazing horizon.

She must sense my eyes upon her. Without moving her gaze, she says, "The sun will set soon— I want to talk to you before it gets dark and we have to return home. Celeste of my soul, I have something to tell you."

My heart takes a tumble . . . "something to tell you" . . . lately nothing happy ever follows those words.

"I am listening, Abuela."

"Celeste, the situation in this country is going from bad to worse. Your parents have gone into hiding so that they don't put us in danger, but . . ."

My grandmother turns at last to face me as I nod hesitantly. How frail my poor abuela looks! But her voice is resolute as she continues, "But the danger creeps closer still. We need, Celeste—we need to send you to live for a while with your Tía Graciela."

Tía Graciela? Tía Graciela! My mother's big sister. I haven't seen her in years. She lives in one of the northernmost parts of the United States, thousands and thousands and thousands of miles from Chile.

Then the actual meaning of my grandmother's words sinks in like a knife. Suddenly I find myself on my feet, clasping my hands and yelling.

"No! Please, Abuela Frida! Don't make me leave! Please don't make me leave! I can't leave you and Nana Delfina!"

I am drowning. They can't send me away! They can't! I throw myself onto my grandmother's lap. She lets me cry and cry until I no longer can.

"¡Ay, Abuela!" My throat burns. I whisper, but it feels like a scream. "What about Mamá and Papá? They could come back soon! And I wouldn't be here! Or . . . what if they need me to help them?"

Abuela Frida wipes sand that has stuck to my face. "Celeste, your parents would want you to leave. We discussed this possibility." She brushes the sand from her gloves and tells me more. "They did not want to frighten you more than you were already, but I think you should know the truth. Esmeralda and Andrés received death threats. And now . . . and now that they have fled, it seems that the government . . ." Abuela's voice grows unsteady, but her eyes hold mine. "Now it is not safe for you, either. Your parents told me to use my better judgment in regards to your safety. I have prayed about this, Celeste. It is best that we live apart for a time. Right now Chile is no place for a young girl to grow up."

I shake my head in disbelief. "But . . ."

"Believe me. I already have too much experience with these sorts of situations."

"I know, Abuela Frida."

She looks out at the red ball of light sinking toward the sea, and speaks to me in German. "My mother sent me away because she didn't want a young girl to be exposed to the cruelty Jews were experiencing in Vienna."

Abuela Frida takes a quick, raspy breath. I hold her hand hard, afraid of her memories. "I remember my mother sewing her jewels into the lining of my winter coat. Then she put it on me and buttoned it all the way up. I didn't want to let go of her, but she pushed me out the door and into the street, where a car was waiting for me. Inside was the young Austrian couple I've told you about. They risked their lives to get me out of the country . . ."

Abuela Frida's voice softens to an echo. "Celeste,

I am an only child like you. I believe that if my parents had known they would die if they stayed in Vienna, they would have come with me. My mother, my father, my grandparents, aunts, and uncles—my entire family died. Only a few months after I escaped, the Nazis raided our house in the night. An Austrian refugee I met in Santiago confirmed my worst fears. He had had his violins repaired by my father, and recognized him among the thousands of people waiting—waiting like animals in pens—for the train to take them to a concentration camp. But I never found out where and when it was that they died."

Abuela Frida takes her handkerchief from her pocket and presses it over her nose and mouth.

"Oh, Abuela Frida!" I put my arms around her, sobbing. "I'm so very sorry."

Abuela Frida takes one of my braids, unbraiding and rebraiding it, for a long time. "So you see, Celeste of my soul, I have to take every precaution when it comes to taking care of you."

I tighten my arms around her slight frame—so tight, I must be hurting her—but I feel I can never let her go.

"Mi amor, I am sorry. You are still a little girl, and it's not right to plunge you into so much sadness. Forgive me."

All I can do is hold my Abuela Frida until my arms tremble. She always tells me to save my tears for joy, but I can't help crying again. Abuela Frida's thin body also shakes and sobs. It seems we could fill the beach with another ocean.

I cry until I fall into a light sleep. And I dream that the ocean opens to form a ring of protection around us. And overhead fly white pelicans, illuminating the night that has sunk into my heart.

"Celeste mía, wake up, Querida. The sun is setting, and Alejandro is waiting to take us home." I open my eyes as she says, "Remember. You'll only be gone for a short while. I have faith that this country will come back to life. But in the meantime you will be safe. I will pray that time passes quickly. And soon you'll return to our house on Butterfly Hill."

A Seashell and a
Green **Shawl**

Sleep is impossible that night. I toss and turn and turn and toss. My mind races with fears—about leaving my family, my friends, my country—and then suddenly the strangest worry will divert my attention.

What if the pelicans start to fly by my window again? What will they think if I'm not here to say good morning? Who will water my dolls' garden? And then another big worry takes over: I don't speak English. How will I talk to people? How will I know what's going on?

At dinner I asked Abuela Frida about not speaking the language. Delfina had made my favorite humitas, but I could barely swallow, let alone taste them. "Graciela will be there to help you," Abuela Frida said with a wave of her hand, as if trying to sweep English to the corners of the kitchen and the far recesses of my mind. "And you will learn. Just as I learned to speak Spanish when I came to Valparaíso. Poco a poco. Little by little."

I finally give up trying to sleep and sneak up to the roof to watch the night sky brighten into dawn. The sea swells turn pink beneath the first rays of the sun. It is beautiful to watch. And as the light reaches my eyes, I bow my head and pray for my parents, Abuela Frida, and Nana Delfina. "Please keep them safe. Let us all be together again soon."

I know it is time to go. My hands tremble as I slip back into my blue bedroom. My throat tightens, but I hold back my tears so I can take one last good look at my wall full of words. "Tears should be saved for happiness," I repeat Abuela Frida's words to myself. I remember hearing them so often as a little girl, when I would trip and fall or spill my ice cream in the grass. "Tears are for happiness, Celeste." Maybe if I save my tears, happiness will follow?

I run my hands over my desk, my chair, my photo album. I didn't pack many clothes in the small turquoise suitcase that used to belong to Abuela Frida. Delfina gave me her green shawl, woven so many years ago by her own mother. "When you put it on, Celeste," she said, "you'll be wearing a hug from Delfina."

I bring a picture of Abuela Frida beside her lilacs, and a portrait of my parents on their wedding day. But none of Delfina—"I want you to only carry Nana's picture in your heart, where you can see it best," she tells me.

I also have the class photo that was taken before I left school, but so many are missing! Lucila. Ana. I will have to keep their faces in my heart as well. And the ones who are still here? What will they think when they discover I am gone? Will Marisol and Cristóbal Williams be hurt that I haven't said good-bye?

Abuela Frida wants me to leave Butterfly Hill so quickly, and without saying good-bye to anyone! "It's safer for everyone if they find out you're gone once you are safe in the United States," she tells me firmly in German, and even though she doesn't even speak German, Delfina nods in agreement! No adiós? No hasta luego, see you soon? It makes me feel like I will never see my friends again! And when I think about how I can't say good-bye to my parents, a new lump of sadness rises in my throat, then one of fear. Will Gloria tell her father once she figures it out? Will she betray me? "Please, amiga," I whisper into the air. "You have been my friend since we were five years old. You will always be my friend. Please keep my secret safe."

There Are No Good-byes, Only **Returns**

The morning of my departure, I open the front door like a sleepwalker. Don Alejandro and his car are waiting for me. The only thing I feel is the knot in my stomach when I think of my grandmother. She has been in bed since yesterday morning, so fragile and wrapped in so many blankets that she reminded me of an onion with its thin, delicate skin. Last night I kissed her good night like I always do, and she said, "See you in the morning, Celeste of my soul," and closed her shiny eyes. I know Abuela Frida can't bear to say good-bye.

"Here, take these." Delfina presses a little brown pouch into my hand. "These are seeds that you should plant in your new land." She kisses my forehead and says, "The wisdom of the Lord will protect you. Have faith and believe in the universe." She runs inside.

I walk slowly down the stone steps. I see my dolls' garden, and my one old pelican hovering above. "No good-byes. Tears are for happiness." I keep whispering these words to myself, hoping they will come true. All of a sudden I hear a commotion in the sky and turn back. The old, slow pelican—my favorite—is squawking and swooping low, banging his wings against the roof.

When I lower my gaze in wonder, I see my Abuela Frida standing at the window. She is wrapped in an enormous orange scarf, waving. Her lips tremble, but I can read them as they slowly move in her beautiful, wrinkled face.

"I love you too, Abuela Frida! See you soon!" I call. Her smile is the last thing I see before Alejandro helps me into the car.

The Road to
Santiago

Dew covers the grasses and wildflowers that grow alongside the highway to Santiago. I have seen snow fall only out in the country, near the mountains, but soon I will see snow fall in a city, and I don't even know how to say "snow" in English. Everything I will see, everything I will hear, will be unknown to me. I only know Tía Graciela. I haven't seen her since I was eight years old. Will she recognize me? Will she have changed?

I try to count the butterflies that fly by, just like I did when I was little: uno, dos, tres, anything to keep my mind still for just a few seconds! Cuatro, cinco . . .

Alongside the valley rises the tallest mountain in all the Americas, Mount Aconcagua. It fills my eyes like a snow squall. "I don't see the ocean anymore, Alejandro."

"The sea is there. She is just behind you now."

Behind me. So much behind me: the sea with its taste of salt; the hills; and the fireflies like big, bright bunches of grapes. Behind me is the roof of my house. And the sky above my roof. Is it the same sky over us now? Will they be the same stars over Juliette Cove, where my aunt lives, or will I have to find a new map of the sky?

"Celeste!"

I jump, startled, as Alejandro's low voice shakes me from my thoughts. "Don't think so much, niña. Right now you have to move forward and not look back. But when you are up there in the North, have one eye see ahead and one watching behind you. Be careful of unknown things, but also have faith, Niña Celeste. God is everywhere. Wherever you go, he is there."

"I'll do what you say, Don Alejandro."

He nods at me in the rearview mirror. "Muy bien, Niña Celeste." I never noticed how strong Alejandro's gaze is before now. "And now something to fill your mind with sweeter thoughts," he says as he slows the taxi and pulls to the side of the highway. Behind a yellow stand with a sign that says MERIENDAS! SNACKS! are a small old woman and a little boy. Alejandro gets out of the car and returns with an alfajor.

"Thank you!" I bite into my favorite sweet: caramel spread thick between two crisp shortbread cookies and covered with powdered sugar. Will I ever find someone on Juliette Cove so good to me as Don Alejandro? Why must we leave someone to realize how much we love them?

Tío
Bernardo

Tío Bernardo is waiting for me outside the airport. I see him as the taxi approaches the curb that says INTERNATIONAL DEPARTURES. He opens the back door and reaches in for me. "Celeste!" He hugs me, and I hang on to his neck as if I could climb him like a tree and escape everything.

He isn't really my uncle, but I call him that because he is my father's best friend. When I was younger, I would call him Oso, because he reminded me of a bear with his broad, hairy arms and scruffy black beard. Papá and Tío Bernardo have known each other since medical school, and like Papá, he works in a hospital for the poor, in Santiago.

I can't bear saying good-bye to Alejandro. "Thank you, Don Alejandro. For everything." Alejandro's eyes fill with tears.

"Gracias a ti. Thank you, niña. Remember, God is everywhere."

I am still clinging to Tío Bernardo, and he walks like that, with me in one arm and the suitcase in the other, through the airport doors. Then he puts me down, and I peer over my shoulder at Alejandro's old taxi rolling away.

"Niña Celeste, you have grown a bit!" I turn back toward my uncle. "How beautiful you look, almost a señorita!"

It's hard to speak. "Gracias, Tío Bernardo."

"This is your first time flying in an airplane, no?" I gulp and nod. He holds me close again. "I promise you will have a good trip. The plane is like a steel pelican." He laughs and then so do I.

I whisper, "Sí, Tío Bernardo." Then I have to ask, "Do you know anything about my parents? Have you had any word from them?"

"I only know that they both are safe."

Tío Bernardo walks me to the gate where I will board the plane. He places a ticket in my hand and gently tugs the passport that dangles from my neck. "I have to leave you now. Just hand the lady your ticket, and when you get on the plane, look for your seat, 14A." I nod, blinking back tears. A woman's voice, so pleasant it seems unreal, announces that boarding for the flight to Boston has begun.

"Please, pequeña, if anyone speaks to you or asks you anything, just say you are going on vacation. Don't say anything else. There are informants everywhere." Tío Bernardo kisses both my cheeks. "God bless you, Celeste! ¡Adiós!"

Steel **Pelican**

I look out the window as the plane rises into the air. The landscape passes quickly. The wide green valleys suddenly grow narrow. The steel wing disappears as the plane enters a cloud. All is white. When we emerge, the ground below is full of shadows. Then sunlight returns to dance over the vineyards. I hear the words of Abuela Frida in happier days: "Wine is a yellow sun in a crystal goblet. One taste of Chile's earth and sky could delight the whole world." And over everything before my eyes, over every voice that echoes in my head, rise the mountains. The Andes. They rise and fall eternally. I can't imagine a place on earth where their peaks don't touch the sky. Yet they become smaller and smaller as the plane rises higher. Soon I won't be able to see them. My last look at Chile. My last look at Chile! I feel a pain like a knife in my heart, and suddenly, finally, after holding back tears all day, I am crying. A moan like from some sad hidden animal comes from inside me. Sobbing and shaking with my face against the window.

The young man in the blue suit and tie in the seat beside me pats me on the shoulder. I turn even closer to the window, hide my face in my hands, and try to contain my sobbing. After a while I feel his hand gently patting the top of my head. I glance at him. His curly blond hair and rosy cheeks make him look like Nana Delfina's statue of the Archangel San Miguel. My sobs slowly sputter out into sniffles. Salty tears dry on my cheeks as I sleep for the first time in days.

When I awake, the plane's cabin is in semidarkness. I glance over at the man beside me and watch as he writes in a notebook. I love the familiar sound of a pen scribbling fast over a blank page. I don't recognize any of the words, but I think they are English. Maybe he is a writer?

Nana is always asking San Miguel for a sign. I think she must have magically sent him to watch over me . . . and remind me of something too! I watch the rosy-cheeked man turn to a fresh page in his notebook, and I lean my head back and make a promise:

I, Celeste Marconi, promise to never forget. I promise that these mountains, so white like the powdered sugar that still sticks to my fingers from Alejandro's cookies, will never be distant. I promise to always return to them in my writing. I will write the

Andes with the thread of the moon that I carry with me all the way north. And this moonlight will guide my pen to weave stories.

I close my eyes to hold on to the memory of all I leave behind.

PART II
In the North

Welcome to the USA

I arrive in the city of Boston, Massachusetts, at dawn. I walk with sleepy eyes from the tarmac to the noisy metal carousel where luggage from the flight is turning round and round. I spot the tiny turquoise suitcase that has just emerged from a black rectangle in the wall and lift it from the conveyer belt, glad that Abuela Frida told me to pack light.

Passing through customs is much easier than I feared. Once I make it to the front of the long line, a police officer with a thick yellow mustache leans over to look at me and then looks at my passport. "Vacation?" he asks.

"Yes," I whisper, my heart beating in my throat.

"Enjoy your stay, Miss Marconi," he replies, waving the next person forward.

I walk cautiously through two big swinging doors, and immediately I spot my redheaded Tía Graciela among the throngs of people waiting. She is jumping up and down, waving her long arms, and calling "¡Celeste, aquí! ¡Aquí! Over here!" I run into her arms, and she greets me in English, "Celeste, welcome to the USA!"

We laugh and she squeezes me tighter. I feel such relief. "How happy I am to have you here, Querida! It's been so long!" Her voice—it's like my mother's yet different, all at the same time.

"Button your coat up, Celeste, and here, wrap my scarf around your neck," Tía Graciela tells me, starting to walk to another set of doors. "We are going outside, and you have never felt such cold as January in New England! We still have to drive a couple of hours to get to Juliette Cove." And she is right! As soon as we walk into the parking lot, a penetrating cold stings my cheeks and makes my nose run like a faucet.

Even my bones hurt, and my voice sounds funny emerging from between chattering teeth: "¡Que frío, Tía! How cold it is!"

"It feels like we're in the North Pole, right?" Tía Graciela laughs. "You'll get used to it, but I have to admit, I am still not completely a fan of this cold!" I watch my breath leave my body like big puffs of smoke.

The Gray of the
North

The roads are empty. In the dim light of early morning I
see only pile after pile of dirty snow and the dark outline
of trees lining either side of the highway. Once in a while
I catch a glimpse of headlights from a car very far behind
us or very far ahead. "Tía Graciela, why is there almost
nobody on the road? Because it's so early?"

My aunt smiles and says, "Celeste, here you almost
never see anyone. I suppose people keep to themselves.
But you will get used to solitude. And the day will even
come when you love it." I watch my hands fold and unfold
on my lap. They are red with cold. Tía Graciela reaches
over with her right hand and clasps both my hands in
her one. She laughs. "Your hands are the same, still so
small!" And then she says, "I remember how on Butterfly
Hill nobody is ever alone. From morning to midnight
people are making noise: talking, arguing, calling for one
another, laughing at jokes, humming old songs. And the
noises from the kitchens! How the pots and pans would
whistle until so late into the night! Remember?"

"It was always like that but not anymore. Now everyone is afraid, and there is such an eerie silence. But even so, Tía, I could still hear the neighbors whisper if I sat very still on the roof and closed my eyes. Even with the curfew, Butterfly Hill never felt as frozen and empty as this."

"Here things are different, mi amor. Something I learned to do—it's very difficult and took a long time—is to braid my own voice into the silence of day and of night. The silences when the sky is dark and when it is light are distinct. I learned that, too. And I learned to speak to them both."

I look at my aunt. She has changed so much. She never used to talk like that, in riddles and poems. I don't understand her, but I am happy to have her. I lean over and kiss her hand, still encircling my own.

"Gracias, mi Celeste. It does my heart such good to have you here with me," she says, and she drives the rest of the gray highway with her left hand on the steering wheel and a smile stretched like a rainbow over her pale, thin face.

I think about what Mamá told me when I was a little girl and Tía Graciela suddenly left Valparaíso without saying good-bye. "She has given her heart away, Querida, and so now she must follow it." My mother's words confused me, but she looked so sad that I didn't ask her to explain more. Instead I crept downstairs late that night and sat under the table, where my parents and Abuela Frida were sipping cognac.

"It's that famous Argentine tango dancer, Guillermo Garela, Mamá," my mother explained to Abuela Frida. "Remember? Graciela and I went to see him perform last month? He ran over to us right after the curtain went down, kissed Graciela's hand, and told her he had been so distracted by her rose-red hair during the entire performance that he'd feared tripping over his own two feet! He invited her to have dinner the next day. She accepted, and has been seeing him ever since."

"Esmeralda! How could you girls keep this a secret from me?" Abuela Frida's voice was unusually sharp.

"It wasn't my secret to tell, Mamá."

"Forgive me, hija. I am just upset. Tell me more."

"Last week Guillermo found out that his dance company is moving on to Canada, and so Graciela decided to follow him to Montreal."

"¡Ay! Why couldn't your sister at least have said good-bye?" my abuela asked.

I heard my father, silent until then, cough to clear his throat like he always does when he is upset.

"I don't know, Mamá. But she promises to call soon. I think she was afraid you would try to stop her."

"Ay, Esmeralda. I know you are my youngest, but oftentimes I feel Graciela is my baby. She has my own mother's love of romance and wanderlust inside her."

"Wanderlust . . . romance . . ." Now, four years later, I am wondering how such exciting words eventually led my aunt to live alone in such a cold and dark part of the world, when she pulls the car off an exit and onto a small stone road full of small hills and sharp curves.

"This is Juliette Cove! Roll down the window, Celeste," Tía Graciela urges. I look at her like she's crazy but do what she says. Immediately the car is filled with icy wind. "Now take a deep, deep breath!"

I close my eyes and inhale. "Oh! Tía!" The smell of salt air, almost like home, enters my nostrils. And something new, a scent so strong and yet so sweet, it tickles my throat.

"That's pine, Celeste. Pine trees."

I turn my eyes toward the sky. Everywhere I see are enormous trees of deep green, covered in what look like shaggy fur coats speckled with snowflakes. I stick my head out the window, suddenly unaware of the cold as we emerge into a clearing and I see the ocean.

"Your first view of the Atlantic, Celeste."

We drive along tall cliffs and small coves with docks where fishermen tie their boats. The small vessels rock back and forth in the gentle morning swells. "They seem to have been sleeping for years and years," I tell my aunt. And I notice that the ships, the sea, the sky, even the snow, everything is a shade of gray. "Tía Graciela, I have never seen this gray before."

"Yes, it caught my attention when I first arrived too. In Valparaíso everything is so blue! But this is the gray of Maine, Celeste mía."

"It seems so sad, Tía."

"Sí, but you will get used to it, and believe me, one day you will even miss it. It is a gray full of mysteries. If you take a moment to look at it, you will see that this gray contains a light. It's a color that promises the sun's arrival. It's a gray that has been part of the history of this coast and that poets and painters have fallen in love with because behind its fragile light lies another light. The lights are waiting for you to discover them too."

We drive the Coast Road a little farther in silence. Then at a green, snow-topped sign with the unfamiliar words "River Road," Tía Graciela slows the car and turns onto a bumpy dirt road that seems no wider than a path through the forest. I reach my hand out the window and touch snow-dusted branches. I lick my fingers to taste the snow. And suddenly we enter another clearing in the forest, and Tía Graciela says, "Welcome home."

I gasp. The small gray house with green shutters is surrounded by a yard full of tall trees. "Those are oak. Wait until you see how beautiful they are in autumn," Tía Graciela tells me excitedly as she parks the car.

"And it's all hidden under snow now, but there's thick green grass that you will love to lie in, and small wildflowers, and I always plant a garden with flowers and vegetables too!" I listen to my aunt's happy chatter as I step out of the car and hop up and down to try to wake my legs up after the long ride. "Careful you don't slip on any ice!" Tía Graciela calls. She has already carried my suitcase to the front door. "I will have to teach you to walk in the winter. You'll need snow boots, and maybe ice skates! Would you like to learn?"

I nod, but my attention is distracted by a gobbling sound from a cluster of oaks. "Tía, what . . ."

My aunt smiles mischievously and calls out, "Come out, you all! Don't tell me you're suddenly shy." One by one a family of wild turkeys emerges.

"Wow!" I count, "One, two, three, four . . ."

"There are eight in all, Celeste. They live in the forest." Tía Graciela laughs. "But really they live in this yard and on the food I sometimes leave out for them. Especially in the winter, it's hard for them in this deep snow." The turkeys are both strange and beautiful at the same time.

"I love the emerald color on their feathers," I say.

"Yes, just wait," my aunt says. "They will grow on you and become good friends. And look over there, by the bushes. That's my shy one—she comes once in a while to have a snack."

My eyes follow my aunt's gaze and land upon a small brown deer. The deer's eyes are like two black moons. "Oh, how pretty!"

"Creatures like this don't live in cities like Valparaíso, Celeste," my aunt whispers, "so maybe you won't mind living here in the country for a while. Now come inside and see your home!" I take one more look at the deer and gulp back tears. I never knew it was possible to feel such sadness standing before something so beautiful.

"Sí, Tía. Gracias."

A Blue Room in the **North**

Tía Graciela sets my suitcase down in the hallway. "First things first! Go see your bedroom! It's up those stairs." The white stairs are shaped like a seashell; they swirl round and round and up and up. My room is so high up that it feels like a tree house. Then I gasp—there is a small window in the ceiling so I can see the tops of the trees that lean over the house. I'll be able to look at the stars from my bed! And then I notice the walls. They are blue! The exact same shade of blue as my bedroom on Butterfly Hill. And my bed has a blue bedspread, and a big blue pillow with green and purple flowers embroidered on it. Oh. Oh!

Tía Graciela appears in the doorway, my suitcase in hand. "Oh, Tía! My room is beautiful! Thank you!" I cry out.

"I am so glad, Querida. Don't you love the skylight? And I painted the walls when I heard you were coming. I want it to remind you of your blue room at home. I want this house on Juliette Cove to be your home, your home away from home, okay?" I nod and run to hug her.

Then I ask her what Abuela Frida was not able to explain to me. "Tía, why did you come to Juliette Cove?"

Tía Graciela goes over to the window and fusses with the curtains, sliding them this way and that. "Oh, one day I just knew it was time to leave Montreal." Her cheerful voice sounds forced. "I looked at a map and saw a name that reminded me of Shakespeare's story about love lasting beyond death . . . and so"—her voice falters—"and so . . . I decided to come here. Simple as that!"

Tía Graciela turns from the window and smiles a smile that is too wide, too bright. It doesn't match the shadow in her eyes. She changes the subject brusquely. "I am heating up some chicken soup for you. Why don't you unpack, and I will come and get you when it's ready."

"Okay, Tía." I turn back to face my blue walls. "Okay," I say again, wiping my tired, teary eyes, and add, mostly to myself, "Maybe I will just lie down on my new blue bedspread a minute and look at the sky before I unpack. . . ."

I must have slept the whole day, because when I awake, the room is in total darkness. I turn on the little light beside my bed and see that my aunt has left a bowl of soup, some brown bread, and chamomile tea on the wooden dresser. It's cold, but I eat it all anyway. Then I search through my bag to find my flannel pajamas, and as quick as I can, jump under the covers. The night air is cold. I wonder what time it is and if Tía Graciela is still awake. I am afraid to wander around a house I don't yet know. I am afraid to walk in the dark and the cold. Afraid to realize that this is my first night half a world away from Butterfly Hill. I lie staring through the skylight—which I have renamed "starlight."

I flew today, I realize. But in a steel pelican. It seems so long ago somehow. Heavy rains have come to visit me. Drops as big as stones knock on my window. *Bang, bang, bang!* Startled, I get up and stand before the window and press one hand against the glass. My hand feels like it is freezing there, so I draw it back. Immediately a white light appears in its shape in the windowpane. And in the middle of that light a butterfly, copper-colored like the hills of Valparaíso, flaps her wings. I walk backward to my bed and sit in stunned silence. I don't even want to blink. I can't take my eyes away from the butterfly. A light that looks like ocean water fills my bedroom. Suddenly I feel a soft wing brush my forehead. It's a push so gentle, yet I tumble down onto the covers, and my eyes close the moment my head touches the pillow. I sleep. And in my sleep I hear a voice that is like water, and also like light. "This is your blue room on Juliette Cove, where everything is so quiet and still that the only sound and movement is the trembling of your heart. Let your heart speak to me often. I am always listening."

Juliette Cove,
Maine

I wake up in the morning unsure of where I am until I peek out the frosty window. Everything is blanketed with snow, and more is falling; the sky seems filled with white feathers. All of a sudden I feel utterly alone.

I put on my socks and creep down the winding stairs just as Tía Graciela comes in the front door, shaking white from her hair and shoulders. When she takes off her big coat, I notice how very thin my aunt has grown. Her waist curves like a violin. Then she sees me at the bottom of the stairs and smiles like my mother. "Good morning! The snow has come to welcome you, Celeste!"

I follow her to the kitchen with its old wallpaper with yellow flowers and a small white table and two chairs. I sit in one of them and watch my aunt float about the kitchen. "Is toast okay?" she asks.

"Of course!" I smile, knowing full well that toast is one of the only things my Tía Graciela can make!

"Today is a special day, so I will try to prepare some scrambled eggs, too."

Tía Graciela chatters excitedly about the red foxes, along with the deer and wild turkeys, who live in the forest surrounding the house. Poor Tía. It must have been so long since she has had someone to talk to, I think. After breakfast she takes me on a tour of Juliette Cove. Tía Graciela's road lets out onto the Coast Road, which follows the rocky beach. The Atlantic Ocean is gray, the same color of the big overcoats worn by the few residents we see walking down Washington Street, which is where the Coast Road eventually leads.

"This is our main street!" Tía Graciela laughs. "Very different from Valparaíso, no?"

I look out the car window at a convenience store, a pharmacy, and an Italian restaurant called Sal's Pizza. "They have great hamburger pizzas, Celeste," Tía Graciela says. We pass the businesses quickly and drive down Washington Street for as long as it takes me to practice the alphabet twice in English, and arrive at another rocky beach. "This is called Saints' Harbor. I think Delfina would like that name, don't you?"

"Oh!" I cry out. "A lighthouse! It looks just like the one I watch from the roof."

How strange that this lighthouse could look almost exactly like the one in Valparaíso Harbor, when they are so far apart—one so north, the other so south.

Tía Graciela seems to hear my thoughts. "There are

lighthouses all over the world, Celeste," she says. "And harbors where sailors find safety and refuge."

I think I know what she is trying to tell me. "Then . . . maybe, Tía . . . maybe there are other things here that are also at home. And maybe I can find those things . . . and try . . . to be happy."

I Call Them
Friends

In Valparaíso, Tía Graciela had many different jobs. She sometimes was an actress in the community theater, and she sometimes tutored students in Spanish at the university. She even worked as a receptionist in my parents' clinic for a while. But here on Juliette Cove she reads tarot cards for a living. I never even knew she could read the cards!

"I kept the tarot a secret from Mamá," my aunt confides in me, "because I was going through my rebellious teenage years. You know the magician at Café Iris, of course?" I nod, intrigued. "Well, he and I were classmates in high school. He taught me just for fun. I never knew just how much it would come in handy!" Tía Graciela's eyes twinkle with mischief. "Good times or bad, I can always find someone with a question about when they will strike it big! Or"—she winks at me—"about their love lives!"

An incredible idea comes to me, and I blurt out, "Tía! Can you use the tarot to tell me what's happening to Mamá and Papá?!"

"Oh, Celeste." She puts her hands on my shoulders and looks deep into my eyes. "I'm sorry, but I can't. Something El Mago taught me is that magic exists, but it is *we* who create it." She laughs ruefully. "How I wish I *could* predict the future!"

"Then how do you . . . ? But your clients . . . ," I trail off, confused.

"The cards, like the stars, serve as guides for the imagination. It's like a picture book. I just describe what I see. It isn't hard to figure out what people need to hear. I see every word light up in their eyes each time I turn over a card."

I remain quiet, unsure of how I feel about everything she's told me. I look around Tía Graciela's bedroom. Every flat surface—the bureau, the windowsill, the night table—is covered with conch shells.

"I began collecting them as a girl in Valparaíso and never stopped." She looks up toward the three pink shells on the doorframe as her head pops from beneath the folds of her long violet dress—the one she wears when she visits clients. I stifle a laugh as she arranges a turban, also violet, on her head. "Can you help me, Querida?" She points to the red curls sticking out in the back. I tuck them in one by one as she now motions toward her dresser. "I keep the cards in that little bag. Isn't it pretty? It's Chinese silk, and the color reminds me of the sky over Butterfly Hill." Tía Graciela is talking a mile a minute. She must have had too many cafés con leche today . . . or maybe she is just excited to see her clients.

"But why do you have to go out to see them? Isn't all that driving tiring?" I ask her, tucking the last tendril beneath her turban. Ever since I can remember, I have walked or rode a cable car to wherever I needed to go, with the exception of the occasional outing in Don Alejandro's taxi. I am still not used to the idea of driving everywhere. To me, Tía Graciela's station wagon is a stuffy, stifling milk carton on wheels.

"It's good for me to get out, Celeste." She sighs. "I have no true friends here, you know. Well, perhaps the mailman—he does visit every day but Sunday!" She laughs at her own joke. Then her voice turns serious.

"Celeste, many of the people whose homes I visit are old. They are old and they live alone. We drink tea and talk, and I don't need the cards to figure out that I am the first person who has listened to them in a long time."

"Everyone likes to tell their stories," I say, remembering everything I heard under the kitchen table on Butterfly Hill.

"Yes, you would know!" Her face brightens again. "I remember what a snoop you were as a little girl! And still are, most likely!" Tía Graciela takes the blue pouch from the dresser and turns to me. "I'll be back in a few hours, Querida! Hopefully you can find something in the fridge that will do for lunch!"

I follow her to the front door and throw her winter coat over her shoulders before she walks out without it . . . which she seems to do a great deal too much in this cold weather. "Good luck with your clients!" I tell her.

"¡Gracias!" She opens the door, and the winter wind rushes in. "But I don't call them clients, Celeste! I call them friends."

As I bolt the door behind her, I wonder if she accepts eggs for payment like my parents. Then I remember that I'm in America now.

Nostalgia

The Juliette Cove firemen know Tía Graciela well. The first time I see them running into the house, all dressed in red, they seem to me like wild balls of fire, and I actually forget how cold I was. You see, I am learning that Tía Graciela's house always smells of fresh coffee and toast, except on the unlucky mornings when it smells like *burned* toast. My aunt gets distracted easily, and in the mornings she has a habit of forgetting the four slices of wheat bread in the toaster as she stirs sugar into her coffee and stares at the swirls of milk like seafoam and tries to see the future. Sometimes the toast turns so black that smoke fills the house, setting off the scary scream of the fire alarm and forcing us to run into the icy Maine air, wrapped only in our bathrobes.

My aunt is moodier than I remember her and is often looking out the window toward the horizon. In the silence of the afternoons I press my ear against the window's cold glass and almost hear the trees sigh as their branches sway.

When I tell her this, she says, "All winter they stand strong against the wind and bear the weight of the snow."

I answer how I think Abuela Frida would. "Then they must have something to teach us. . . . Is that why I find you at the window so often?"

My aunt doesn't answer my question and instead tells me, "Celeste, show me precisely how to put my ear against the window so that I can hear the trees sigh too."

"I'll bring you something happier!" I say, and scurry upstairs. I return with the pearly conch shell Nana Delfina gave me. "Listen!" I urge my aunt. Tía Graciela puts the shell to her ear.

"The Pacific!" she gasps. Her face brightens, and her head sways ever so slightly to the rhythms she hears inside. She looks so happy that for that moment I forget my own homesickness and say, "You keep it, Tía! You've been away from Valparaíso so much longer." Then I quickly leave her alone before I change my mind.

Sometimes I hear Tía Graciela sing to herself. Other times I hear her crying, not over a pot of potatoes but into her own hands. I run to her room. "What's wrong? Can I help?" And one day I hesitantly ask her, "Do you miss Guillermo?"

But Tía Graciela never talks about the boyfriend she followed all the way from Valparaíso to Montreal, Canada. And Abuela Frida warned me that she wouldn't.

"Oh, little one, it is just the nostalgia." Tía Graciela sniffs into a tissue. "If I let my tears flow, they will finally dry up." I kiss my aunt on the cheek and taste a tear so salty, it's as if it held the entire sea.

I return to my own room and sit on the bed and think. *Nostalgia.* I never liked the sound of that word, and now I know what it means because I have it too— it's missing someone so much that it becomes a part of you, a constant ache. It's getting through another day—waking up, eating breakfast, getting dressed, even taking a walk—while all you think about is the past. I have nostalgia for my parents, my grandmother, and Delfina, who must still be sweeping the doorways with rose water to scare bad spirits away from the house. I miss Cristóbal Williams, too. I hope he is managing to stay awake and keep his magic pendulum hidden! I wonder if others are asking for me, like Marisol and Gloria. And have they found out where Lucila is? Is she hiding like my parents? Or is she safe in some faraway country like I am?

I miss waking up in the morning and saying hello to the pelicans. Have they come back to Butterfly Hill, or are they in hiding too? I hope they're all right. I wonder if they know I'm gone.

I wish I could send a letter, or even better, receive one. ¡Sí! A letter from my parents, and another with news of my friends, and another wrapped with blue yarn from Abuela Frida's scarves. Can't somebody, anybody, tell me anything?! Not knowing drives me crazy. But Tía Graciela says it is too dangerous to send mail to Chile, and even more dangerous to send it here, because the police in Chile read everything.

I rummage through my dresser. Inside the bottom drawer I find a map of Chile I brought from home. I pin it on the wall, next to the calendar I use to count the days since I have seen my parents: sixty-five.

Juliette
Cove Middle
School

On Sunday evening Tía Graciela takes me out for dinner at Sal's Pizza. Not since the plane landed in Boston have I been surrounded by so many strange sounds. Hearing people at other tables speak English without being able to understand it is a scary feeling. It's like being a baby again, not being able to express myself in a way that everyone will understand. It makes me feel trapped.

"Celeste. Earth to Celeste!" Tía Graciela smiles at me between mouthfuls of a hamburger-and-onion slice. "Querida, I want to talk to you about something important. It is time for you to go to school."

School! I don't want to think about going to school here. I don't want to go to school anywhere else but Juana Ross in Valparaíso. It makes everything seem too real. It makes being *here* real. Not just a visit. Not a vacation, like I told the airport security people. I wish that I could keep pretending, but Tía Graciela insists on school. And she insists that my parents would insist.

So the next day I wake up early on Juliette Cove and

eat a bowl of cold cornflakes that make my stomach ache. I walk to the end of River Road wearing Nana Delfina's green shawl over an orange winter coat Tía Graciela found at a secondhand shop. It is way too big for me, but I don't care. With my ears and face wrapped in my long blue scarf, I pretend no one can see me. Maybe the bus driver will just keep going, and I won't have to go to school? But soon a bus the color of a sunflower pulls to the corner where I stand. A young blond woman opens the door for me. I climb on board without looking at anyone, sit in the empty front seat, and pray for a happy day.

Every time the bus stops, the kids get in and run all the way to the back. I am afraid to turn around, but I can hear a lot of laughing and shouting back there. And a lot of English I don't understand. Finally we arrive, and I run off the bus and toward the school with my head down before anyone can notice me.

Juliette Cove Middle School is too dark, as dark as the gray day that seems to be the color of Juliette Cove and the color of Maine. Gray houses, gray umbrellas, gray smiles.

The first thing I notice is that no one wears uniforms, and they chew gum all the time. I tell myself, this is America. One girl offers me gum, and so I start chewing. Her name is Kim. Like me, she is from a faraway place. She is from Korea, and when she speaks,

I think she must have swallowed a bird. I like her a lot, and even though we hardly speak the same language, we become friends.

I spend all day trying to understand the English and watching the mouths of students who seem to never stop chewing gum. They look at me and don't talk to me. When I pass through the school yard at the end of the day, I hear a group of girls making fun of me. I don't understand everything they say, but I feel how mean their words are.

Words like "Latina" and "ugly coat."

Their peals of nasty laughter sting my eyes. I take a deep breath and tell myself, *No llores!* Don't let them see you cry! I pass by them pretending not to hear. They shout after me, "Does she wear that stupid apron with her name on it all the time? Are they sure she belongs in sixth grade?"

Before I turn down the street, I look for Kim, but she seemed to disappear as soon as the bell rang. My feet feel so heavy. The last eight hours—the first day of school—flash through my mind. During math, which I thought might be easier because I am good at math and I don't need to speak English to solve an equation, a loud boy named Charlie kept making fun of my name and imitating my accent every time the teacher turned his back to write on the blackboard. And all those nasty girls exploded into their nasty laughter behind their hands with shiny pink nails.

The teacher is named Mr. Turner. The school is so small that he teaches all the sixth-grade subjects, not like at Juana Ross, where I saw a different teacher each time the bell rang. I liked that, because if I was caught daydreaming or passing notes to Marisol in one class, I could always start fresh in the next. Mr. Turner seems kind, but he speaks in a low drone and seems to make the entire class either sleepy or fidgety. But for half the day I join Kim for special English lessons at the back of the classroom. The English teacher is named Mr. Kendall. He is very old and doesn't seem to like children or teaching at all. He is impatient and doesn't wait to let Kim and me sound out words until we get them right, the way Abuela Frida taught me to speak German. He snaps the answer to us as if he is angry. I've never felt stupid before, and I keep reminding myself what my father once told me: "No one can make you feel inferior without your consent, Celeste."

I wish I could tell Kim this, but I don't know how yet. She shakes like a leaf when Mr. Kendall asks her a question or makes her read out loud. At the end of class I see inky smudges on Kim's worksheets where tears have fallen.

Soaps

Since Mr. Kendall is not much help, I mostly learn to speak English after school by watching the television. I watch it a lot, although I never liked to in Chile. We watch what Tía Graciela calls "my program" when I get home from school. It fills the pit that is always in my stomach, at least for a little while. "This is how *I* learned to speak English," Tía Graciela tells me. She is addicted to *General Hospital*. It is a type of show with a funny name: soap opera. But I know what they are; we have lots of these telenovelas in Chile. I listen to the way all those blond, glamorous-looking Americans speak, and try to make the same gestures. I am good at moving my hands, but my voice sounds like a stranger to me. "But your accent is getting better, Querida!" Tía Graciela encourages me every day.

"Here it is just English, everywhere you turn. But in Valparaíso you heard so many foreign words and voices all mixed together. Remember Madame Lamoreux, who would always speak to us in French?"

Tía Graciela smiles. "It was your mother and I who gave her the nickname Madame Roquefort, like the cheese!"

"And now the whole neighborhood thinks that is her name!" I almost choke on my spaghetti because suddenly I am laughing a real, deep laugh, something I haven't done since I left Chile. "Why did you and Mamá call her after such a smelly cheese, Tía?"

"It wasn't because she smelled. Actually, she always smelled like Chanel perfume. But it was because she thought she was so much more elegant than everyone else on Butterfly Hill. She put on too many airs."

"When I was little, I thought she was called Roquefort because when she came on Tuesdays to have coffee with Abuela Frida, she always brought cheeses wrapped in purple cellophane and tied with a pink ribbon. On Abuela Frida's birthday last year she brought Austrian cheese, and Abuela ate it all in one day!"

Tía Graciela smiles again as I continue, "Madame Roquefort was always telling Abuela Frida that I should learn English. Señora Atkinson, too. Now it seems they were right. But I wanted to learn German."

"I am glad your grandmother taught you, fräulein." Tía sounds funny calling me "little miss" in German. Her accent is terrible! It makes me feel better about my accent in English.

"Everyone is always learning something new," my father would remind me when he checked to see if I was doing my homework and found me gazing out the window at the stars. "If not, why be alive?"

A Winter
Birthday

Winter lasts too, too long on Juliette Cove! I am tired of what feels like months upon endless months of snow blanketing the ground. The yard is like a blank sheet of paper, but instead of imagining stories to write on it, the only words I find are the names of everybody and everything I long for. The snowflakes that fall from the sky remind me of Abuela Frida's hair. How I would love to brush it for her again! My hands, always cold, search for sunlight as warm and bright as Nana Delfina's gap-toothed smile. The cold makes me miss the warm smells of Sunday empanadas and fresh-picked cilantro from the herb garden.

In winter it feels sadder that I have no one at school to talk to. On my hands I draw map after map of the long and thin land whose name reminds me of a bird, and rock myself to sleep saying, "Chile, Chile, Chile."

On February 28th I wake up to frost on the windowpane. The crystals remind me of the stars over Valparaíso Harbor and the hours I would spend on the roof, looking out over Butterfly Hill. I bury myself deeper beneath my comforter. It's cold, and part of me doesn't want to get up because I know what day it is. At home many people would gather around our table to celebrate my birthday, but today I am guessing that only one person will knock on our door—the mailman, Mr. Carter.

How strange to have a birthday in the wintertime! When I was born, it was summertime in the Southern Hemisphere. "All the flowers were blooming that morning," Mamá always told me. February 28th was one of the only days of the year when my parents wouldn't go to the clinic. Nana Delfina would always fill her hair with orchids and copihues, the national flower of Chile. They are like delicate pink bells with yellow clappers inside them, and they looked like earrings hanging from her ears.

Delfina would proudly walk through the entire neighborhood with the enormous birthday cake she stayed up late into the night baking, enticing everyone to our home. All of our neighbors would come to drink té and café con leche and eat that beautiful cake with endless caramel layers, that cake called mil hojas . . . a thousand leaves. That was the one day I could have a mug entirely full with strong coffee, with as much sugar as I wanted. Friends brought me presents like fresh cheese, chocolates, flowers, and hard-boiled eggs. And Abuela

Frida would sing "Happy Birthday" to me in German with a shy, girlish smile on her face. I was always so happy that day, and maybe every day, and yet I didn't realize just how much until now. And here I am so far away, and I can't even call my mother because I don't know where she is. But I know that she is thinking of me, and my father, too. I know that.

I hear the old springs of Tía Graciela's bed creak as she rolls to one side and then the other. That's the sound of her waking up. Will she remember what day it is? I must have dozed off for a moment because the next thing I hear is Tía Graciela knocking on my bedroom door, and then I see her walking toward me wearing Abuela Frida's smile and carrying a little white cake with a blue candle on top. "¡Feliz Cumpleaños! Happy birthday, Celeste! Make twelve wishes, one for each year!" I close my eyes for a long time, and then I blow out the candle.

"I can tell they were good wishes." Tía Graciela pulls a fork from her bathrobe pocket. "Breakfast in bed, señorita. Have a taste—it's something new for you." I take a big forkful and sigh as the tastes and textures of cinnamon, carrots, and cream cheese dance in my mouth. "Carrot cake," she tells me. This cake doesn't have the heavenly vanilla scent of Nana Delfina's, but it tastes just as delicious. Maybe even better, though I would never tell Delfina that.

I Search for
Myself in
Spanish

My English must be getting better, because Mr. Turner asks me to write about my family in Chile and to read my essay aloud. My classmates don't even know where my country is located, and they say "Chilly" instead of Chile. They don't know the capital cities of South American countries either.

I search for myself in Spanish and always repeat in my mind some of my favorite words like "libélula," "luciérnaga," "lluvia," "euforia" or "dragonfly," "firefly," "rain," "euphoria." Sometimes when I repeat the word "euphoria," I feel great sadness, which is the very opposite of the meaning of the word. But I can't imagine feeling euphoria until I am back in Chile with my family and friends.

Charlie, who seems to bully everyone, asks me if my family lives in a hut and if we have refrigerators.

"Charlie"—I struggle to get the words right—"my country has highways, airplanes, *and* refrigerators. But more important, Chile has poets, and people fill entire stadiums to hear them." Suddenly I feel brave, and I toss my head. "I know poems by heart. Do you?"

He looks at me, surprised, then shrugs and pretends like he didn't hear me. I walk home with a huge smile on my face. On the side of the road I notice the tip of a daffodil bulb emerging from the ground. I search for myself in Spanish. But today I took a stand, and found myself in English.

A **Basket** of Blueberries

I try to make the time pass by learning at least ten new English words, and writing them in my notebook, every day. And somehow the time *does* pass, and when I count the days on my calendar, I see that it soon will be winter in Valparaíso. Summer has come to this half of the world, and Juliette Cove Middle School let out yesterday. I am glad! I didn't have anyone to say good-bye to but Kim, who surprised me by giving me a little hug at the back of our classroom before running out the door.

Today, to celebrate the summer, Tía Graciela takes me blueberry picking at a farm down the road from the lighthouse in a town called York. I've never seen—or tasted—blueberries before! They look like sapphires all wet with morning dew and glistening in the sunshine. And the taste! Yum! I can't seem to stop stuffing handfuls of the tiny, tangy sweet jewels into my mouth.

"Celeste, you are eating more blueberries than you put in your basket! How will you ever make a pie?" Tía Graciela teases me as she pops some berries into her own mouth.

"Do you really want to make a pie, Tía?" I ask, anticipating yet another visit from the fire department.

"No, personally I don't want to make a pie. I want *you* to make it!"

"Me?! But Nana Delfina doesn't even let me near the stove! I have never baked anything in my life!"

"Until today, Querida. Until today. There is always a time to start."

I look at her skeptically. She must be joking.

"Celeste." Tía Graciela's voice is suddenly very serious. "I want you to get busy. I have decided to give you chores like American kids have. You spend way too much time upstairs in your room. I have left you with too much empty space to fill with sad thoughts. It's a bad habit of my own, and I don't want to teach it to you. Working with your hands will be good for you."

"But . . . so . . . what . . . ?" Flustered, I don't know what I want to say.

Tía Graciela smiles. "Didn't you have your imaginary dolls' garden on Butterfly Hill?" I nod. "Well, here I have a real garden that needs tending, and meals that need to be cooked."

I nod and feel my mouth gaping open. Part of me doesn't believe she will make me follow through with it, and the other part of me hopes she does.

I hesitate, then ask, "Can I plant parsley and basil so

I can learn to make spaghetti sauce like Nana Delfina's?"

"Of course! I will take you to the library to find books about gardening, and then you can plant whatever you like." Suddenly I feel so excited. "Provided," Tía Graciela continues, "it will grow here in this crazy northern climate."

"It will, Tía! I promise it will!"

Tía Graciela nods. "That's my girl. Come on now. I will race you to see who can fill their basket first! Someone's got a pie to bake!"

"¡Ay! I wish Nana Delfina were here to help us!" One stop at the lighthouse, two cones at the ice cream stand, and three long, flour-covered hours later, I am in the kitchen, Tía Graciela peering over my shoulder. I wave my hand at the smoke pouring from the oven and take out the pie.

"*Your* pie that *you* made, all by yourself!" Tía Graciela says proudly, squeezing her nose shut with her fingers.

I poke a fork inside the pie, wave it around to cool it, and tentatively take a bite. The insides are still sweet and yummy!

"Here, taste!" I hand my aunt a fork heaped with warm blueberries. "I'll just cut off the crust and leave it on the porch for the wild turkeys."

Tía Graciela shakes her head. "Oh no—they are much too refined for burned leftovers! I bet you they turn their wobbly beaks up at it."

Then she takes me by the hand. "Come on. Let's have pie in the living room for dinner tonight. I have a treat—your Abuela Frida's favorite movie. It was the first movie she saw in the theaters after arriving in Valparaíso. And I found it on sale in the drugstore, of all places!"

"Only in America!" I imitate my aunt, who pokes me in the ribs. She says that a lot, especially when we are in the long, wide aisles of the grocery store trying to choose a breakfast cereal or watching hour-long TV commercials for frying pans with spatulas that flip pancakes automatically.

Mesmerized, we curl up on the couch and watch all three hours of *Gone with the Wind* while our mouths turn blueberry-blue. Then I crawl up the stairs to my room and hope I have a dream about Rhett Butler as I remind myself that, like Miss Scarlett said, "Tomorrow is another day."

When I open the front door the next morning, I find that my aunt was right about turkeys and their snobby palates. An army of ants, however, was not so picky and is piled atop the crust. Pretending I can hear my own red petticoats rustle, I quickly run to get the broom and scatter the feast into the grass before Tía Graciela sees!

I imagine I am Miss Scarlett gazing out at the red earth of Tara. "After all"—I drawl with an elegant curtsy to the ants, still clamoring over one another in a race to carry home crumbs twice their size—"tomorrow *is* another day!"

Year of the
Tiger

Tía Graciela was serious about me doing chores. "Unlike your grandmother, I want to see dirt underneath your fingernails!" she says, laughing. In the garden I plant fuchsias to fill the vase on the table, rosemary for fragrance and seasoning, and tomatoes and mint to make what I have named Celeste's Super Summer Salad. I also borrow a book about herbs from the library and read about growing parsley and basil. But before I learn to cook sauce, I teach myself to boil pasta. I try all different kinds: penne, fettucine, linguine, orecchiette. Tía Graciela tells me, "Celeste, one day you will wake up and find you have turned into an enormous noodle. Eat something else." But I will never get tired of pasta.

   With something to do each day, my first summer on Juliette Cove passes quicker than I ever thought it would. The evening before the first day of school, Tía Graciela takes me out for hamburger-and-onion pizza at Sal's. When I place an order, in English, for the two of us, Tía Graciela beams. "Celeste, just look at you! You've grown up so much this summer! How much more confidence you have! What would everyone on Butterfly Hill say now if they could hear you speaking English? If they could see you in the kitchen—cooking pasta, washing dishes, and sweeping the kitchen floor all at once? I think you have some of Nana Delfina's magic! And you learned to do laundry—"

"Sort of," I interrupt my aunt, raising my eyebrows in amusement.

"You *did!*" she insists. "I like pink shirts and socks better than white any day!"

"Gracias, Tía." I smile. It's true that I've grown taller and stronger, and as of yet I have not turned into a noodle. And digging in the garden all summer will sure make me better at shoveling snow this winter. Suddenly the thought of another winter here makes me miss Abuela Frida. I close my eyes and see her shoveling snow outside her house in Vienna. She is about my age, but she looks like an angel.

On the first day of seventh grade I am surprised to find that I understand a lot of what people are saying. I feel less afraid of speaking English, and less afraid of my classmates. Plus, I like my new teacher, Miss Rose, with her curly blond hair and gentle smile and her hands that are always moving. And how her name reminds me of the yellow rose that Nana Delfina wore in her hair when she arrived at our house under a black umbrella.

Miss Rose often comes to the back corner of the classroom to help me and Kim. She is patient and explains things in a way that I understand. Miss Rose looks so happy when I finally begin to pronounce the *TH* and *W* sounds correctly that I find myself starting to like English.

One Friday afternoon Miss Rose calls me up to her desk and tells me that she speaks a little Spanish. "¡Un poco!" she says, smiling. "Celeste, how about we set aside an hour every Friday so that your classmates can learn some Spanish, too?"

"Yes . . . ummm . . . thank you?" I nervously stumble over my words. I don't know what to say. I'm not sure I want to teach the class Spanish.

But Miss Rose continues on excitedly. "You are the teacher now, Celeste," Miss Rose says as she sits in my seat. "Why don't you sit on my desk so that everyone can see you?"

I look at her, surprised and hesitant. But already some hands are raised, and Charlie shouts from the back of the room: "Celeste, how do you say 'basketball' and 'recess'?"

"Celeste, how do you say 'to have a crush on somebody'?" Charlie's twin sister, Meg, asks with a sly grin. My brain does somersaults as I try to write all the answers on the blackboard. I help them pronounce difficult words like "amarillo"—"yellow"—and "ferrocarril"—"train"—and tell them how important accent marks are. I teach them the alphabet in Spanish, and how to roll the tongue to pronounce the letter *Rrrrrr*. That is especially hard, and all sorts of strange gurgling sounds can be heard coming from classroom number 44.

I tell them to practice by repeating the English word "kettle" and feeling the way their tongues tickle the roofs of their mouths. They laugh, but it starts to work!

Miss Rose also asks me to tell the class about Chile. I tell them about geography. "Chile got its name because of how our birds sing. The Spanish heard them say 'chile, chile.' Chile has the sea, mountains, grass, and a desert called Atacama. Flowers—purple and yellow—grow there in the sand." I realize how much I love talking to the class about my country. Suddenly I feel a big smile stretch across my cheeks. And then, amazingly, I see that same smile beam back at me from some of the desks!

Miss Rose always tells the class how wonderful it is that Kim and I are able to speak in two languages. I know she is trying to make us feel better, but it makes me squirm and slide down lower in my seat because I can see the popular girls rolling their eyes behind their books, whispering, "What goody-goodies! What babies!" I want to shout out that I actually was raised to speak *two* languages perfectly—Spanish and German—and I even know some Hebrew and a few words in Mapudungún! But what good would it do? This isn't Valparaíso, where it seems like everyone has at least one grandparent who came as an exile from somewhere else, where I've listened to the magician at Café Iris read palms in Russian and even Arabic! They would just think I am even stranger than they do now, and have one more thing to tease me about.

Today Miss Rose asks Kim to share some words in Korean about New Year's, because she saw the Chinese New Year celebrations in New York City on *Good Morning America*. At first Kim looks confused, and I raise my hand to correct Miss Rose: "Korea is *not* China!"

But before I can, Kim says softly but firmly, "We celebrate New Year at this time in Korea, too, but we call it Seollal." This year is the Year of the Tiger. A good year to try something new . . . maybe . . . try something that scares us. I look at Kim. At this moment she reminds me of Delfina. Kim never seems to boil up with frustration the way I do inside. She has that same simple dignity as the elderly Mapuche woman so far away whom I miss so much. Miss Rose smiles her beaming smile, and Kim shyly returns her smile and bows her head.

"Thanks to you, Kim, and to Celeste, the whole class can become bilingual, and that," Miss Rose says with a flourish of her chalk-covered hands, "is the future."

Kim's House

On a cloudy Friday in March when the snow finally has begun to melt and everything is all gray and slushy, I leave early for school so that I can walk instead of taking the bus, which tends to make me dizzy. I enter the coatroom, and there I find Kim, slouched in the corner, her head on her knees. She is sobbing without making a sound. "Kim?" I approach her and put my hand on her head. She looks up, and I know that I shouldn't leave her alone.

"Kim, I am coming over to your house after school today."

Kim nods. "Yes."

That is the only word she speaks all day. Kim holds her head down and won't respond to anyone, not even to Miss Rose, who thinks she is ill and sends her to the nurse.

I am distracted in school. I worry about Kim and suddenly realize that none of my classmates have ever invited me to their homes. None of the girls have invited me to the pajama parties I always hear them talking about. And Charlie might give me a piece of gum now and then, but he never talks to me at recess or asks if I want to do something after school.

I sigh and peek at the clock over the classroom door. Ten thirty a.m. The morning drags on and on. Is sadness so heavy, it slows down the clocks?

Kim stays in the nurse's office all day, but when the dismissal bell rings, I run to find her waiting for me outside. She gives me a shy smile and walks toward the road, motioning for me to follow alongside her. We walk in silence. Every time a car speeds around a corner, we jump into the slush and wait for it to pass. Finally at the end of the road I see a small grocery store. In its nearly empty parking lot is an old run-down taxi. Its windows are grimy with dust and dirt, but I see a slight figure in the backseat. Then the door opens, and a small woman with hair as black and shiny as onyx and a tired but gentle smile emerges. She reminds me of the jade goddess Kim wears. It is her mother.

We get into the taxi, which Kim takes to and from school when the weather is bad. She speaks a few soft words to her mother in Korean. Her mother reaches her hand out for mine. Her palm is rough but warm. She smiles, and her brow furrows in concentration before she speaks. "Hello, daughter friend."

"Hello. My name is Celeste."

"Pretty. Me, Sae Jin."

I like the sound of her name, like something electric. "It means 'jewel.'" Kim speaks to me again for the first time all day. "Jewel of everything." Kim struggles to explain to me. "Of land, of sky, of sun, of trees, of people, of stars in black sky, planets far away. Especially faraway stars."

"The whole universe?" I ask.

"Yes!" Kim actually smiles a bit. "Sae Jin. 'Jewel of the Universe.' My mother."

I remember Delfina's nickname for my mother. Joya.

"My mother is a jewel too," I say as I reach my hand out to Kim's mother, who takes it in her own hand with a kind but confused look on her face.

Kim speaks again to her mother in Korean. It is amazing to hear Kim speak so naturally in her own language, when English is still such an effort for both of us. Jewel of the Universe. Sae Jin wears jeans that are too big for her, and a threadbare pink sweater so tattered at the elbows that I wish my Abuela Frida could knit her a new one. At her feet is a big yellow bucket with strong-smelling cleaning products, a toilet brush, and rubber gloves inside. I feel carsick. I want to say something that makes Kim and her mother laugh until they shine like emeralds, but my insides are sad and silent. I watch the scenery—thick trees interrupted by the occasional house, pub, or convenience store—as the taxi rumbles down a bumpy road that seems to go on forever.

Finally we turn down a small dirt road that leads to a clearing in the woods. It is a parking lot filled with trailers. We get out of the taxi and zigzag our way through the rows of trailers until we stop in front of a small brown one, and Kim's mother takes a key from her purse. "Welcome," she says as she opens the door. The trailer is small, but it fits two cots and a little table with a photograph of a man with a serious face. Kim sees me looking at it. "My father."

"Does he live here with you?"

"No. He was." Once again, tears fall down Kim's face. Her mother puts her arms around her daughter and looks over at me.

"He left to Korea," her mother says. "Yesterday. My son now is man of the family."

My throat goes dry, and I feel my own eyes begin to burn with tears. "I am sorry," I say, wincing. I don't ask why because I am afraid the answer will mean Kim will leave next.

Kim motions to me to sit with her on one of the cots. "I sleep here with my mom, and Tom—that's my brother; he's working now—he sleeps over there." I sit cross-legged on the thin mattress, my back against a pillow Kim has propped against the wall. We sit in silence. The trailer has only a few small windows. It is dark and the walls are bare. In Chile I saw poverty, but I never felt its grief like I do now. Maybe because the poor families were all together to share what little they had? I can't imagine suffering from hunger, but I do know what it is like to suffer from loneliness. Both together would be unbearable. I look at the small burner where Kim's mother has begun to stir something in a pot.

"I make dinner. You like rice?"

I nod and say, "Yes, thank you," and wonder if Kim always has enough to eat.

Kim's mother serves us tea and steaming bowls of white rice. The three of us eat quietly, but just being there helps me understand Kim and her shy ways more. Once we have finished our meal and are sipping our second cups of tea, Kim's mother points out the tiny window. "Sky darker. Your mother worry."

I think of my mother in hiding somewhere at the bottom tip of the world. "Mamá, don't worry," I want to call to the southern winds.

Kim shakes her head at her mother and says a few quick words. Sae Jin puts her arm around my shoulders. "Oh, your aunt waiting. But you come again. Visit my daughter?" I reach up and give her a kiss on the cheek.

"Yes, señora. Thank you."

The same taxi brings me home. I watch the darkening sky and the bare branches that line the road for less than half an hour until finally we pull up to my driveway. I walk toward the door, where Tía Graciela waits for me in her bathrobe. She takes my face in her hands and kisses my forehead. She doesn't ask any questions. Maybe she sees the reflection of a lonely mother and daughter in my eyes and understands.

I climb the stairs to my bedroom and stand in front of the map of Chile before throwing myself onto my bed. Once again, I count the days and anticipate my return, until I fall asleep. I dream that I am trapped alone in a trailer in the middle of a snowstorm. Ice has frozen all the doors and windows shut. "I can count my way out!" I scream, and begin, "Uno, dos, tres, cuatro, cinco," until a low voice interrupts me: "Celeste, how can you number the unknown?"

Kim and I have gone from being the two girls who smiled at each other shyly to being good friends. Miss Rose always says, "Kim and Celeste, you are two little peas in a pod!" And she tells us what a peapod is, and all of a sudden I am in the kitchen shelling peas with Delfina. Magically the scent of parsley fills the back of the classroom where Kim and I sit while the rest of the class learns something called phonics that seems very boring.

It's true we are like little peas. Kim is just as small as me, and sometimes when we see each other in the morning, we trade something we are wearing for the day. She loves the forest-green shawl Nana Delfina gave me, and I love the red ribbon she always ties around her neck. It has a beautiful jade stone in the shape of a goddess dangling from it.

I show Kim the advantages of being tinier than the tall kids with their long legs who always run fast and tag us out in baseball. We both dread gym class, and

sometimes we hide under the teacher's desk while the rest of the class goes to the gymnasium. We sit back-to-back so we can lean on each other and take a nap.

Other times we feel like having some fun, so we tiptoe to the empty locker room and swing back and forth on the doors of the bathroom stalls. *Creak, creak, creeeeeak!* Their rusty old hinges threaten to give us away! We fly, our legs dangling in the air, until we can't contain our giggles or our arms give out. Then we hide in a shower until the class comes back from gym to change. We get strange looks and snickers from the girls, especially the popular girl Meg, but we get that anyway. "They maybe think we are too stupid to understand gym," Kim whispers to me. So we just play along and join them as they march back to classroom number 44.

I think that Miss Rose never notices. But Kim shakes her head at me. "She knows. She just doesn't say." That makes me love Miss Rose even more.

We are both learning English much faster this year, and Kim's face lights up with happiness when she learns a new word. I hear her laugh when she reads that funny-sounding word with a surprising and beautiful meaning. "Butter fly . . . ? Butter . . . but it flies? Wait! Oh! I know! *Butterfly!*"

I say, "Kim, you are like a comet."

"Butterflies are my favorite."

"Me too. That is the name of the hill where my

house is in Chile. What is the name of the place where your house is?" But Kim just shakes her head and turns her eyes down to the list of vocabulary on her desk.

When Miss Rose lets us out for a recess that always seems too short, our teeth chatter as our four feet in tall boots kick through the frozen leaves covering the playground. "My fingers feel like they might fall off!" I say, and watch a big *poof* of white smoke escape from my lips.

"Do you think our hearts can freeze too?" Kim asks me with fear in her eyes.

"Let's run to the top of the hill and lie under that pile of leaves and pretend it's a blanket!" I answer, and pull her by the hand because I don't know what to say about our hearts.

But Kim is smiling again as we crunch, crunch, crunch up the hill. Something Kim especially loves to do is find leaves that resemble letters. One day Kim makes a beautiful shape by placing leaf stems on the pavement. Her name in Korean. Then she teaches me how to do mine. "That is the name for sky. That is where *she* lives"—Kim points to her necklace—"at the gate of the sky, watching us. Her name is Kuan Yin."

Kim's language sounds so strange. I ask her to teach me the word "friend" in Korean. Kim tells me, "Celeste, you are my chingu. Friend." Then she says, "Young won hee!" Her bird eyes sparkle. "That means 'forever.'"

Watching
the Sky

I wake up this morning the way I often do, imagining that Tía Graciela's alarm clock is the doorbell, and that I hear my parents' voices saying, "Where is our little star? Where is the celestial Celeste?"

But more and more, there are good things to look forward to when the morning comes. Now that spring is almost here, Kim and I like to lie in the grass just to look at the sky. Sometimes her older brother, Tom, comes along. The ground is still cold, but the air around us is warm. We watch the clouds drift by in comfortable silence, and once in a while blurt out the shapes we see.

"You always see an angel, Celeste," Kim says, laughing. "I think what you see is *you*. My mother says the sky is my mirror."

"And a messenger," adds Tom. I think about that and wonder if Abuela Frida is thinking of me right now. I almost see her looking out the window from her old chair, with her knitting on her lap, watching for my reflection in the sky.

"Tom, Kim! I just realized the air has no borders. Someone in Seoul and someone in Valparaíso see the same sky right now!"

"You need to bring your notebook with you when we watch the sky, Celeste." Kim puts her elbows in the grass and, with her chin on her hands, looks at me with her dark eyes. "It talks to you."

"You like to write things down? You have a bad memory?" Tom laughs. Kim gives her brother a little shove in the rib cage and scolds him in Korean. "Ow! Okay!"

"Celeste is going to be a famous writer. My friend will make many people happy with her books. I know."

"Kim, I think you are one of the angels I always see in the sky. The shy one who always flies away with the wind."

Tom closes his eyes and pretends to snore. "You girls are strange. No, funny. Different countries but made from the same clay."

I am learning that Tom is a lot like Kim. He is quiet, but he likes to laugh and tease more. I am the talkative one, the "chatterbox," as Miss Rose sometimes tells me with her finger to her lips during math quizzes.

The early April sky begins to turn shades of pink and purple. The sun is setting, and Tía Graciela must be on her way to pick me up. Suddenly I don't want to leave my friends. I realize that we aren't like the kids who grew up here on Juliette Cove, who have been friends all their lives and probably will know one another forever. We are from faraway places that we dream of returning to.

"Someday we'll all go to Chile," I tell them. "I'll take you to see Cape Horn, at the southern tip of South America. So many old sailing ships were shipwrecked there that people say the whole island is filled with the ghosts of sailors!"

They smile at me. "Are those ghosts as loud as you?" Tom laughs. Kim jabs him in the ribs again, but I am laughing too. It feels so good to laugh after so long that I don't want to stop.

"You'll have to come to Chile and find out," I say, "but beware, we are a country of tale-tellers, cuenta-cuentos!"

Tom is chuckling softly to himself. He stretches his hands behind his head. "I love the colors of the sun going down," he says. His voice goes serious. "The sun going down . . . until west becomes east again . . . all the way back to Korea—"

His sister interrupts him. "Tom, why do you say sad things when everyone is happy?" She doesn't pause for an answer as she turns to me. "Celeste, I'll make tea so we can get warm before your tía comes." Kim brushes the grass off her legs and, with her gait that is more like a pony's trot, heads toward the trailer park.

I've never been alone with Tom before. Strangely I find myself feeling a bit nervous. The silence feels different without Kim in between us. I search for something to say.

"Why did you leave Korea?"

"For political reasons. And you? Why did you leave Chile?"

"For political reasons."

We laugh. Then softly I feel his hand move closer to mine. My body shivers a little, but as his hand brushes mine, I feel I know him. And all of his pain. In the stillness of the evening our eyes search and find each other, blinking like two timid butterflies.

Dreaming
in English

That night I dream that Kim and Tom come with me to Chile. We fly all night atop a colorful blanket like the ones Delfina wove on rainy days. I breathe in the soft salty air. I feel so happy to be once again at my house on Butterfly Hill. All of a sudden I hear Delfina calling me. "Celeste! Celeste!"

"I'm here on the roof, Delfina! That's my nanny," I tell my friends.

Once again, Delfina's voice like big silver bells: "I have been so worried about you! Where have you been for so long?" My Nana Delfina is speaking to me in English! *When did she learn that?* I wonder, but Delfina continues, "Your mother is looking for you! I am sending you a silver seashell to fly to her!"

A seashell appears beside me, and I climb inside. The seashell rises into a sky filled with stars and flies toward the Southern Cross, so small in the distance. Are we going to see my parents?

"Little Star, where are you?" a sweet melodic voice beckons from the south.

"Mamá?!" I hear myself talk in my sleep and wake myself up. Then I realize: "I just had my first dream in English!" I shout down the hallway to Tía Graciela, my heart beating with joy.

Daydreaming

Miss Rose is talking about when the United States was an English colony and writing things like "Samuel Adams," "Benjamin Franklin," and "Live Free or Die" on the board. Everyone around me is scribbling away in their notebooks, jotting down notes so they can memorize everything before our final test of the year. Summer vacation begins in two weeks, and suddenly everyone is worried about the grades their parents will see on their report cards. Even though Tía Graciela always tells me that knowledge can't be measured in numbers, I want to do well and I want to show Miss Rose how much more I can do this year because she has helped me so much with my English. But I just can't seem to concentrate. Even the Boston Tea Party with its interesting name can't hold my attention.

I let out a sigh and gaze out the window. Kim glances over at me with a question mark on her face. Yesterday she told me, "All week you are like a cloud. Floating."

What if I told her, "I can't stop thinking about

your brother"? But I'd rather keep it secret inside me, as if even saying his name would make my daydreams crumble like a sand castle.

I don't know much about Tom. He doesn't talk much, but he chuckles to himself a lot. Kim is my best friend here on Juliette Cove, I remind myself. Of course, *she* is the reason I visit the trailer park so often. But when Tom and I lie together in the grass and look at the sky, I feel a tingle in my throat.

I sigh again. I wonder if he's thought of me at all. Celeste, soñadora, what a dreamer you are.

The Empty
Seat

For the seventh graders in Miss Rose's class, the last week of school is full of exams but also excitement. Everyone can't wait for the summer, and my classmates remind me of kernels of corn bursting into popcorn in a hot oily pan, the way they can't stay still in their seats and wriggle this way and that to ask about plans for summer vacation. Everyone is giggling with their hands over their mouths and passing notes about meeting at the beach tomorrow, the last day of school.

Charlie reaches back across the aisle and pulls my braid to ask me, "Hey, you're coming with us to the beach, right?"

"I don't know yet." Normally I'd look to Kim before answering. I still don't feel like I completely belong with the rest of my class.

"Hey," he says, his voice coaxing, "I'll even let you borrow my boogie board and teach you to ride the waves."

Charlie and I have become friendly, but he isn't

always this kind to me. It makes me nervous because he seems to be trying to console me, and I don't want to think about the reason why. I smile at him, but it feels forced. I see him glance over to the empty seat beside me and then back again at me. His eyes look to me to tell him why Kim's place is empty. All I can do is shake my head and look back down at my English grammar worksheets. My eyes burn, and my throat feels like invisible hands are squeezing it tight. I start to cough. I don't want to cry. It's not that I care so much about crying in front of Charlie, or the whole class for that matter. It wouldn't be the first time. It's that crying would make my fears true. Charlie has gotten up and grabbed a tissue from Miss Rose's desk. "Here. Nobody noticed."

He looks over again at the empty desk and says, "Come with us to the beach tomorrow, Celeste. Everything will be okay."

"Thank you, Charlie," I whisper as he turns to face forward in his seat because of Miss Rose's sudden gaze in our direction.

And now I can't hold my tears back any longer. They rain on my worksheet, blurring the words I try so hard to learn, and making the ink run like dark, sad rivers. All week Kim's place beside me has been empty. On Tuesday I walked to the supermarket where Tom works to ask him if she was sick, and the manager told me that he hadn't worked there since Friday. Where have my friends gone?

Why didn't they tell me anything?

Will they be back?

I feel like I am in Valparaíso again, when everyone began to go missing.

The seats in the Juana Ross School emptied one by one until half of my class was gone. I remember when I realized that they wouldn't be returning. It was the day I sat alone on the bench outside, where all of us friends would gossip and share snacks like sugar-coated almonds. Even in the winter the bench would stay warm from the heat of all our bodies crammed together. But that day the bench beneath me was an iceberg. Today feels just the same. The June sun shines through the classroom windows, and I am buried in icy dread. "Nana Delfina, if you can hear me, please help!" I clasp my hands tight and pray, "Send me some of your magic. Tell me, where have they gone?"

"No More Pencils, No More Books"

Today is the last day of school. I watch the cereal Tía Graciela has poured for me grow soggy. My throat feels too tight to swallow anything. "Tía, can you drive me to school so I can get there early?" Tía Graciela peers up from her tarot cards, surprised.

"Celeste, for almost two years now you have never seemed eager to spend more time at school than you had to."

"I—I want to say good-bye to Miss Rose," I stammer, "without anyone else around. She has helped me so much this year."

"Está bien, niña," my aunt says, agreeing to drive me so I can arrive early enough to talk to my teacher alone.

As Tía Graciela pulls her station wagon away from the curb in front of the Juliette Cove Middle School, I can hear throngs of sixth-grade boys running around the playground chanting: "No more pencils, no more books, no more teachers' dirty looks!" Last year Kim and I heard that song, and we could barely understand it. We just looked confusedly at each other and burst out laughing. Now I know what the words mean, but it still seems strange to me. Strange and sad: a school with no pencils to write with, no books to read . . . no Kim, my best friend.

I run through the playground and up the front steps of the school. The halls are mostly empty because it is still ten minutes until the first bell. I turn down the corridor that leads to a door with a sign that says FACULTY. I have always wondered what the teachers say and do inside that office, when none of their students are watching. I wonder if they are more like their real selves and less like teachers. Students aren't allowed in this office, but I gently knock on the door anyway.

When it opens, the eighth-grade teacher Mr. Gary opens it. He looks down at me in concern. "Hello there! Can I help you?" Behind him I see a bunch of teachers at a table, chatting and laughing, drinking coffee and eating doughnuts.

"Yes. Can I speak to Miss Rose, please?"

Mr. Gary calls over his shoulder, "Theresa, one of your students is here!"

Miss Rose comes to the door. "Celeste! What a surprise! I will be out in one minute. Wait for me there." I nod. Mr. Gary smiles and shuts the door.

Soon my teacher emerges with a bag of books and papers over her shoulder and a doughnut in her hand. "It's butternut." She holds it out to me. "You look as if you need a little treat."

"Thank you, Miss Rose." I've tried doughnuts before, and I don't like them very much, but I bite into it to be polite, and I am surprised to find there is something soothing today about its doughy sweetness. As we walk down the corridor, the click-clack of Miss Rose's high heels makes a comforting echo that somehow steadies my heart and makes it easier to speak.

"Miss Rose, why hasn't Kim been in school all week?"

My teacher puts her heavy bag down and turns to look at me. "Oh, Celeste." She puts her hands on my shoulders, and I watch her kind eyes try so hard to blink back tears. "I don't know. I have called the contact number we have on file for her, and the principal has checked with the police, and all the hospitals, to see if there have been any accidents. Then I found out that her brother has not been at school this week either, which makes us suspect that Kim and her family have moved on to another place."

My hands begin to shake. "Oh! No, not Kim! Why? Why? Why do people disappear?" My head spins until I am nauseous, and suddenly I am back in the halls of the Juana Ross School, and so many of my friends are disappearing, and I don't know if it is Miss Rose or Señorita Marta Alvarado holding me tight in her arms. I want to howl and scream, but no sound comes out. I can't get myself to stop shaking.

Miss Rose pulls some tissues from her pocket and wipes my face, guiding me toward the classroom. I hear the noisy banter of my classmates who are already inside. Miss Rose turns to me at the doorway and speaks in her most serious "teacher voice."

"Now, you walk in there with your head held high, Celeste, and be proud of who you are today and always. You are my student, Celeste, and if you never remember anything I taught you, please remember this: Have faith. So much faith that you have faith in faith itself. And never, ever give up."

Solidarity

"Celeste! Aren't you coming to the beach?" Charlie calls after me as I run fast as I can out the door when the final bell lets school out for summer, to the roaring cheers of students in every classroom. "If you do, I'll teach you to boogie-board!"

"Another time, Charlie, I promise!" I call over my shoulder, and catch a glimpse of him in the hallway. For a second his face looks glum, but then he smiles and becomes teasing Charlie again.

"Okay, Macaroni, but you're missing the ride of your life!" he calls back as I wave and continue to run. My mind is racing even faster than my feet. *I could take a taxi to the trailer park. Or maybe I should go home first and tell Tía Graciela. She could help me look for them.*

I decide to run home.

Tía Graciela is sitting on the front steps reading a book about palmistry. "Happy summer vacation!" she calls out when she sees me.

"Tía, I need your help."

"¿Qué pasó, mi amor? What's happened?"

I take a shallow breath, and my voice sounds raspy as I finally speak those awful words: "Kim and Tom haven't been to school all week!" Tía Graciela sets down her book and springs to her feet.

"Can we go look for them?" I ask.

"Hop in the car!" my aunt says without a moment's hesitation.

As we drive through the leafy woods, she gives me a sidelong glance from beneath her sunglasses. "Celeste, I wish you would have told me sooner. I am always ready to help. And not just to help you but to help others. Remember, I belong to what Chileans call 'the generation of solidarity.'"

I nod. "Papá said that a lot, but I don't understand what it means."

Turning onto the bumpy road that will take us to the trailer park, Tía Graciela explains, "When the government elected by the people was toppled, and the military began to persecute everyone for having their own opinions or for their long hair and jeans, it made everyone very frightened, and unfortunately, people you thought were your friends turned into enemies, and neighbors betrayed neighbors. But that is only half the story. Many Chileans began to help one another. They hid people in their homes, or found hiding places outside the city and brought them food, like the people who are helping your parents. Even if our own lives are in danger, we don't abandon others. That is solidarity."

"That's how I'll be, Tía Graciela."

"That's how you are, Celeste."

The trailer park is as dark as the clouds accumulating overhead. It has been a while since I last visited Kim and Tom at the trailer park. Everything looks so different, so empty. The grass is dry, and there are no longer any bicycles, children's toys, lawn chairs strewn around the trailers. In fact, there are hardly any trailers left. *Where have they gone?* And of the half dozen or so left, where are all the people? Huddled inside, waiting for the storm to pass? I clutch Tía Graciela's hand and lead her to Kim's trailer. The door is open, waving back and forth with a bang bang bang that goes straight to my stomach.

I glance at Tía Graciela and she nods, so we climb the rusted stairs and step inside. "There's nothing here!" I cry. "Tía, something must have happened to them!" Gone are the cots they slept in, the clothes they wore, the table where they served me tea and rice. All that remains is the smell of incense and orange blossoms.

"It looks like they left in a hurry, Celeste. Is there someone we could ask about where they went?"

"Tía Graciela, I don't think anybody knows them." All of a sudden I can barely breathe inside my friends' empty home. I run down the stairs and into thick raindrops that have started plummeting from the clouds. Tía Graciela follows me.

"Let's ask the neighbors. It doesn't hurt to try." We knock on every door. Most of them remain closed. "Hmmmm, maybe they are at work . . . ," my aunt says in a light voice that is meant to encourage me.

Then we come to a silver trailer parked under a tall pine tree. The door opens, and a white-haired woman with a gap-toothed smile greets us. "Can I help you?" A little boy peeks out from behind her pink bathrobe. "This is my grandson, Jimmy. He's a bit shy. I'm Bess."

"Hello, Jimmy. Nice to meet you, Bess," my aunt says. "We are looking for some friends."

"A Korean family," I pipe in. "A girl my age and a boy in high school. And their mother."

"Ah yes. Kim and Tom, right?"

I nod eagerly.

"Yes, I saw them around sometimes, but I never met their mother. They seemed to keep to themselves. Didn't speak much English. Aren't they in their trailer?"

"No, ma'am. Not anymore. But thank you anyway," Tía Graciela says.

After we thank Bess and walk away, I stutter in protest, "But . . . but . . . they left no tracks. No traces of them at all, Tía." Suddenly I think of Cristóbal Williams.

Did he say the same thing about me when he visited our house on Butterfly Hill with his magic pendulum and found I was no longer there?

Tía Graciela puts her arm over my shoulders and leads me to the car. "But they did, Celeste—they left traces of themselves in our hearts."

"Is this what it means to be an exile? To become invisible to this world, to become just a memory?"

Tía Graciela starts the car, sighs, and turns in the direction of our house. "Exile, Celeste, is a complicated topic. Our planet is full of exiles, refugees and immigrants—all of them find themselves where they are for different reasons."

"And what about us, Tía Graciela? Are we exiles?"

"Celeste, we are a bit of everything. But above all, we are two women from Chile. A country like a rose petal—remember the poet Neruda said that? And to Chile we will someday return."

We drive in silence. In my mind I see the empty trailer. I see Kim's dark eyes and feel Tom's warm hand. I taste Sae Jin's tea. I hope they are somewhere where people are kind to them. A place like my home, like Butterfly Hill. I imagine them walking up the path that leads to my house. The garden is in full bloom. Nana Delfina opens the door with a smile. "We've been expecting you," she says, and she reaches her arms out to gather them into her green shawl.

Somewhere
to Keep Her
Sorrow

When we arrive home, I run upstairs and lie on my bed. I listen to Tía Graciela walking this way and that all over the house, and dropping things and picking them up again. She does that when she is thinking too much.

Then she bursts in. "I've ordered hamburger-and-onion pizza for us tonight, Querida," she says. "I feel too clumsy to cook."

"Okay, that sounds safe to me."

Tía Graciela sits down on my bed. I notice a bunch of letters overflowing from the pockets of her purple skirt. "I've been thinking more about exile. What it is."

I drape Nana Delfina's shawl over my aunt's shoulders. "I am listening," I tell her.

"Mmmmm, I can smell my old nana's parsley and rose water." She tucks the edges of the shawl tighter around her thin waist.

"You know, Celeste, I still miss the light, the aromas, the familiar words, and above all, our family. But"—she looks at me with eyes like sunlit lakes—"I've grown accustomed to living this way, each day waiting for the mailman to arrive with a letter. Over time I've adjusted to my loneliness, like the Andes root themselves deeper into the stilled earth after a tremor has rocked them off balance."

"But why—" I take a deep breath as I prepare to ask something I've always wondered but was afraid to mention for fear of upsetting her. "Why didn't you go back to Chile when . . . I mean, after . . ."

"After Guillermo and I broke up?" my aunt finishes my question.

I nod, biting my lip. It's the first time I've heard her say his name.

"I'm not sure I know exactly." Tía Graciela looks down at her hands for a long while. "I guess I stayed because I liked the freedom of being in a place where nobody knew me—"

"Anywhere but Valparaíso?" I interrupt her.

She nods. "I think I wanted to be anonymous."

"It's hard to understand, Tía," I tell her. "Maybe because right now I miss my friends and neighbors on Butterfly Hill so much. I can't imagine *not* wanting to be surrounded by people who know me and care about me."

"That's because you have always been so sure of who you are, Celeste," Tía Graciela says. "It's taken me longer to know who I am." I want to tell her that I feel confused and scared nearly every day, but Tía Graciela continues. "At the university, Celeste, I studied to be a lawyer. I wanted to help the poor by fighting for their rights to food, to medicine, to an education. I had all these big ideas—your mother and I even dreamed of building a community center where people could come for medical checkups and legal advice. But when I graduated, I found that thinking about something and actually *doing* it are very different. All the poverty and injustice in the country was just too much for me. I knew that as much as I worked, there would still be more to do. I felt like I was drowning."

"I think I understand, Tía," I say, remembering how overwhelmed I felt when I went with my parents to the outskirts of Valparaíso after the big rainstorm.

"So I tried different things—I acted in community theater, I worked as a receptionist for your parents, but most of all, I wanted to travel. I wanted to live in exotic places. I wanted to feel free. So I followed Guillermo on his dance tours for a while, all over Chile, Argentina, Brazil. And when he was invited to join a dance troupe in Montreal, I was thrilled by the chance to move to Canada. But soon after, we broke up." Tía Graciela grows quiet, and I wish I could think of something to say. Instead I reach for her hand. She squeezes my own hand and smiles gratefully.

"Then what happened, Tía?"

"I moved to Juliette Cove because I needed some place, any place, to be alone and recover from my heartbreak. I picked this spot because the name reminds me of my favorite Shakespeare play, the one about a love that lasts forever. And I did recover . . . slowly . . . and I think I grew to like being in a place where I can be just as eccentric as I please . . . even though the price of freedom is loneliness."

"But can't you be yourself in Valparaíso?" I feel sorry for my aunt, thinking that it's either one or the other. It doesn't make sense to me. It's been hard for sure on Juliette Cove, but I've been myself here as much as I have been at home in Valparaíso. Because there's nothing else I *can* be.

"I can," she concedes. "But it's very hard for me. I find I am braver here, among strangers. Isn't that strange? It should be the opposite. You see, my dear, there are always challenges we need to overcome. We never stop growing. . . . In fact, I've learned a lot from watching you."

Tía Graciela's voice quiets to a whisper. She looks very tired as she leans over to kiss my cheek. "Now get some sleep, Querida. Buenas noches."

"Buenas noches, Tía. Thank you for sharing with me. And I won't forget to root myself like the mountains when I am lonely."

As Tía Graciela slips from my bedroom, I open my journal and write: *Now I know why Tía Graciela collects conch shells. She needs somewhere to keep her sorrow.*

Maybe They're
Smiling
Together

I wake just after dawn, my notebook beside me. I stand at the window and see the pale crescent moon. It is a slight, fading sliver, waiting for the sun to completely erase it from the sky. I look for a long time at the crescent shape, until in it I see my mother's smile. Or is it my father's? It has been so long since I have seen either of them. . . . Could it be both of them smiling together . . . wherever they are?

I turn from the window and crawl back into bed, pulling the sheets up over my head. I think about Mamá and Papá, Abuela Frida and Nana Delfina, about Lucila and Ana, about Marisol and Cristóbal . . . about Kim and Tom. I think about the people I love who I can't be near, and soon my head throbs and my heart feels sore.

I must have fallen asleep again, for I wake to Tía Graciela placing her hand on my forehead. "Celeste, you've been asleep all morning! It's nearly one in the afternoon! Are you ill, Querida?" Her hand is cool and soothing, like Delfina when she checks for a fever. . . .

And then the tears come.

"Oh, Tía," I sob. "I miss Kim! I am so worried about her and, and . . ." My voice falters. "And her whole family!" I cry and cry—and finally I draw a ragged breath and ask, "Tía Graciela, what does the word 'love' mean to you?"

She smiles. "Love for one's parents? For brothers and sisters? For friends? For a puppy? A favorite book?"

I know she understands perfectly well what I asked. She is trying to get me to smile, and somehow it works and I feel a bit better. "No, Tía Graciela! The love you have for someone like your boyfriend Guillermo."

She sighs. "Well, to love another so much that you build a life, a home, and a family together is something so beautiful, but that—that is almost impossible for me to describe like your parents could." She turns her face toward the window for a moment. "For Guillermo and me it didn't work out like that."

I squeeze her hand. "I am sorry, Tía, if I . . ."

But she quickly turns back to me. Her eyes are sad, but her voice is light as she teases me, "Hmmmm. I don't need the tarot cards to know that my little niece isn't so little anymore. And that you are maybe asking more about a first love." She pauses dramatically, and her eyes turn from sad to sparkly. "About Tom, maybe?"

My heart leaps and crashes when I hear his name. I whisper, "Sí."

"Oh, my first love. So long ago, but I see him so clearly. I remember how I felt that my entire skin seemed to breathe in and out. I laughed and sang all the time without knowing why. Oh, Celeste, whenever I saw Daniel Lombardi, I would blush as red as those baby tomatoes we used to see in the markets of Valparaíso. Remember?"

I find myself smiling. Tía Graciela sounds so much like how I felt after that day Tom and I held hands beneath the sky.

"But you must also know that love can mean letting someone go, too. The person you love must be free, and if he returns to you, it's a gift from heaven. And if he doesn't return, you are still happy to have had the chance to know and love him."

So that's the only thing I can do about Tom. Let go. I fear I am getting good at missing the people I love most. Not that it hurts any less. Tom. I will think of him when I see the clouds in the sky and hope that maybe someday I will see him again on Juliette Cove. Or even on Butterfly Hill.

At the
Lighthouse

The summer seems like a string of multicolored pearls. White, black, blue, pink—different lights, different shades mingle to form one long necklace. I never know quite what day it is, especially because Tía Graciela never uses a calendar. For the past few weeks all I have wanted to do is eat my breakfast as quickly as possible, run to the oak tree in the yard, and open the book Miss Rose gave me at the end of the school year. "Here, Celeste," she said as she handed me a thick book with a picture of four girls in old-fashioned dresses on the hardcover. "This was my favorite when I was your age. I think it will be a challenge for you, but your English has improved so much that I want you to try." The book is called *Little Women*, and I can't put it down. Of course, I imagine myself as Jo, who wants to be a writer and is always saying things that people think are strange, and always getting into mischief.

"Celeste Marconi! I do believe that the roots of this tree are going to wrap around you and keep you for their own. Which I suppose you think is fine now, as long as you have a book to read, but you're going to be awful cold there buried in the snow in the winter!" I laugh and drag my eyes away from the page.

"Hola, Tía."

My aunt reaches her hand out to me.

"Help me get out and have some fun! Let's go to the beach and have a picnic!"

I snap the book shut and hop up. "By the lighthouse! Let's bring lemonade and cheese puffs!"

My aunt rolls her eyes. "Ay, Celeste, cheese puffs? They don't even taste like cheese! Nana Delfina is going to have some harsh words for me if I send you home with a taste for American junk food!"

The lighthouse stands at the edge of the rocky harbor. We stretch on the sands beside it and gobble our lunch of lemonade, tuna sandwiches, cheese puffs, and chocolate pudding. Between bright orange mouthfuls I tell my aunt, "I love lighthouses—they're always there—giving us light and keeping us safe." I pause, then add, "And I imagine all the ports in the world and their lighthouses lit up like a welcome, and I see myself sailing to so many places someday. I want to find the earth's heartbeat in the middle of the sea."

"Ay, Celeste. I hope you are writing all these beautiful

thoughts down in a book. I want to read them all!"

My cheeks turn pink. I don't tell her that I've already started.

As Tía Graciela and I walk on the beach, it grows misty. I look back at our footprints in the sand. Sometimes they go in straight lines, sometimes they curve, and sometimes they circle around each other and form knots. But Tía Graciela likes to look ahead at the sand before she steps.

"See these cracks and holes?" She falls to her knees and peers down one excitedly. "There must be some creature like a clam or a crab underneath, and that's its airhole. Did your mother ever tell you how when we were little girls, we would sit by these holes for hours and hours, waiting for a pearl to pop up? We would both keep our hands very near and ready, each trying to be the first to catch one!" Tía Graciela laughs. It is a sound that's contagious. I laugh and scoop some seaweed up and drape it over her head.

"Now you can dance with the mermaids, Tía!" I shout, and begin to twirl around in circles right where the seafoam meets the shore. I close my eyes and spin faster. Then I hear a voice, not Tía's—younger, American.

I open my eyes and see Valerie from my class, the girl who is always tagging along with Charlie's sister, Meg. Valerie always seemed snobby to me but not nearly as scary as Meg. "Oh, hi!" I say. I'm instantly embarrassed. But Valerie smiles. "Do you take dance lessons?"

"Ummm, n-no," I stutter. After a summer alone with Tía Graciela, English drops like clumsy stones from my mouth. Valerie smiles again and steps closer.

"I take ballet lessons. I want to dance in *The Nutcracker* ballet in Boston someday. My mother used to take me and my sister every Christmastime before she got sick."

Her smile fades, and I don't know what to say. I reach out my hand and touch her wrist. "I didn't know that, um, that . . ."

"My mother has cancer," Valerie completes the sentence. "I didn't want everyone in our class to know. I was . . . afraid . . . they would look at me . . . differently." Her blue eyes lower to the ground. "But maybe . . . maybe you know how that feels a little bit too. I am sorry, Celeste."

"I am too," says a voice approaching from the mist behind Valerie. It is Meg, the queen bee of the class herself, with her twin brother, Charlie, a few steps behind, a sheepish half smile on his face.

I take a deep breath and glance over at Tía Graciela, who tells me, "I'm ready for a rest. I'll go sit on that big rock for a while, Celeste. You go with your friends." I take another deep breath. My stomach is doing somersaults. Friends. *Are* they my friends? Or will they laugh at me? Find a way to remind me I'm not one of them?

Instead Meg shouts, "Let's play hide-and-go-seek tag! Boys against the girls! Too bad, Charlie, you are all alone and you're IT!" We all laugh as we scatter through the mist and hide behind rowboats and the huge berry bushes that grow high on the dunes. We play until we are huffing and puffing and tumble onto the cold sand to catch our breaths.

"Macaroni, I have been telling these girls for a while," Charlie says, "you might be a bit strange, but you sure aren't boring."

"Thanks, Charlie. I think."

Charlie smiles a real smile, and then he gives my braid a tug before bounding up from the sand, yelling, "Catch me if you can!"

"Oh, I am too tired to chase him!" Valerie yawns.

"He can be such a pain," Meg says to me with a roll of her eyes. We laugh, and suddenly Tía Graciela is approaching us.

"Girls, would you like to come to the house for empanadas?" she asks with a warm smile. "Celeste made them herself." I blush, embarrassed, pretending to be absorbed in turning a seashell over with my big toe.

Valerie and Meg exchange quizzical glances.

"Empanadas—they're like little pies filled with meat and onions and raisins and all sorts of yummy spices," I tell them. "We eat them in Chile like you eat peanut butter sandwiches here. And I am so tired of peanut butter, by the way!"

They laugh. Again, a friendly laugh. "Okay, why not?" says Meg.

And Valerie nods and shouts, "Charlie, come on. It's time to eat!"

"That should have him back in a flash," she adds. "I call him the trash compactor."

That afternoon I watch as my new friends each tentatively try an empanada. I hold my breath. The empanadas are, as always, a little too dark along the edges. Oh, why can I *never* take anything out of the oven on time? But I watch, amazed, as they eat another and another, licking their fingers and asking for more. Tía Graciela peeks into the kitchen with a Mona Lisa smile on her face, and I can tell she is just as pleased as I am.

Dinner Party

That night I find Tía Graciela in bed early, reading her worn copy of Neruda's love sonnets.

"Tía?"

"Hmmmm?" She lifts her eyes from the page reluctantly, propping her pink reading glasses atop her wavy red hair.

"Tía, I want to have Valerie, Meg, and Charlie over to the house again. I want to make them dinner. May I?"

Her smile is so bright, and she looks so pleased, that I have to grin back at her.

"I think that is a wonderful idea, Celeste! What will you make?"

"Spaghetti de verdad, Tía. True, authentic pesto the way we make at home. They will love it! They hardly ever get homemade food. Did you know that? Their parents all work, and they almost never sit around the table with the whole family. Charlie and Meg usually eat frozen pizza watching TV."

"So, this will be a real treat for them, Querida." Tía Graciela seems to have borrowed some of my energy.

"How about Friday? You can pick some flowers from the garden. And I will try to find a pretty tablecloth when I am in town so everything can be elegant!"

"Gracias, Tía." I give her a hug. "And velas, too?"

"Oh, yes. What is an elegant dinner without candles?"

All week I am absorbed in preparations—trying to remember Delfina's recipes, looking up the words for ingredients in English to make a shopping list in my notebook, scouring the aisles of the grocery store with Tía Graciela, and watering the blue hydrangeas in the front yard every evening so that they bloom into the perfect table centerpiece. It feels good to have something to look forward to, and to be so busy. Working with my hands seems to quiet the ever-present question in my mind—where are my parents?—at least for a little while. I look for more and more to do, and think of Abuela Frida and her constant knitting of scarves. I can't learn to knit overnight, but maybe there is something I could make . . . ? On Thursday I walk the beach and find that, once again, Nana Delfina is right: "Nature always provides the answers."

Friday evening arrives in no time. Meg and Charlie's mom drops all my guests off at once. "Hola! Dinner is almost ready." I lead them into the dining room. "While you are waiting, open these. I made you each a present!"

Valerie gasps in surprise.

"You didn't have to do that, Celeste!" Meg says. "It's not our birthdays or anything!" But I can see she is excited too.

"I know," I explain as I hand them each a small package wrapped with tissue paper and ribbon Tía Graciela cut from an old hat she no longer wears, "but where I come from, we like to give little presents for no reason at all, not just at birthday parties and holidays."

"See, didn't I always tell you that Macaroni was a little weird—okay, *very* weird—but totally awesome?!" Charlie grins at me as I give him his gift. "Hey, this is heavy. How'd you lift this, spaghetti arms?" he teases me—which I now know is his way of saying "Thank you" and "You're my friend" and many other things that maybe I will one day teach him to say—as he unwraps the rock I found on the seashore. The waves had polished it perfectly smooth into a round and curvy shape with what looks like a tail at the end that reminds me of a whale. It is a deep, dark gray color, the color that will always make me think of Maine. On one side I carefully painted in a black eye and marked where his flippers are, and put a shy smile on his face. And on the other side I wrote the word for whale in Spanish: "Ballena."

"It's a whale!" Charlie laughs.

"And it's a paperweight," I tell him. "Because your papers are always falling off your desk in school."

Charlie looks at me without the mischievous smile he always wears. And his dark eyes grow very wide. "You see *everything*, Celeste!"

"I try."

For Meg and Valerie I found pretty pinkish shells and strung them on purple ribbon so they could wear them as necklaces. Meg gets up from her chair and throws her arms around my shoulders in a big hug. And Valerie follows and puts her arms over both of our shoulders.

"Celeste, I am sorry that I was so nasty when you first came here," Meg murmurs with her head bent low.

"Me too," Valerie adds, her blue eyes wistful.

"Me too, Celeste," Charlie pipes in. "You saw *me*, but I didn't see *you*. But . . ." He hesitates, then adds, "Now I do!"

Tears of happiness and relief fill my eyes. I can't speak. I just look at them all and nod and smile. For so long I felt so alone without Kim. And even when I had Kim and Tom by my side, there was a certain loneliness still because we were all outsiders—we were united by feeling like outsiders and missing where we come from. But now I feel like the ground beneath my feet is the steadiest it's ever been since I came to Juliette Cove.

My mind flashes back to Butterfly Hill, and I feel Lucila, Marisol, and Cristóbal with me. Somehow, in my new home with my new friends, I feel so much closer to home.

"Awwww. Enough of this mush!" Charlie finally returns to his old grumpy self. "Macaroni, I am starving. Let's eat some of your people. . . . I can't believe you boiled spaghetti, you cannibal!"

We all laugh.

Then Valerie asks shyly, "I've always wondered: What is in that notebook you always carry around with you? You're always writing in it at recess, at lunch, even during gym class!"

"Macaroni, read us something! I double-dare you!" Charlie says.

I pause. Charlie's eyes are so bright, I know he truly wants to know. So I decide I can be brave, and get my notebook.

"Okay. I usually write in Spanish. But sometimes I try English because Miss Rose says it's good practice. So, this is my first poem in English. I wrote it a few days ago in the woods." I pause again, unsure, but they are nodding at me, so I say, "Well, here it goes."

I take a deep breath and find the pages are shaking in my hands. *Don't be nervous, Celeste. These are true friends. You were given a gift so you could share it with others.* From far away I hear my mother's voice, soothing and guiding me.

I Walk Barefoot

I walk barefoot through the forest
To feel the grass, the soil, the moss.
My toes buried beneath the ferns
Search the roots of the forest
And find the roots of me.
Step by step I make a path.
Step by step I discover myself.
How could I know the trees are my sisters
When my roots began in a faraway soil?
Until I took off the shoes I wore yesterday
And buried my feet beneath the forest,
Beneath the same eager earth
That the whole round world calls home?

"Wow, Celeste, that is so good! I can't believe you wrote that in English!" Meg exclaims.

"No kidding," says Charlie. "Macaroni, you should be a writer someday."

I feel myself blushing. I am not sure what to say, but finally a strong smell reminds me: "Let's eat!"

I run to the kitchen and take the pot of pesto sauce from the stove—and not a moment too soon. The pesto at the bottom of the pot is burned! "¡Ay, no!" I groan as I skim a spoon over the top of the sauce, say a little prayer, and taste what is left of my creation. Phew!

I heap each plate with a generous serving of pasta and sauce, cross my fingers in my imagination that my friends will like it, walk to the dining room, and announce, "Pesto a la Andes!"

I hold my breath as Charlie dives in. "Yum! This is awesome! You really cooked this yourself, Macaroni?" he asks with his mouth full.

"Really yummy!" Meg slurps up tendrils of pasta that have escaped from her fork.

I let out a sigh of relief and take a bite myself. It really *is* yummy! "What's your secret ingredient?" Valerie is licking pesto from her fingers.

"At home my Nana Delfina—she is like my nanny, and she was even my mother's nanny when she was a girl—well, she cooked for the whole family."

"Like a maid?" interrupts Valerie.

"Yes . . . well . . . that and so much more," I try to explain to them. "She's not just some servant who eats her dinner in a tiny back room. She is also a member of the family. She has her own bedroom next to mine. She cooks our meals, but then she sits at the table with us. She loves us and we love her."

But their faces still look puzzled. It's *just* so different here!

"So . . ." Meg's voice is a mix of curiosity and envy. "She does everything in the house? You don't have *any* chores? Your mother doesn't even have to cook?"

I shake my head. "Not really. Mamá is kind of a bad cook anyway. She always burns the food, like my Tía Graciela." I lower my voice so she won't overhear us from the living room, where she is writing letters.

"Not like you at all, then!" Charlie says to me with a wink. I blush. He noticed!

"No, not—at—all," I stammer, then give a conspiratorial wink back. Valerie and Meg are too busy gaping at each other to notice.

"No chores!"

"Wow, you are so lucky!"

"You mean you didn't even have to make your bed?"

"Well, of course I made my bed!" I say with my mouth full of pasta. I take a sip of grape juice, which I poured into wineglasses to look fancy, and gulp. "Abuela Frida, my grandmother, says that a lady makes her bed and braids her hair each and every morning."

"Do your friends have chores?" Valerie asks me.

I shake my head. "Not really. Well, Cristóbal Williams had to help his mother at her fruit stand, but they were poorer than most of the families at my school. Papá told me a lot that we were the lucky ones in Chile, and because of that, he and Mamá wanted me to spend my time reading and studying, and also getting lots of exercise outside and sleep on school nights." Then I add, as an explanation, "They are doctors." My friends nod and exchange curious glances.

Questions

There is a long silence. But I feel their questions in the air like an approaching thunderstorm. Then all at once they rain down on me, hard—all the things I don't want to talk about.

"Celeste," Valerie begins nervously, "I don't want to make you sad, but . . . what happened to your parents?"

"Do you get to talk to them on the phone? Will they visit?" Meg adds.

"Why are you here when they are back in Chile?" Charlie looks at me intently.

I take a deep breath. Talk to my parents? It has been so long that sometimes I get scared that I won't remember their voices. "No," I say simply. "It is too dangerous to talk on the phone. But only my grandmother and nana are there, anyway, at Butterfly Hill." I look up. Six wide eyes stare back at me. Three silent, open mouths. "My . . . my parents are in hiding." My voice falters.

Valerie reaches for my hand. "Don't cry. Everything—"

"But why?" Charlie cuts her off, so insistent, he sounds almost angry. "Hiding from what? Did they do something wrong? And are you hiding too? Is that why you are here?"

"Well, yes . . . I guess so." Me, in hiding? I had never thought about it that way. "I feel more like I am waiting . . ."

"But where are your parents hiding, Celeste?!" Meg asks impatiently. "Why aren't they with you here?" Good question. Why aren't they? I had never thought about that either. Why *couldn't* we have all come here together?!

There is so much confusion in my mind, so much sadness in my heart, but I try to tell them what I do know. "My parents had to hide quickly," I say, squeezing Valerie's hand hard. She squeezes back. "They left when the president was killed and a general took power, because he was making people like my parents—people who help the poor and believe everyone should be equal, like in this country—disappear."

"Disappear?!" They say the word in unison.

I nod. "Disappear." That awful word. That question mark that dots itself with the point of a knife in my head. That constant ache. "Some people are kidnapped and locked in jails somewhere. Some, the lucky ones, already escaped and went into hiding like my parents, or are exiles in faraway places like me. And some"—I hesitate—"are killed."

They blink at me in utter silence. How can they understand what I am telling them, if I can hardly understand it myself?

More silence. Finally Valerie tries to change the subject. "I like what you said in your poem about the trees listening to us." Her fork plays with the last strands of pasta on her plate. "Don't laugh, Meg"—she gives her best friend a quick glance—"but when I was little, I used to talk to the trees."

"But why did you stop?" I ask. "Keep talking to them! What I wrote I really believe," I say. "Since the forest is alive, it must hear us in some way, and know us. Just in a different way from how people know each other."

Meg casts Charlie a sidelong glance. But Charlie avoids his sister's eyes and looks at Valerie.

"Celeste, so you think there is another world out there, like ghosts and witches and things like that?" Valerie asks, her blue eyes round as the plate set before her.

"My Nana Delfina always talked to me about the spirit world. She says it is natural, and nothing to be afraid of. In her culture what we call witches are not scary but wise women, medicine women who take care of people. She told me sometimes spirits stay behind to help us who are still living here." I give Valerie's hand another squeeze. It is cold despite the humid summer evening. I know she is thinking about her mother. "And our loved ones stay close to us to be our guardian angels."

Valerie smiles gratefully at me.

Meg begins to giggle and then tucks in the corners of her mouth.

"What do you think, Macaroni?" I don't hear one drop of sarcasm in Charlie's voice.

"My Abuela Frida always told me that the important thing was to have faith—that we live what we imagine. And that is how I know I will see my parents again. I imagine it every day."

Eighth Grade

Since reading my poem to my friends, I now imagine one day seeing my poetry in a bookshop in Valparaíso. Tía Graciela says that dreams only come true with effort, so I decide to write every day for the rest of the summer. Every evening I walk through the woods to a circle of trees with a perfect sitting stone in its center. And there I write in my notebook. "Even if you just write one word, Celeste," Tía Graciela encourages me, "you come that much closer to filling a page." Sometimes I think of only small things like: *There is something delicious about summer evenings in Maine, cool and sweet like a dish of strawberries.*

When I see the fireflies with their bright little lanterns floating around my face, I know it is time to go home. I can see the house lights shining through the trees. Tía Graciela turns them on so I can find the house . . . like a ship finding the harbor.

Tonight I stay out a bit longer and imagine the flowers starting to peek from the ground on Butterfly Hill. I hope they are not afraid to bloom. Even though the General still rules Chile, even a dictator can't stop the springtime. But here in the other half of the world the days are getting shorter and the nights longer and cooler. Autumn is coming, and tomorrow is the first day of school.

The eighth-grade teacher, Mr. Gary, is a tall man with light blue eyes, salt-and-pepper hair, and a picture of his daughters on his desk. He seems like a kind and gentle man. He says that my English is so much better that I don't need extra help. "You will learn even more quickly when you have no other choice," he says, smiling at me. He speaks so much faster than Miss Rose! I look back at him nervously. "Trial by fire." He smiles again, encouragingly. "Extra credit if you figure out what that means by the end of the week!" Oh gosh, is that extra credit or extra homework? How will I ever keep up in class?

I like Mr. Gary, but I try to visit Miss Rose's classroom whenever I can. When I show her some of the poems I have written in English, she hugs me. "Celeste, I am so proud of you!" Then she pulls a piece of lined paper from her desk and hands it to me. "I found this in Kim's old desk while I was cleaning my classroom this summer."

There is just one sentence on the paper, written in Kim's careful penmanship: *Celeste is my forever friend.*

I read those words, and it's like having her next to me for a moment. I see Kim's hands making paper birds.

Her eyes with the look of yearning for home. "Miss Rose," I say, "I promise that I will study hard to improve my English and make this year my best ever on Juliette Cove. I will do it for Kim because she always tried so hard, and now she can't be here herself. And someday I will become a writer and she will read my stories, wherever she is."

Scraps
of Life

The day after Halloween there is no school. I sit with Tía Graciela at the kitchen table, but I don't have much of an appetite for breakfast after eating so many caramel-filled chocolates the night before. Meg and Charlie invited me to go trick-or-treating for my first time. I tried to say no at first—I was feeling blue—but Charlie insisted. When I finally agreed, he said "¡Gracias!" in Spanish, so I dressed like a snowflake, something I know will be falling from the sky soon. I wore all white clothes and glued cotton balls over every inch of me. I even had a white cap covered with cotton balls on my head! And Tía Graciela sprinkled me with silver glitter and gave me a little pumpkin to carry to keep any mean spirits away.

"Did you have fun last night, Querida?" Tía Graciela asks me. I push the round toasted oats, a cereal I have finally come to like, back and forth in my bowl and watch them slowly expand like sea sponges in the milk. "Mm-hmm." I did have fun, but today I feel tired and down. Maybe it is because all morning Tía Graciela has been telling me news of Chile she has received from her friends living in other countries, like Spain, where it is easier to get news from South America. She is always taking the same letters out and rereading them. Sometimes it makes me frustrated to hear words like "censorship" and "hunger" and "disappeared" over and over again.

I pick up a piece of yellowed paper folded in threes near the bottom of the pile and scan a few lines. I read aloud: "'My brother asked the government permission to throw a party for his son's seventh birthday and was denied . . .'"

I remember how Abuela Frida forbade me to walk in the park with large groups of friends. "No more than three of you, or they'll call it subversive! They could arrest you!" Even in memories the fear in my grandmother's voice still sends chills up my spine.

Subversive. I remember Gloria saying it as well. It sounds sinister, all twisted like a serpent. I don't ever want to write it down. I hear myself let out a long sigh. My chest feels tight.

"But listen." Tía Graciela's voice brightens. "There might be a change soon! My friend says that exiled Chileans as well as French people have been standing outside the gates in Spain every day for a whole two weeks!" She reads on, and I watch as hope lights up her face. "They hold signs with the General's face crossed out with a big red X. And other signs that say: '¿Dónde están?' Where are they?"

¿Dónde están? ¿Dónde están?

"Where are they?!" I cry out, unable to hold any longer the question I carry with me every day. "Where are Mamá and Papá? Where are Lucila and Ana? Where is Principal Castellanos?!" I fold my arms over my chest and stare at Tía Graciela. "And how many more have been disappeared or had to leave like I did?" I demand. Suddenly I hear myself shouting, "I don't want to think about dark jails and the people I love in them!"

I can hardly breathe, and my hands have scattered all the letters to the floor. My aunt reaches to hug me, but I pull away.

"Celeste, Querida mía," she says soothingly. "There are many people who don't want to recognize what is happening to our country because they don't want to be reminded of pain. They are afraid of pain. But you are not one of those people, Celeste."

I sniffle and look at my aunt with some disbelief.

"No, Celeste. If you never knew pain, how could you recognize joy?"

Then it all tumbles out of me at once.

"I want to hear the sounds of Butterfly Hill. The sirens of the boats coming and going from the harbor, the creaking of the swings, Señora Atkinson's piano . . ." I gasp for air. Tears run hot down my cheeks. "But, but, I wouldn't care if I never heard anything again if I could only hear Mamá's and Papá's voices!"

"Oh, Celeste." Tía Graciela pulls me into her arms, and this time I let her.

"How do they get food? Are they cold at night?"

For some strange reason I remember it is getting warmer and warmer there, as it gets colder and colder here. But then the thought just reminds me of how far away I am from my parents. Not just miles, but days. So many *days* between us. I make a decision.

"Tía Graciela?"

"¿Sí?"

"Will you take the calendar off the wall in my bedroom when I am at school tomorrow and throw it away?

"Are you sure, Celeste?"

I nod. I finally understand why Abuela Frida doesn't like calendars. I have been using the calendar on my wall to count the days since I left Chile. 647. Since day ten, Tía Graciela has told me I am being stubborn and hanging on to sadness.

"I want to measure time according to the seasons, like Abuela does," I tell my aunt, who is wiping her own eyes and looking so relieved. "Seasons are so much larger than days. Only four a year."

"Mamá taught me and Esmeralda that each season is an instrument," Tía Graciela tells me, and motions for me to sit down. "She would tell us how she always knew it was spring when the piano keys rang like little bells as her old music teacher Mr. Leschetizky played Liszt's *La Campanella*."

"Then autumn on Juliette Cove is a burnished viola bursting with the sounds of yellow, orange, and red," I say. Suddenly I feel relieved too. For now it is enough to imagine. *No more counting, Celeste,* I tell myself. *Be like the seasons and just keep going.*

The Mailman
Mr. John
Carter

Tía Graciela powders her face with the fine rice powder Abuela Frida gave her. Then she puts on red lipstick and turns her head to the front window like a swan. She does this every day around noon because that's when the mailman comes by.

At first they only exchanged a courteous hello, but as months turned into years, Tía Graciela and the mailman John Carter became friends. I like how Mr. Carter is always ready to smile and how his big laugh sounds so genuine.

"He is nice to chat with," Tía Graciela tells me. "Before you came, he was the only person I had to talk to besides my clients—I mean, friends," she corrects herself. "And *they* only want to hear about themselves!" she continues, and I laugh. And just then we hear Mr. Carter's familiar TAP-tap-tap-TAP upon the door.

"Mail's here! Letters from abroad, Miss Graciela. And a package!"

My aunt receives letters from all over the world,

from places as far away as Russia, because so many of her friends are exiles.

"Tell me, Graciela, how do you have time to answer all the letters you receive?" he asks. "They are from so many places!"

"I find time every day. It's my only way of talking to my friends. So many of them are living in other countries now—Spain, England, Germany, México, Russia. I have a friend in Alabama and others in California, Texas, Chicago . . ." Tía Graciela's voice trails off. "If Celeste and I didn't have our letters, we would feel so alone. And, of course, we always look forward to seeing your smile and hearing you say, 'Mail's here!'"

I hand a plate of chocolate-chip cookies to Mr. Carter. "I made them myself!"

"Look!" Tía Graciela whispers, and points at something behind Mr. Carter's left shoulder.

"Oh!" My breath catches in my throat. A slender brown deer stands in our front yard. She seems to be looking right at us! Then she moves her head up and down four—no, maybe five—times! "It's as if she's nodding yes!" I whisper.

Mr. Carter tips his hat to both of us and returns to his mail truck. The deer scampers into the woods. And we watch until Mr. Carter, too, has faded into the whiteness of winter on Juliette Cove.

An Entire Sky
Inside

I wake up in the middle of the night to the smell of salt water, cilantro, and cinnamon. "What a strange dream!" I rub my eyes. In my sleep I stood aboard a small wooden sailboat with billowing sails whiter than the moon. I was skippering the boat, following a large flock of pelicans flying low over the water. Suddenly my friend the old pelican turned back to look at me and started heading south, as if leading me home.

BOOM! A gust of wind slams the shutters back and forth. A storm must be coming. I glance toward the window. The branches of the trees are waving so fast. *It's as if they are trying to get someone's attention.* Just then Tía Graciela opens the door to my bedroom. Her face is flush—a look I've never seen before.

I hear a branch fall to the ground as my aunt sits beside me and takes my hand. She takes a deep breath. I do too—waiting to hear what has her acting so oddly. It can't be the storm. . . .

"I received a call from a friend in Spain very late last

night." Her voice trembles in disbelief. "The General is dead. Celeste, we are going home!"

I stare at her. "Dead?"

"Dead."

"We're going home?" I echo.

"We're going home!" Tía assures me, her voice cracking.

Shaking with surprise, disbelief, and joy, I hardly know what to do with myself. I walk downstairs, put my winter jacket and boots on over my pajamas, and wander into the front yard. The night is still and cold, as if the storm never happened. How strange! I just heard that smash of wind! That branch falling! I look up at the stars and see my breath rise like smoke to greet them. They twinkle like little lighthouses. "The Big Dipper, the Little Dipper, Orion the Hunter." I whisper those names as I find the shapes that Tía Graciela showed me during my first week on Juliette Cove.

How funny, I think, *to realize only now that I love the stars of the Northern Hemisphere almost as much as the constellations of the South.* Shivering with cold, I turn to go back to the house. Suddenly a bright light from above shines in my eyes. An orb I have never seen before—so big and bright that it must be a planet— radiates a soft, green light, shining brighter and brighter, until it makes me think of an emerald. Esmeralda!

PART III

Only Returns

The **Refuge**
Against
Oppression

Tía Graciela lets me stay home from school. We sit on the couch in front of the TV all day, waiting for any mention of what has happened in Chile. We watch the morning news, the lunchtime news, and finally—just when I think that friend in Spain was mistaken—our country is mentioned on the evening news.

The news anchor says that Chile will begin a peaceful transition to democracy. The screen then flashes to—*could it be?*—the streets of the capital: parades of children and their grandparents emerging from behind locked doors. Men kneeling and weeping while women dance with the colors of Chile—red, white, and blue—all through the streets.

It's the first time I have seen my country in three years. Mouth open in shock, I keep pointing to the screen and then turning to look at Tía Graciela to make sure I'm not dreaming.

Tía Graciela's face is soaked with tears. "Oh, thank you! God is good."

The TV now shows a reporter interviewing citizens of Santiago. How wonderful it is to hear the *shhhhh* sound of their accents, like soft waves rolling onto the sand. Each voice holds a slightly different story—there seems to be more than one version of how the Dictator died. My aunt's brow is wrinkled in concentration.

Some people believe that the General died drinking his own poison. Others point to the rumors that he suffered from long bouts of colds, until two days ago, when he sneezed so hard that the roof of his bedchamber crashed all around him, trapping him cowering under the covers. And others say the earth conspired to end him and began to quake, but just in his own palace. In no other part of Santiago was even the slightest tremor felt. Not even a leaf fell from the trees.

Much, *much* too soon, the reporter from Chile says good-bye. The anchor moves on to another story.

"No! Wait! Please stay!" I reach my hands toward the television set, wishing I could grab those sights and sounds and hold them safe in my arms.

Tía Graciela continues to cry, but she is also laughing.

"We are free, Tía Graciela! All of us! I can hardly believe it! We are free!"

"We should sing, Celeste." And no sooner has she uttered the words than we move to our feet as one, put our hands over our hearts, and sing:

"Pure, Chile, is your blue sky . . . Either you be the tomb of the free or the refuge against oppression."

Tía Graciela pulls me into a tight hug. I feel so happy, yet at the same time I am very afraid. I fear to see what has happened to my city, to my family and my friends. Who will be there and who will still be missing? I tremble at the thought of everyone and everything I know having disappeared.

I look up at Tía Graciela, who seems just as lost in her own thoughts. Maybe . . . maybe . . . we should just stay here. . . . I am finally getting used to Juliette Cove. . . . I've made friends with the shadows that live in the woods and the vast silence of the snowy fields. . . . It's like I have one foot on Juliette Cove and the other on Butterfly Hill. . . . But then I imagine the blue sea and sky of Valparaíso. I see myself arriving at our house on Butterfly Hill for my birthday. Delfina is lighting the candles on my "thousand layers" cake and singing in Mapudungún. My friends and I run down the hills and water all the buganvillias in Valparaíso that shriveled and have refused to bloom since the day Presidente Alarcón was killed.

Traveling
Light

The next morning we hover over the radio and drink café con leche. After her third cup Tía Graciela stands up and turns the radio off. "That's enough. Celeste, we can't sit here all day listening to the announcements from Chile. You need to get ready to go home!" My aunt trots over to the cluttered closet in the hallway, and I follow slowly. I'm not sure I heard her right.

"Tía?"

"Hmmm?" Her head is hiding inside the closet.

"Why did you say 'you'? Aren't you coming too?"

My aunt pulls her head from between the winter coats and sits on the hallway floor. I sit down to face her and reach for her hands. They are cold, and her face suddenly looks pale and listless. "Celeste, I was up all night thinking about returning home to Chile." She pauses and stares down at our entwined hands for a moment.

"I am not proud to admit this, but despite my happiness I am filled with so much fear. I don't know if

I am ready to return. I left Chile to be with Guillermo, and it didn't take long for that to fall apart. But then I was too ashamed to go back, because everyone had told me I was crazy to give up everything for a man I had only known for a few months. And . . . and . . . I always hoped he might come looking for me. . . . So I stayed awhile, and then a while more. And I always felt, well, guilty for leaving my country for what I sometimes feel was a selfish reason, just before the time Chile would need me most. I don't know if I can face the truth when I return. That some of my friends and neighbors have been disappeared, that my own sister might be . . ."

I pull away my hands and draw back in horror. "No! No! No!" I yell. "Don't you dare say it! Don't you dare even think it!"

I run outside into the cold. I have never felt anger like this. I feel like I am tangled in my aunt's fears as well as my own, and I hate it. The fears are like thick cobwebs, and the more I try to escape, the tighter they become. I run over to the garage and kick the old oak door until it cracks with a snap. "Ay! Owwww!" I fall backward and clutch my foot. It sears with pain. I rock back and forth, rubbing my foot.

"Celeste, mía."

I feel Tía Graciela behind me. She puts a hand tentatively on my shoulder. I shrug it off.

"I am sorry, Celeste. Please forgive me. You always have been so strong. Actually, you have been my strength these past two years. I am not like my tiny young niece with a heart as big and brave as a chorus of angels."

I turn to face her. "Tía Graciela?" I say her name like a question. As if the woman standing before me is all the questions I couldn't answer.

"Celeste, you will make Mamá and Nana Delfina so happy with your presence. And I know you will find Esmeralda and Andrés. I know you will find your parents."

"I know I will too, Tía."

"Forgive me, Celeste?"

"Sí. I love you, Tía."

"I love you. Celeste, you are the daughter I never had. Now come inside. There's much to do."

"Let Your **Voice** Be Heard"

The first snows of the year have put the yard to bed in billowy sheets of white. I sit at my bedroom window, my face pressed to the glass. It's hard to believe that this is one of the last times I'll look out at the forest. In a few days I leave for Chile. I don't know where to start. When I arrived here nearly two years ago, I never thought it would feel so hard to leave my second blue room and return to my first.

But first I must say some good-byes. First is the mailman John Carter.

The chimney of his small red house pours forth smoke like a locomotive. We ring the doorbell, and a few seconds later Mr. Carter appears wearing a flannel bathrobe and slippers. He's carrying the crossword from the daily paper in his hand. Of course, it's Sunday, every mailman's day off! "Graciela! Celeste! To what do I owe this pleasant surprise?" His eyes dance behind his bifocals. "I don't have any letters today."

"Mr. Carter, I came to say good-bye. I am leaving for Chile soon."

The mailman takes off his glasses and rubs his eyes. "Really? Just like that? Oh, Celeste, I will miss you!"

I swallow hard.

"I want to thank you for being such a good mailman and always taking such good care of the letters that mean so much to us."

Mr. Carter clears his throat. "Maybe you could send me a letter from Chile? And I will be sure to write to you from here. What is your address?"

"Butterfly Hill . . . Wait, let me write it down for you." Mr. Carter hands me the crossword and pulls a pencil from his bathrobe pocket. Beneath the black-and-white grids that always remind me of train tracks leading to no place at all, I write: Cerro Mariposa, Valparaíso, Chile, 2-370835.

"No house number?" he asks.

I shake my head and smile. "In the hills everyone knows where everyone else lives."

Mr. Carter nods. "Ahhh, no wonder you and your aunt are always so friendly to your neighbors! And yet, I suspect that just as some things at home are simpler, others are more complicated?" He gives us a knowing look.

"Yes," I say. "If you visit my city someday, you will ride the cable cars that take you up and down the hills.

They are almost a hundred years old, and half the time they don't work. But just when everyone is ready to give up on them, suddenly you can hear the big wheels at the tops and bottoms of the hills start turning and pulling the cars up and down on pulleys, and then all day you can hear the cable cars rattle over the hills."

Tía Graciela throws up her hands and adds, "And you hear the voices of the people inside them, who are happy with our cable cars once again and swear they would never want to get rid of them!"

Mr. Carter chuckles. "I understand. It is like that sometimes with the mail service." His face becomes serious, and he puts his hands on my shoulders. "And I understand, Celeste, why it is time for you to go home. If the cable cars are working again, you need to be one of the happy young people aboard them. Let your voice be heard."

He gives me a big hug. "Write to me and tell me all about it."

"Good-bye, Mr. Carter."

"Good-bye, Celeste."

"And Miss Graciela? What will you do?"

"I am staying here, Señor Carter. Please don't forget about me."

"Never! Tomorrow I will be at your door . . . hopefully with a letter from Chile."

"Gracias, Mr. Carter!" my aunt and I speak in unison as we wave good-bye to a man whose kindness I never will forget.

Tía Graciela and I are quiet on the short ride home. But when we turn the corner onto River Road, I realize that tomorrow is Monday—a school day—my last on Juliette Cove. My stomach flip-flops. I wish it were my usual end-of-the-weekend blues. But this is a feeling of dread.

"I think saying good-bye is the most awful thing in this world," I tell my aunt.

Tía Graciela sighs softly in agreement. "But remember, Celeste, something your Abuela Frida taught us all—in this family there are no good-byes, only returns."

"Tía, life is so strange and unexpected! Now that I finally have friends to miss, now that I am used to living here with you, why does everything have to change so suddenly? I know that I am going home, and I am happy. But a part of me feels like I am leaving home too. A part of me is sad."

"Oh, Celeste. Por eso se llama exilio. That's why they call it exile. You belong everywhere and nowhere at all."

I think about what my aunt has said. Maybe once you are an exile, you always are an exile. Always missing somewhere else, always carrying a bit from here and a bit from there, and always with a bit of a broken heart.

"I'll Be **Seeing** You with My Heart"

I sit in school with a secret. I can hardly bear to look around the classroom. I keep my head down, scribbling *Good-bye, Juliette Cove* and sketching wild turkeys in my notebook.

"Celeste, you are so quiet today!" Mr. Gary is saying something. I jerk my head up toward the blackboard. "Are you feeling well?" I fight back tears and shake my head. "Do you want me to call your aunt to take you home?" I shake my head again.

Home. Home is where I am flying tomorrow night. And Home is also what I am leaving. "No, Mr. Gary, I will be fine."

"Okay, then why don't you read the next paragraph, which begins, 'Abraham Lincoln wrote the Emancipation Proclamation . . .'"

At the end of the day I walk down the hallway to my favorite classroom, number 44. Miss Rose is bent over her desk, squinting through her purple reading glasses and grading papers.

"Miss Rose, I am going back to Chile."

She looks up at me confusedly. "Celeste Marconi! Hello! I hope I heard you wrong! You didn't say you were leaving, did you?"

"Yes."

"When?"

"Tomorrow."

Miss Rose puts her hands to her heart. "So soon? Just like that?" She snaps her fingers. "In the middle of the semester? I don't understand." Her face looks pained.

"Me either, Miss Rose."

Miss Rose stands up and holds her arms out to me. I hug her, and she says, "I have never known a more courageous girl. Thank you, Celeste Marconi. You have taught us all so much."

My tears wet the front of her pink sweater. "Thank you," I sniffle. "Thank you," I try again, "for being so kind and patient. Thank you for teaching me English. And thank you for giving me books to read. I am taking *Little Women* home with me, and I know I will read it again and again and think of you."

Miss Rose wipes her eyes and smiles. "Celeste, I will never forget you. You arrived here so small and timid and sad, with your eyes always turned to the ground. And now you are a flower that is always in bloom. I will miss hearing your beautiful laughter fill the corridors."

I give her one more hug. "I should go. I told Valerie, Meg, and Charlie to meet me at the lighthouse. I have to say good-bye to them, too. Will you tell Mr. Gary and the rest of my class for me tomorrow? Tell them that I promise to write from Valparaíso?" Miss Rose nods, gives me one more squeeze, and lets go. I turn around quickly and run out of her classroom, all the way down the long corridor, and push through the heavy double doors into the cold winter air.

I find the big black boulder in front of the lighthouse, but the sun is setting, and the cold fog rolling in from the Atlantic makes it hard to spot my friends. Then suddenly I hear Charlie. "Celeste! Over here!"

"Charlie, where are you guys?"

"Here, three steps in front of your face!" A hand reaches out from the mist and grabs my wrist.

"Meg!" I cry, startled. She pulls me toward her, and she and Valerie hold on to me and hug me all at once. Charlie stands close by with a sullen look upon his face and drags a piece of driftwood through the seaweed.

"Oh, Celeste, tell us what is going on!" Valerie pleads. "You have been acting so strange all day. And we just saw some kids in the school yard who said they saw you crying and that they heard a rumor you were leaving!"

I look at them and can't say anything. But I don't have to.

"But . . ." Meg shifts from one foot to the other in the sand. "But we've only just become friends." She looks at her brother, who scowls even more. "Charlie, can't you say anything, or are you just going to stand there like another dumb rock?" She turns back to me. "I know my brother. He tries to be a tough guy when he really is sad."

"It's not fair!" Charlie yells. "Is that what you want to hear? Because it's not!" He comes closer to us, and we all sit down in cold, damp sand. He looks at me, and his voice turns soft: "It's not fair." Meg scoots closer to her brother.

I hear myself asking them, "Remember just now, how I couldn't see you in the mist? But I could hear your voices? Well, I think that saying good-bye is like that. When I am in Valparaíso, we won't be able to see each other with our eyes, but we can talk with our hearts. I'll be close by, just in another way."

Valerie nods and presses at her eyes with the end of her fuzzy yellow scarf. Meg bites her lip, and Charlie looks out to the ocean. "You always were so strange, Celeste," he says. "That's why I teased you in the beginning. And why the girls stayed away from you."

"And we were so stupid!" Valerie talks over him. "We are so sorry!"

"But . . ." Charlie takes a deep breath and continues. "You were always so great at being yourself. You never changed to try to fit in. The only thing you did was learn English, and I used to think, 'Wow! That girl works so hard! She's tougher than I am!'"

We fall into silence and listen to the waves roll in and out as the sky grows darker. A soft halo of light surrounds us before the sun sinks fully to sleep in the sea. "We should go," Valerie says as she lifts her long ballerina limbs from the sand. "We are happy for you, Celeste," she adds in a rush. "Don't think that we aren't. We are just sad to lose you."

"I want you all to visit me in Valparaíso someday," I tell them. "And in the meantime you can visit me with your imaginations. And I will visit you on a boat my Abuela Frida named the Ship Called Hope."

They burst into laughter.

"Oh, crazy old Macaroni, I will miss you!" Charlie gives me a sheepish smile and a hasty hug.

"It's true." Meg elbows him in the stomach. "Celeste's Abuela Frida always says, 'To imagine is to believe.'" The girls and I begin to run toward the end of the beach, with Charlie tagging slowly behind.

Suddenly he runs off in the other direction, down the beach and toward the water. "Celeste Marconi!" he cries. "I'll be seeing you with my heart!"

Of Flights and
Faith

On the ride from Juliette Cove to Logan International Airport in Boston, I can't stop braiding and unbraiding and rebraiding my braid. I don't dare think about my parents—about where they are and if they will return. I am also afraid to think of my friends. I force myself to think of the things that *will* be there: my home on Butterfly Hill, Abuela Frida, and Nana Delfina. I won't let myself think about saying good-bye to Tía Graciela. It's a day as cold as the one on which I arrived. I lean my head against the icy windowpane and let out a long sigh.

After a long silence as heavy as the wet snow that would block the door of the house on Juliette Cove, Tía Graciela pulls the car to the side of the road.

"Celeste, I think now is a good time to give you something."

"What is it, Tía?"

My aunt pulls a conch shell from her pouch. "This was the first one I found on Juliette Cove. Right by the lighthouse." She places the peach-speckled shell into my hands. "So you carry the voice of the ocean of Juliette Cove back home with you. And so you have something of mine to connect us always, no matter where we go. Listen to it whenever you need help, Celeste—this conch will help you hear the voice of your heart."

"Thank you, Tía Graciela!" I whisper. I hold the shell to my ear and listen to a murmuring cadence that soothes me like a lullaby.

Tía Graciela glances at her watch and pulls the rickety station wagon back onto the road. "I don't want you to miss your flight." Her voice is trembling. I can see the city of Boston, its buildings twinkling in the light of early dawn, on the far horizon.

When we arrive at the airport, Tía Graciela parks the car and waits with me at the gate. We don't say much until the flight attendant announces it's time to board. Then I spring to my feet and look down at them, unable to move any farther.

"Do you know how much I will miss you, Tía Graciela?" My aunt's eyes fill like deep green lagoons.

"Remember there are no good-byes in our family, only returns," she whispers as she kisses my cheek.

I join the line of people boarding the plane to Santiago. The seat next to me is empty. I wish Tía Graciela were in it. And just like that, the plane takes off. "Good-bye, Juliette Cove. Gracias. You will always be my friend."

I must fall fast asleep, because the next thing I know, I imagine I hear a far-off cry, almost like a squawk. I rub my eyes and stretch. I hear the cry again. A few of them in unison. It reminds me of something, but I am not sure just what. I must still be dreaming. . . .

I open my eyes wider and raise the window shade. Oh! I almost lose my breath. We are crossing the Andes. The Andes Mountains! Am I not dreaming?! Am I really flying over Chile?

And what are those in the sky? I rub my eyes again. Could that really be?! Yes! I see a flock of pelicans! Seven pelicans, flying through the cloudless sky. I imagine them crying out once more. They are here to greet me!

The plane descends slowly. I can hear the mountains whisper:

"Welcome back, Celeste Marconi, child of mine. You are Home!"

The Road
to Butterfly Hill

I'm shaking as I make my way through customs. "Chilean citizen?" a young woman asks me as she opens my passport and stamps a page. I see the word in green ink: "Return." I can't keep back my tears.

"Sí, señorita. I am a citizen."

"You have been gone a long time." Her voice is kind and her dark eyes understanding. "Welcome home."

I see Alejandro instantly. He stands outside customs with a big bouquet of red copihues, our national flower. Shaking, sobbing, and laughing all at once, I leap into his arms. "How good to see you, Niña Celeste!" he says with the shy smile I remember. "God is good to bring you home to us safe and sound." I am so happy to see Alejandro, but in the daydreams I've had for the past two years, everyone I love has been waiting at the airport to welcome me home to Chile. ¿Dónde están?

Alejandro sees me looking around and puts his hand on my shoulder. "Your Abuela Frida and your Nana

Delfina are waiting for you at home, Niña Celeste, and are so excited."

I nod. "Oh, okay, Don Alejandro."

But Alejandro looks pained. "Your abuela . . ." He clears his throat, searching for words. "Your abuela . . . she is not quite as you may remember her. Two hard years have made her body weaker. But"—he pats my shoulder—"her spirit is as strong as ever!" My stomach tightens into knots. I look at Alejandro in confusion. Abuela Frida! Is it sickness? Nostalgia? Something terrible that has happened? It's too much all at once!

"Come, Niña Celeste." Alejandro changes the subject and leads me toward the car. "Delfina has been preparing a stew all day that is fit for a queen!

"How little you brought home!" Alejandro says as he puts my suitcase into the trunk. "You travel light like your grandmother. Maybe she will get out and about more now that you are home," he continues. "She is always afraid that the wind will blow her hearing aids away! But last week Delfina and I convinced her to let us carry her down Butterfly Hill to sit for a while in the sun. She has grown so thin that she fits inside a picnic basket!"

I shake off the idea of my grandmother getting old, and try not to think of weakness or hearing aids and all the other changes I fear facing when I arrive home. So I look out the window at the sights of Santiago. Empanada stands, street singers, children running down the sidewalks, signs in Spanish everywhere. Spanish! How strange to be speaking my language with everyone and not just Tía Graciela! I chatter to Don Alejandro and hope he can't tell I am trying so hard to sound carefree: "Tell me about Butterfly Hill, Alejandro! What has happened there? How is the magician at Café Iris? And Señora Atkinson and her teacups and the piano she plays on rainy days?"

Alejandro casts a grim look my way in the rearview mirror. "Niña Celeste, here so much has happened, so much has changed, so much has been lost, and yet so many of the little everyday things have remained. They are a blessing. During the darkest days they were all we had. But the most important thing, Niña Celeste, is that when I saw you, I realized that the years of pain truly are coming to an end. Forgive me if I drive faster than usual today. It's just that Doña Frida and Delfina have been waiting so very long to hug you." The Andes Mountains rush by in a blur, but they still look like they are topped with Chantilly cream.

"I had actually forgotten how steep and curvy the road to our house is, Don Alejandro!" My hands begin to tremble as we pass through thick forests of eucalyptus. I dreamed of their intense scent so many times before. All of a sudden we pass by Bismark Square, at the bottom of Barón Hill. Children are playing marbles and running around. On one of the benches there is an old woman with a face so wrinkled that it looks like onion skin. I wave to her. We round another corner, and Butterfly Hill comes into view. Unable to contain my excitement, I roll down the window and sit up on the door ledge with my hair flying in the breeze so that I don't miss seeing a single flower or neighbor, or hearing the cable cars make their familiar bumps and thumps. Alejandro looks at the backseat with a worried brow. "Cuidado, Niña Celeste!"

"Then may I get out and walk from here, Don Alejandro?" He smiles, and his smile is even kinder than the memories I kept of his goodness. "A fine idea, Niña Celeste. I will drive up with your luggage. I know you have been waiting to take this walk for a long time." I step out of the car and back onto my native soil. I feel Tía Graciela with me as I climb Butterfly Hill. Then, as I turn a familiar corner, I see the blue-and-yellow house I have dreamed of every day. The windows are open, and I see a huge pink scarf flying out from the balcony like a flying carpet. I hear the call of pelicans. "Oh, Abuela!"

Abuela Frida begins to run down the stairs with her arms open wide. My feet root to the earth and pull me down upon it. I watch with tears running down my cheeks. My Abuela Frida running down the stairs like a young girl, with her nightgown on and a long pink scarf trailing from her neck! She has covered her ears, I suppose so her hearing aids don't fall out!

With surprising strength she pulls me from the ground and holds me tight in her arms.

"Celeste, how beautiful you are! Let me touch your hair, just like Rapunzel's braids! You are home! And your hands have not changed." Abuela Frida puts her hands in mine and squeezes them tight. "Celeste, how much I have missed you!"

We hug each other for a long, long time. Then slowly we start climbing the rest of the hill, holding hands. I feel that her hand has become smaller. Before it was so big that mine fit inside it and could get lost in it. Her gait is slower. And she is so thin! Her face is so small, almost childlike, hiding behind layers of rice powder, but her blue eyes twinkle like always. We walk up the path in silence, and I watch my house grow larger and larger. Every so often Abuela Frida squeezes my hand and pulls me to a stop. She looks up at my eyes and tells me what life has been like on Butterfly Hill while I've been away.

"Every night I thought about faith, the very thing I always told you to have," she says, "and I confess that sometimes I wondered if it was just a word. Delfina and I were so lonely without you. I played cards a lot. Solitaire, mostly. But on rainy days Leslie Atkinson would visit for

tea, and we played bridge with her English cards. And sometimes after dinner Delfina and I played poker with your Abuelo José's old Spanish cards. We gambled for buttons." She winks at me.

Abuela is so much older that she is almost like a little girl. I don't know whether to laugh or cry. I am happy, frightened, and sad all at the same time. I never imagined that returning home would be so overwhelming.

I walk through the long grass toward my dolls' garden. The gardens are overgrown, and the flowers have grown so much, they resemble giant trees. They almost totally disguise the house. Abuela Frida reads my thoughts and points to the lilac bush outside the window where she rocks and knits. "Somehow they made me feel safe, hidden. It was dry and withered all these years you were away. And this morning I looked and it was in full bloom!"

As I walk through the front door, I am greeted by a special quiet, the quiet of sadness and waiting. *I wonder where Delfina is?* I find her in the kitchen shelling peas, mumbling, and looking through the window at the sky as if she is praying or searching for someone in the clouds. Then she looks at me. We hug and do not say a word. I only hear the music of her heart.

Like **Old** Times

Nana picks up my suitcase and heads for the stairs.

"No!" I shout.

She looks back at me, surprised. I, too, am taken aback. "I mean, ummm. I can do it myself." Why am I so jumpy? I should be happy—I am finally home! But for some reason I want to rediscover the house on my own. But most of all, I want to climb up to the roof.

Delfina, as always, understands me even when I don't. "Delfina will be warming the stew in the kitchen," she says.

I climb the stairs, creakier than ever, and stand at the threshold of my blue room.

My first blue bedroom. Sometimes I sat in my second blue bedroom and tried to imagine just how the quilt on the bed, or the brass handles of the dresser, looked. Now things seem strange to me.

I put my suitcase down. It seems like things haven't been touched for a long time. My old school uniform is folded on the bed. The dresser is covered with dust, as is

my reflection in the mirror that hangs over it. I look back
at a girl whose eyes are too sad and serious to be Celeste
Marconi's. And I suddenly realize that I don't have to
stand on tiptoe anymore to see myself!

I sit down on the bed and run my fingers over my
uniform. It looks so small! Nana must have ironed and
left it there for me, hoping not too much time would
pass until I returned. I put my head down on the scratchy
fabric and catch the slightest scent of rose water, which
she always sprinkled on our laundry.

Then I spring from the bed and run down the hall
toward the stairs. "Delfina! Abuela!" I call to them the
way I used to when I arrived home from school in the
afternoons. "I'm home!"

I find them both in the kitchen. These two little
women, they fill the room like sunshine. Abuela Frida sits
at the table, beaming at me above a bowl of untouched
stew. And Nana Delfina sings a song in Mapudungún
as she ladles out my own stew. She looks up as I enter.
"Delfina is giving you extra gravy—your favorite."

"You remembered after all this time! Thank you,
Nana."

Delfina looks at me in mock shock. "To think, Niña
Celeste, that Delfina could forget one thing about any of
her girls!"

"I'm one of her girls too." Abuela Frida's smile is

like a little girl's. "See"—she holds her bowl up for me to see—"extra potatoes."

I sit next to my grandmother and scoot my chair over to be closer to her. It is so very good to be home and yet still so very unreal to me. I've dreamed of a moment like this—a meal like this one—for so long, and now I don't quite know what to do with it, or with myself.

Abuela Frida seems to read my thoughts. "Time to eat, Celeste. Just taste one bite at a time."

Oh, Abuela, how I missed you!

Suddenly the doorbell rings. I jump out of my skin. Half in excitement, half in fear. Could it be my parents? Or could it be the police?

I hold my breath until Nana Delfina comes back smiling. "A special visitor has arrived for you, Celeste," she says excitedly. "Nana Delfina's favorite young gentleman—with blue eyes and a big appetite, and who loves Nana's cooking! Can you guess?"

"Cristóbal!"

I run down the hall toward the front door.

"Celeste!" None other than Cristóbal Williams shouts my name as he lifts me up and spins me around in a big hug.

I watch as Cristóbal reaches into his knapsack and pulls out a bunch of wildflowers, purple, red, and yellow. "I picked them on my walk up Butterfly Hill, one by one, until . . ." His voice trails off, and I watch as his cheeks turn from pink to bright red. I feel my own face flushing too. He pushes the bouquet toward me and finishes by saying hastily: "Here, Celeste, like old times."

"Gracias, Cristóbal."

I smile at him shyly. Cristóbal looks different. I guess, like me, he is older. But there is something else. His eyes are no longer cloudy with dreams. They are alert, and his face has grown sharper, thinner. Everything about Cristóbal is watchful. What happened to that drowsy boy I left behind?

I take his hand and lead him to the kitchen. "Come in and say hello . . ." I look at him curiously. "Wait—how did you know I was home? Your pendulum?"

Cristóbal blushes. "Well, yes . . . partly. And partly because your Abuela Frida called me on the telephone."

"He's been coming quite often to check on us ladies," Abuela Frida pipes up as we enter the kitchen. "Hola, Querido Cristóbal." She smiles at him as he kisses her cheek.

"Buenos días, señora."

"Let's go take a walk. All right, Abuela?" I ask.

"Sí, Querida, you two have much to catch up on," Abuela says. "Just stay on Butterfly Hill."

"Cristóbal, keep her safe," Delfina adds, beaming in Cristóbal's direction.

"Thank you for coming and visiting them," I say as we shut the door behind us.

"De nada. It was nothing." He brushes it off and takes a deep breath. "It's a beautiful day. You must have missed days like this on Butterfly Hill." He gives me a sidelong glance.

"I did. I especially missed my walks with you."

We walk in silence, close to each other, for a while. Then, tentatively, I say, "Tell me about our friends."

Cristóbal stares down at his feet, and we walk a bit longer. Then he pulls me down onto a bench and looks into my eyes. "Lucila and her parents. We still have no idea. I am sorry, Celeste. It has just been me and Marisol for a long while. I should have brought her with me, but I wanted to see you for myself. . . . Ana moved with her family to México."

It's too much to comprehend. I feel like a machine as I ask, "And Gloria?"

"Her father moved her to a private school, just a few weeks after you left. I haven't seen her, but Marisol saw her once in a dress shop."

"And what happened?"

"Marisol can tell you the details—"

"I'll stop by her house first thing tomorrow. I'm dying to see her," I interrupt him. "I'm sorry, Cristóbal. Go on. What happened then?"

"Nothing much, I guess. Gloria's mother just grabbed her hand and rushed her out of the store, but Marisol said that she caught Gloria's eye and she looked sad and frightened, but then Gloria looked down at her hands, and when she looked up again, her eyes were hard like she had never known Marisol."

"Poor Gloria! Poor Marisol!" And I ache to think of Lucila. Just trying to wrap my lips around her name feels like a hand choking my throat.

"Celeste, be careful if you see Gloria, please." Cristóbal takes hold of my arm. "So much has gone on here while you've been away. Her father was working for the Dictator, in the Ministry of Justice, and he rose to a really powerful position. Even now everyone fears him."

"Maybe even Gloria herself," I answer him. "The smartest student in the entire school! Don't tell me she doesn't know the difference between right and wrong!" And all of a sudden I feel angry and luckier than I had ever realized to have the parents I have. "Cristóbal, as much as the way my parents lived their lives worries me and causes me to miss them every minute now, I couldn't imagine fearing them, or disliking who they are."

Cristóbal nods. "I know. I am so glad my mother is my mother too, with her vegetable stand. Oh, did I tell you she branched out? She is selling roses now too! She told me to bring you some, with her love."

"And I bet you forgot!" I laugh. "Is *that* why you picked me wildflowers?"

Cristóbal shrugs his shoulders with a sheepish smile and yawns. "Maybe. . . . You'll never know." And for a moment it *is* like old times.

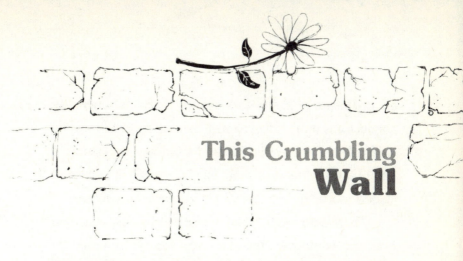

This Crumbling
Wall

That night Nana Delfina tucks me into bed like I am still a little girl. "Niña," she says, "you must make a promise to Delfina that you won't go any farther than Butterfly Hill on your own." What?! After being away from Valparaíso, after dreaming of seeing my friends and favorite sites and sounds for so very long?

"But, Nana, why?!" I protest. "I have been taking the cable cars all over the city by myself since I was ten!"

Delfina is stern. "It is still dangerous out there, Celeste. There is confusion and violence. The Dictator's soldiers are angry. And the people of Valparaíso are angry. Abuela Frida feels that it is no place for a young girl. Your grandmother doesn't need to worry any more than she does already."

"Sí, Nana." And so I promise, mostly because I am too frustrated, confused, and oh so tired to argue with her more.

The next morning I wake up to a basket full of memories. The rain outside sounds out of tune, like an orchestra of flutes and bells and violins when the conductor is away. I feel almost like a stranger in my own blue room. Even in this house. I look out the window. I don't have the heart to shout like I used to, but I whisper, "Good morning, Valparaíso! Good morning, pelicans!"

There's no answer. I know the pelicans are watching over me somehow, but they still haven't returned to Butterfly Hill.

I wrap Nana's green shawl around my shoulders and tiptoe downstairs. No one else is awake yet. I turn the radio on softly. A deep, low voice tells me that the entire country of Chile has become a giant cemetery. I hear something about graves that sends icicles through my heart. I am scared of my own history. I shiver and walk to the kitchen to make myself some coffee with a bit of cinnamon and warm milk.

After I drink my coffee, I write a note for Delfina: *Out greeting Butterfly Hill, Nana!* I put on my mother's raincoat. It is much too long for me but still carries her scent. My head becomes full with just four words: *Mamá, where are you?* I blink hard and step outside.

I walk the winding streets of Butterfly Hill, pausing to look at the old houses, big and small, purple and yellow. I turn a corner and find a concrete wall that used to be like any other old wall. But now it is painted with indigenous faces, baskets filled with fresh bread, even the face of the murdered Presidente Alarcón.

This crumbling wall, I realize, has become a notebook where people tell their stories.

I walk a bit more and come to a tall house with a balcony facing the harbor. Its orange paint isn't as vibrant as I remember, and it's cracked in some places. I take a deep breath and knock on the door. After a few seconds I hear footsteps, and the door opens—just a crack at first, and then it widens. There stands a girl with long black hair. Tall and curvy in tight brown pants and red boots, she definitely looks like she's in high school! She stares and looks surprised for a moment, and then her dark eyes widen in recognition.

"Celeste?!" she gasps. "Is it really you?" Marisol throws her arms around me, and we hug each other for a long time in silence. She smells like her mother's Chanel No. 5!

I laugh and say, "You're still stealing dabs of your mother's perfume?"

Marisol sniffles and giggles at the same time. "Can you believe she just bought me my own bottle for my birthday? Ay, amiga! Can you believe we are *thirteen*? It has been so long!" She hugs me again. "Celeste, I have missed you so much! Too much!"

Marisol suddenly looks much older than her fourteen years. "Too much has changed, Celeste. Even you, a little bit. You look so serious! I probably do too, I guess . . ."

I put my arm around her. "Walk up with me to my house, Mari, and have lunch with me!"

Marisol nods excitedly. "Let me just leave a note for Mamá. She is working with the pescadoras, cutting up fish to sell in the market, to make some extra money these days. Can you imagine my mamá letting herself get all smelly and covered with fish guts?" Marisol smiles ruefully. I try to picture the elegant Señora López like that and shake my head. "Papá didn't want her to, but she insisted. He hasn't had steady work ever since the General . . ."

She looks down as she puts her own raincoat on. "But enough of that! It's all anyone talks about! I am so sick of thinking about it! So sick of living in it!" She looks at me, her eyes welling with tears. "Celeste, don't be mad, but sometimes I envied you being so far away from Valparaíso!"

I look down. "Sometimes I envied you for being here," I admit.

As we leave, she locks the front door, which used to be always open so anyone could come in and say hello.

Perched on
Invisible Things

The next morning I am awakened by a nightmare.

I was running down the beach, chasing my parents and calling their names, but they dove into the ocean and disappeared.

I drag myself downstairs to the kitchen, feeling I will go crazy worrying about Mamá and Papá. The light through the windows is so bright! I squint, letting my eyes get accustomed to the rainbow palette of colors all around me. I didn't realize how much more dim and muted the light was on Juliette Cove.

I have to distract myself! "Delfina, let me help you!" I insist, and begin to list off all the chores I learned to do on Juliette Cove. "Sweeping, dusting, making spaghetti . . ."

"My niña Celeste, so independent now! Just like a good American," she teases, and hands me a knife to chop basil. She knows that chopping basil next to her is my favorite thing in the world.

Even though I am happy to be with Abuela Frida and Delfina, a whole day at home seems like a very long time, especially when I can't leave Butterfly Hill and so much is going on in the city below us! But Abuela Frida doesn't want me to go to school until my parents return. "Too many changes at once," she explains to me in German, which she now speaks more than Spanish. "Too many questions from too many people." Abuela Frida's gaze has become like a weightless bird that perches on invisible things. Her blue eyes are so pale, they remind me of Kim's paper birds.

Part of me is afraid to go back to school, so I don't protest too much. I don't want to upset my grandmother. I suspect she is keeping me close by because she still can't quite believe that I am really home.

So I sit by her on her favorite green velvet sofa. The blue yarn is limp in her hands. She snoozes off much more often than she knits now. Her soft snores will forever remind me of a bumblebee. Before lunch I read to Abuela Frida from Papá's copy of Neruda's *Odes to Common Things*. She especially likes the poem about the onion. "It makes my eyes water just hearing your voice, Celeste of my soul! Can't you smell the room thick with onions, or is that just Delfina's potato soup?"

And now in the afternoon I read to her from the thick copy of *Little Women* that Miss Rose gave to me, translating as I go. Abuela beams as I read, "'Christmas won't be Christmas without any presents.'" I have read *Little Women* cover to cover two times. The youngest,

Amy, with her curly yellow hair, reminds me of Gloria. Where is my old friend now? Are we even friends anymore?

From behind the closed parlor door I hear the faint ring of the doorbell. It is probably Señora Atkinson wanting some tea and gossip. I turn my eyes back to the heavy book in my lap and reread the part when the girls' father comes home from the Civil War: "'Mr. March became invisible in the embrace of four pairs of loving arms.'"

And what about Papá? I think. *Why hasn't he come back to us?*

Delfina pokes her head in and motions for me to come. "Niña Celeste, you have a special visitor."

"Oh, Delfina, could it be? Is it Ma—"

"No, Querida," Delfina interrupts me, the smile suddenly falling from her face. "It's Señora Atkinson. She's come to say hello."

Two Roads on the Map of My
Heart

I can't just sit here anymore and not do anything. I am going crazy without Mamá and Papá. At least Cristóbal comes to visit almost every afternoon. Today we sit on the swings in the backyard, and Cristóbal tells me how he set up a table next to his mother's in the market. "After school I go there and use my pendulum, or read tarot cards and people's palms. These days so many people are searching for the truth. The truth is only starting to come out in the newspapers, and people have been desperate for answers for years."

"Abuela Frida tells me that everyone has to go to the Red Cross offices or the courts to ask about their loved ones. And hardly anyone gets answers. Everyone is searching for signs."

"You wouldn't believe the people who come to me. Men in suits with stern faces. Ladies with fur muffs and ruby bracelets. People who never before believed in what they called folk or peasants' magic will come to my table and ask me to give them a reading. I am glad they come to me. I believe in what I do, and I charge a fair price. Because other people are taking advantage of all this fear. They are pretending to have answers that they don't and are taking all of the people's money. I guess it is because they themselves need money. It is getting harder and harder for some families to eat."

Cristóbal begins to scoop up handfuls of sand from under the swings and watch it fall through his fingers. "I tell the people who come to me that I am only there to help them understand what they know in their hearts already. That the answers don't come from me or anyone else, but from them. People give away their power so quickly when they are scared, Celeste. Being here during the dictatorship taught me that. I think that these horrible two years wouldn't have happened at all if people had had more faith in themselves in the first place."

I stare, mouth agape, at my friend. Drowsy no more, Cristóbal has just spoken more words to me than he ever did in the eleven years we were friends before I fled to Juliette Cove.

"Show me, Cristóbal, please! I have felt so scared and confused since I got back here. I think if I have to look at my parents' empty places at the table one more time, I will go crazy! Tonight, though, you will sit next to me in my father's chair, okay?"

Cristóbal smiles his gentle smile, nods, and picks up

my hand. He turns my palm over to face him and, with his fingers, brushes away the sand. A little shiver runs up my arm. I try to shrug it away and cast my eyes out to the harbor.

"When people started disappearing, so many of my mother's friends showed up at our doorstep," he murmurs. "They knew I'd had these special abilities since I was a little boy. Then word spread among neighbors and co-workers, until there was sometimes a big crowd outside my door. My mother thought that was dangerous, and she was right. So she told people to come to her vegetable stand instead. People would buy vegetables from her, and if they wanted a consultation with me, they would buy roses. That is how she began selling flowers. All kinds of flowers, but people knew that roses meant they wanted a reading. And white roses meant an urgent case.

"And Mamá would wrap the roses up in papers with the colors of the flag on the outside and the slogan the Dictator always said, 'For God and Fatherland,' as a disguise. That always made her sad, she said, to have to cover the beautiful gifts of the earth in hate and lies, but it was good protection for us. And deep inside one of the roses that had not yet opened its petals, she would put a tiny piece of paper with a date and a time on it. That told the person when they should come see me at our house. That way we never had a crowd, and I was able to help some people make the difficult decisions they were facing.

"It was so hard, Celeste. Imagine having to decide whether to flee or whether to hide, or whether to keep living your life in the open. Young parents wondering how to protect their small children. Or old parents desperate to find their grown children. Can you guess what color roses Mamá sold the most?"

"White." It feels like there is sand in my throat. Cristóbal begins moving his fingers again, softly up and down the lines on my palm. I've never noticed how varied those lines are. Some are faint and some are deep canyons. Some cut sideways and some branch into two rivers.

"See, your palm is like a map, Celeste. It's a map of your heart. I can read yours easily because your heart is very open. And your heart holds the answers you need. It might not hold every answer you wish for, but every one that you need at this very moment. And just like a heartbeat is followed by another, each answer leads to the next question, and then another answer. It is like that until the day we die. What I read here on your palm is like a Morse code from your heart. I believe anyone can read it if they learn. It's just that somehow no one ever had to teach me. I just knew."

I smile at him. I never realized how wise my friend

was. "Cristóbal, could you read my palm like a map?"

"A map of Chile?"

"Sí. A map of Chile."

"Well, is Chile in your heart?"

"You know it is."

"What do you want to see, Celeste?"

"The road that leads to my parents! Please, Cristóbal, will you help me find them?"

Cristóbal continues to trace his fingers on my skin. Then he lifts my hand up very close to his eyes. "There are two well-worn paths here."

Two paths? My heart starts beating hard. "What do you mean?" My voice wavers.

"Your parents aren't hiding together anymore. You have to choose one first."

"You know I can't choose!"

Cristóbal Williams looks at me carefully. "Yes, you can." His voice is stern. "Sit quietly and listen to your heart." Then he starts to draw a map of Chile in the sand. It is a very long and narrow map, surrounded by sea and mountains, totally self-contained. I sit and watch him for what feels like an eternity. The back of my mind mumbles something about before dark, dinnertime, Delfina . . . but I push that away. I want my mind quiet so I can hear my thoughts! Oh, why is my mind always full of so many words?

"Look! Listen! Know what is right there in front of you," Cristóbal says.

I glance at him. He is intently tracing the tip of Patagonia in the sand. Then he looks up and repeats his words.

"Know what is right there in front of you! Celeste, you can!"

Where did this stern voice come from? It is a man's voice. And then that tender smile that follows it. Just like . . .

"My father!"

I leap to my feet, sand raining all over the map of our country.

"My father! Papá! Cristóbal, do you know where to find him?"

Cristóbal smiles his old smile. "I know where to start. Remember, it's you who just told me."

The Squash of
Gold

"Abuela Frida?" She raises her light blue eyes from her bowl of thick eel-and-potato soup. I am nervous, my voice high like a little girl's. From the corner of my eye I watch Delfina leave the simmering pot of tomatoes, onions, and rice on the stove and sit next to my grandmother, whose eyebrow is arched like a bow, waiting for what I have to say.

"Abuela Frida, you have always told me that anything is possible if you can imagine it. That the yellow of a squash could transform into the yellow of gold. You've told me how you came here to Valparaíso with nothing but faith. Now it's my turn."

Abuela Frida and Delfina remain silent, watching me intently. I take a deep breath. "Abuela, I don't know if I can convince you to let me, but I want to go look for Papá!" I hear my grandmother suck in her breath. The lines on her forehead deepen.

"I would go with Cristóbal Williams. Tomorrow, if you let me. We would travel south by bus until it's time to get out and look for Papá." My words come out in a jumbled rush. "When Cristóbal read my palm, he saw that Mamá and Papá are hiding in different places now. I have dreams that Mamá is near, but Cristóbal's pendulum has told us where we can start to look for Papá. I can't explain how I'll know where to find him, but I believe that I can do it."

Delfina clears her throat and glances at my grandmother. My nana's eyes are the ocean on a starless night. These two women who have lived together nearly their whole lives gaze at each other for a long time, and then they nod in unison.

Abuela Frida finally speaks. Her words are slow and wear a thick German cloak, as if the *zzzzz*s that live in her mouth are heavier at this moment. "Celeste of my soul, my grandmother's heart wants to keep you by my side always, but it would be wrong to stop you. You are still young, but you are no longer entirely a child. If you feel deep inside that it is right to make this journey, then you must do it. I have faith in you."

Abuela Frida runs her wrinkled hand over the top of my head. "Delfina, please, go into my old wooden chest and find the hat I used to wear when my girls were just babies. The one you decorated with feathers that you said would bring me wisdom."

Delfina returns to the kitchen with an old-fashioned

gray hat with a wide brim and a navy-blue satin ribbon. In the ribbons are stuck three owl feathers. "Screech owl," Delfina tells me with a smile. "They are loud enough for you to hear their messages anywhere."

Delfina places the hat on my head, and I spin around for them to both admire it. "Oh, thank you both so much! What do you think?"

"I zzzzzthink," Abuela Frida says with a smile, "that you will return with your father quite zzzzsoon."

The Long and
Narrow Search
for **Papá**

Cristóbal and I embark on our search before dawn. We
carry backpacks stuffed with a blanket, bottles of water,
two of Abuela Frida's blue scarves, and six of Nana
Delfina's avocado sandwiches. "Now, don't eat these all
at once, Cristóbal." Nana Delfina winks at my friend as
she says good-bye to us in the bus terminal near the port.
"And take care of Delfina's girl!"

Cristóbal and I climb aboard the rickety green bus
and sit in the back. I'm rearranging the windblown
feathers on Abuela Frida's hat when a man's booming
voice from a few seats behind catches my attention. He
is telling his companion about a group of women in a
town in the north who've lost their husbands, children,
grandchildren. . . . "Every morning they go to the
sand dunes with fine-toothed combs. They kneel there
for hours, running the combs up and down the sand,
searching for fragments of bone . . ."

I begin to imagine them, the women with the sun
on their foreheads. They are women searching for signs

of human life, maybe a hand or a leg. A few years ago I didn't know what such cruelty was, and now we are reminded of it everywhere. I lean my head on Cristóbal's shoulder. "I could never imagine searching for my father with a comb!" I whisper. As the bus lurches toward the south, I close my eyes and begin to pray Abuela Frida's Hebrew prayers in my head.

The rickety bus makes its way south along the narrow coastal road. We ride for almost the entire day without stopping. My legs ache, and Cristóbal's elbow is jabbing into my ribs. But he is sound asleep, and with his dark hair all messy over his eyes, he looks like a little boy. So I stay still and count distant volcanoes crowned with billows of smoke. The bus screeches to a halt just after I reach number ten. "Thank goodness! Wake up! Wake up, sleepyhead!" I shake Cristóbal. He rubs his eyes and looks to the front of the bus after me. I am already halfway out the door.

"We'll be resting here in Quinchamalí for an hour, ladies and gentlemen," the bus driver announces. "Please take this time to use the facilities and eat your dinner. We'll meet back here at eight o'clock sharp!"

At the bus stop women dressed in white from top to bottom are selling candies. A crippled Mapuche lady with an ancient face hobbles close to me and waves a caramel in my face. Cristóbal takes a peso out of his pocket and buys it.

"Gracias, amigo, but I don't have much of an appetite."

"Just take a nibble and I'll eat the rest. I need the sugar to wake up."

"Let's go down to the beach." I grab Cristóbal. I am so anxious to run, to move, to see anything that might give me a clue about my father. Am I crazy to try to find him? I look at Cristóbal. "Were we crazy to come here?" I ask him. He tips his head back and laughs and laughs.

"What? What? Cristóbal!" I punch him on the arm. "Tell me!"

"Ay, Celeste, of course you are crazy! Me too. That is why we have always been friends. And that is why we will find your father. We are crazy enough to listen to silence, to see where there is nothing, and crazy enough, like your abuela always says, to have unshakable faith. Now let's walk."

Quinchamalí is a little fishing village on the edge of a rocky shore. We head for a spot on the beach close to the water, where we can watch the colorful boats bob up and down and fishermen repair their nets.

A man and woman I recognize from the bus are strolling the beach near us. We watch them stop and speak to each group of fishermen. The couple seems to be about fifty years old, and the woman looks frail in her black dress with her hands constantly writhing a white handkerchief. I walk closer to hear what an old fisherman is saying to them.

". . . Many prisoners were brought from here to Chiloé's main island on their way to more isolated islands far off the coast. They say some prisoners escaped to those tiny, uninhabited islands out beyond the prison islands. I myself have tried to reach them. The conditions on those seas are hard." The fisherman looks down at his thick hands. "As you can see, I am an old man. I was forced three times to turn back."

The man in the couple nods his head and begins to walk away, but the woman in black clings to the fisherman's elbow. "Can you tell us anything else, Señor . . . ?"

"Oviedo. My name is Oviedo. And no, I am afraid I can't tell you anything more other than what I tell everyone who comes here in search of the disappeared: be like the fishermen—have patience and trust in the sea."

The Sea like the Heart of Man

I watch the old fisherman turn back to his nets. Cristóbal begins to walk on. "Come on, Celeste," he says, yawning. "The candy wasn't enough—let's go see if we can find some coffee around here." I tug on his sleeve.

"Wait, Cristóbal. Something tells me we should talk to this man."

I take a deep breath and call out, "Señor! May I ask you about my father?" His back is still turned away. It seems like he hasn't heard me. We walk down toward the shore. "Señor Oviedo, excuse the interruption, but I was wondering—"

"Did you hear what I told that couple, señorita?" He answers with a brusque voice and doesn't turn to face us. I notice his shoulders are stooped under the weight of the big nets.

"Sí, señor, I did hear you. But I want to ask a different question. But wait, maybe we can help you with your nets?" I push Cristóbal forward.

He stumbles up to the boat, saying, "Here, señor, let me give you a hand."

The fisherman looks at Cristóbal warily, turns to face me, and then turns back to my friend. "Thank you, young man. I used to have my sons to help me, but . . ." His voice falters. "I don't have to tell you. So many are gone."

We begin to walk up the beach, lugging the heavy nets. In the distance I see a row of rainbow-colored houses lifted high above the ground on stilts. Señor Oviedo turns to me. "So many have come here searching, Señorita . . ."

"Celeste. My name is Celeste Marconi. And this is my friend Cristóbal Williams. We have come here from Valparaíso in search of my father."

We approach a small stilted house the color of ripe raspberries. "This is my home," Oviedo says proudly. "Since the time of my father's father, men have been fishing here and building homes in the air so that we can stay dry during high tides and survive the storms. We live according to the laws of the sea. It is a great force, just like the heart of man, with its ability to do both good and bad." His eyes are nearly buried in wrinkled skin, but a bright light shines through his gaze.

"Celeste Marconi, the islands where the prisoners were kept are where the sky meets the sea. I have tried to sail out there and had to choose turning back or death three times. It is impossible to get out there, and it would be a miracle for any of those wretched souls to make it back here."

Cristóbal pulls me aside a bit and whispers into my ear, "Celeste, the bus will leave without us!"

"I think we should go with Oviedo, Cristóbal."

"Is that what you feel?"

"Yes."

As if he hears my deepest thoughts, Oviedo swings around to face us. "You are young and strong." He looks from Cristóbal to me. "But do you have faith in the sea? Would you put your life in her hands, like some put faith in the will of God?"

"Always. My nana taught me that."

"And you, young man?"

"I believe in Celeste."

"Good. Then I will try to help you find your father."

The tide rises as the sun sets, and we go back for Oviedo's boat so it won't get washed to sea. He ties it to one of the stilts holding up his house. Then we climb the stairs about eight feet up to enter his house. I marvel at the simple genius of those four thin wooden stilts. The house is simple, no more than a bedroom and a kitchen. But it is fresh and airy with its cheery yellow walls and sky-blue curtains in the windows. Oviedo sees my smile as I look here and there. He waves his hand in the air. "My wife," he says, "Clara. She loved colors. She used to say that what we see the first thing in the morning and the last thing at night is as important to our health as the food we eat." He chuckles fondly. "Some people here called her eccentric, but my wife was a very wise woman."

Oviedo clears his throat abruptly and motions for us to sit on the front porch. He goes into the kitchen and soon emerges with lentils and a fried egg for each of us, and mint tea and tiny pink apples for dessert.

"Who are you searching for, Señor Oviedo?"

He looks at me with a mix of surprise and suspicion.

I tense up and jump back a bit. "I am sorry. I didn't mean to pry. It's just that you told us how you had tried to sail out to the islands where prisoners are kept."

"I don't remember. Are you sure you weren't snooping?" Relief floods my body when I see he is smiling despite his accusation.

"Yes. I am sorry. I was snooping a bit. It is a bad habit, I know." My words pour out in a rush, but at least they are true: "I want to be a writer, so I am always looking for stories, ever since I was a little girl. I used to hide under the kitchen table to listen to the grown-ups."

Oviedo throws back his gray-haired head and lets out a raspy laugh. "Well, now that I know your story, Señorita Celeste, I guess you and your shy boyfriend here can stay with me as long as you like." Oviedo reaches inside his pants pocket and pulls out a damp cigarette. He holds it up to the wind for a long while to let it dry. "Patience," he says, and winks at me. Then he lights the cigarette and blows rings into the air. The smoke envelops us in a circle, somehow pulling us closer together, making me feel safe.

Night has fallen. The fog is enclosing the harbor, and even the stars have decided to go to sleep. The three of us sit out on the porch in silence for a long time. I yawn and lean my head against Cristóbal's shoulder. "Come," Oviedo says with a groan as he lifts himself from his rocking chair. He leads us into the little house and points to the floor below the small woodstove. "These blankets will keep you warm."

Cristóbal and I sleep back-to-back on the floor, and from where I lie, I can see the stars through the open window. A warm breeze flutters the burlap curtains. "Look! The Southern Cross!" But Cristóbal fell asleep long before I began naming the stars.

I say a prayer: "Mamá, wherever you are, please help me to find Papá. Help me to trust myself like you taught me. I just need to open my hands and let go of fear, and all sorts of good things will begin to happen."

Patience

I wake at dawn when Oviedo closes the door to his house. I glance over at Cristóbal, still snoring with his mouth open wider than a hooked sea bass. I make my way off the floor and tiptoe out the front door onto the porch. It's high tide, and the sea is all around us.

"Good luck today, Don Oviedo," I call down to the old fisherman, who is untying his boat. "I hope you catch lots of fish and sell even more!"

Oviedo shades his eyes with his hand.

"You are an early riser, Señorita Celeste. You'd make a good fisherwoman. Tell you what, when the tide goes out, you and your friend walk the beach and gather up mussels and seaweed for me. This evening I will make you a stew you will never forget."

"Thank you, Oviedo . . ." I hesitate, then have to ask, "But what about looking for my fa—"

Oviedo puts his finger to his lips. "Patience. All in good time, young one. Have patience and you'll get what you came for."

His words leave me bewildered and frustrated. I should be combing the beach for signs, not seaweed! I have been so busy asking for faith that I forgot to ask for patience. That is something I have always needed more of. Maybe I can borrow some of Cristóbal's.

I tiptoe back into the cottage and watch my friend sleep. Who would have thought we would end up here together? My oldest friend. Yes, Cristóbal was never in a hurry, and yet he always showed up at the right time.

When Oviedo returns in the late afternoon, we put down our baskets of seaweed and rush to help him with his nets. "Sit down, young friends!" Oviedo smiles a nearly toothless smile and sits down in the sand with a tired sigh. We sit next to him and listen as he begins to speak:

"I have tried three times to reach the outer islands. But I always encounter a sudden strong current that pulls me to the one place I want to avoid, and I am forced to turn back."

"What is this place it pulls you to? Is it very dangerous?" Cristóbal asks, and begins to trace patterns in the sand.

"It is a rocky island cut into pieces by narrow gorges with rushing water that could smash a wooden boat like mine to pieces. It's always covered with a fog that would choke you. The last time I tried to reach the outer islands was three months ago—the waters rushed wilder than ever."

Cristóbal and I stare at each other. My limbs shake as I gather the courage to ask, "Don Oviedo, would you tell us why you keep going back to the outer islands?"

Oviedo grabs a piece of driftwood and pokes at the sand.

"Like you, I am searching for someone. My daughter-in-law, Javiera. My sons Tomás and Moisés were killed when they were traveling inland to sell fish in the first days of the military coup. There was no reason for their deaths except that they were in the wrong place at the wrong time."

"We're so sorry, Don Oviedo," Cristóbal speaks up as I shake even more. I sit on my hands—hoping the fisherman won't notice that I'm shivering with dread.

"Soon after, they took my oldest son, Ramón, from Quinchamalí. He was a fisherman like all the other men in our family. He was born into this life. But he also was a painter. I regret I didn't encourage his talent, because I knew he had it, but I didn't want to lose him. I reminded him constantly of his responsibilities to the family."

The old fisherman covers his eyes with his thick ruddy hands. "I realize now what a fool I was. My own father feared losing me too young to the sea, but I feared losing Ramón to a way of life I don't understand. During

Alarcón's presidency Ramón began painting murals on the walls of Quinchamalí. Pictures of children, families eating in community kitchens, and people reading books. Words in rainbow colors that said things like: 'Equality for all means liberty for Chile.'"

He presses his palms to his forehead before continuing. "I don't read, but when the soldiers came for Ramón, they told me what he had written. They said his art was poisoning the minds of the villagers. They said his words were dangerous and subversive. The villagers told me that Ramón didn't resist. He just looked at the soldiers defiantly, and they dragged him away. That's exactly how my son was. His belief in himself was always stronger than his fear."

"Have you had any word about Ramón?" Cristóbal asks. "Have you seen any signs?"

Oviedo looks up at the sky. The clouds are darkening to a deep shade of violet, and the gulls turn in circles overhead, looking for their evening meal. "Thank God his dear mother wasn't alive to bear his loss. You see, youngsters, I felt in my heart soon after that Ramón was dead. The waves on the shore were an empty sound in my ears. But when the soldiers took Ramón's young wife some months later, it was different. Javiera was carrying my grandchild, and I heard two heartbeats in the waves. I still do. Listen."

Cristóbal closes his eyes to hear better, and I do too. I let my body open to the drumming of the tides. The beat is doubled, like the rhythm when two people dance cueca.

"It's true!" I exclaim, grabbing my friend's arm excitedly.

Cristóbal is wiping his eyes. "You are right, Don Oviedo," he says. "First I heard the crash of the waves on the bigger rocks and then a sort of echo on the stones."

Oviedo gets up from the sand and picks up the seaweed we gathered. "That echo is my grandchild." His voice is swallowed by the salty wind.

Fergus Bacon

Cristóbal and I follow Oviedo to his house. As we walk, he tells us, "Today I bumped into one of Queltrahu's newest and strangest figures. He only appears in the village every month or so. He has a funny-sounding foreign name, Fergus. He is a sailor and doesn't speak any Spanish save a few words he uses to barter and trade. But he knows the inlets and coves like nobody else."

"Do you think this sailor could help us locate Celeste's father?" Cristóbal asks.

"I do." Oviedo nods. "In fact, I took the liberty to speak to him of your plight, Señorita Celeste."

"¡Gracias, Don Oviedo!" My heart begins pounding with a strange mix of hope and fear.

"De nada, child. Those islands are impenetrable prisons, caged in by fog and angry seas. They don't even need bars! But Fergus is a strange old sailor. He only comes to shore when the fog is thickest. He says he was taught the ways of the sea by a blind uncle, and so he learned to navigate with his eyes closed, relying on his other senses. I don't know if he has great instinct or a touch of madness, really. I would almost be afraid of him if I hadn't already lived so many years and seen so much."

Oviedo begins to boil eggs on the stove. "To feed the sailor," he explains. "I invited him for dinner so you could meet him. He told me to boil as many eggs as I could so that he could take them back with him."

"Let me help you, Don Oviedo!" I look at the jars of dried seaweed, sea salt, and oregano on the shelf above his stove. "Do you have any parsley? That's what my Nana Delfina sprinkles on top of everything to make it delicious . . . except café con leche . . . but she even puts parsley on eggs!" I laugh.

He squints at me, and I realize that his eyes are not good.

"My father is a doctor," I tell him. "He will examine you when we find him, and we can send you glasses from Valparaíso."

"I hear much pride in your voice, young Celeste." Oviedo nods approvingly. "Respect for your elders. That is good, that is very good."

Just then a booming voice rises up to us from the sands below. "Oviedo! Oviedo! I've arrived as promised! Come down and greet Sir Fergus Bacon!"

"He's speaking English!" I exclaim.

"Can *you* speak English, Celeste?" Oviedo looks at me in disbelief.

"Yes, I can—I was an exile in the North."

"Well, I'll be, señorita. You sure aren't a typical young girl, are you?"

"No, señor." I smile. "I guess I'm not."

The voice booms up again. It nearly drowns out the roaring of the waves. "Come greet Sir Fergus! And bring the little miss down with you! I am curious to meet her."

I look at Oviedo and Cristóbal hesitantly. "Come on, Celeste." Cristóbal takes my hand. "Go talk to him. This may be your chance to find your father!"

As we descend the stairs, my throat goes dry and my tongue twists in knots, just like every time I speak English to a stranger.

The man belonging to the crashing voice reminds me of pictures of Viking warriors that Señorita Alvarado showed us in history class. He has long red hair and a fiery beard as thick and unkempt as the autumn forest on Juliette Cove. He wears tall black boots, and his yellowing shirt is ripped in several places, revealing even more thick hair and sun-blistered skin. Around his waist he wears a belt, from which hang a knife and a coil of rope.

I swallow my fear as the man approaches me. He seems like a giant, like two Cristóbals stacked atop each other. "Come closer, missy," he commands with his strange accent. I step forward.

"Hello . . . sir?" I stumble over my words.

"Ah, so you speak a bit of English, do ya?"

"Yes—sir—nice—to meet you," I stammer on, breathless.

"Sir Fergus," he tells me with a smile. His teeth look as big as boulders. "Fergus Bacon, descendent of the pirate Sir Hamish Bacon, and of the noble MacGregor clan of the Scottish Highlands, a castaway from the strange and fearsome land of my birth, Australia."

"Oh." That's all I can say, dumbfounded. Cristóbal nudges me to say more, but Fergus kneels down in the sand to look in my eyes. "Your color is different, but you have the look of him, missy! It's that melancholy brow. Unmistakable."

"Who? Who do I look like, Sir Fergus? Are you talking about my father? Have you seen him?"

Fergus puts his thick red fingers to his thick red beard. "You can't be a sailor if you don't have patience."

Fergus turns to Oviedo. "Well now, do you have my eggs? I regret to say I shan't be stayin' for supper. The fog is thick, but there is an east wind that threatens to blow it away. Missy and I need to be off now. I need the fog to sense where I'm goin'."

"What did he say, Celeste?" Cristóbal sounds tense.

My legs start to shake. "That he wants to take me in his boat. Now."

Oviedo runs into the house and emerges with a burlap bag full of eggs. "God bless you, Celeste," he tells me as he puts the bag in my arms.

Fergus begins to walk toward the shoreline. A wooden dinghy bobs in the water, the top of its slender mast swallowed by fog. "Here we are! Just wade over and hop in, missy! No time to waste!" He chuckles. "Hope you weren't expecting to stay dry!"

"Yes, sir, I'm ready." My voice shakes, but I take Cristóbal's hand, ready to sail out to find Papá. But Fergus shakes his head at Cristóbal. "You stay here with old Oviedo, boy. We'll be back soon enough." He turns and lumbers to the shoreline. He quickly reaches the dinghy and starts to pull it from the beach into the water.

I stand frozen in the sand, shaking my head. *What did this crazy man just say? I'm to go with him alone?! I can't leave—can't do this—without Cristóbal!*

"Sir Fergus," I protest. "Please, Cristóbal and I need to stay together."

As an answer Fergus hops into the dinghy and lifts a big burlap sack of potatoes from the bottom.

"Afraid I can't, missy. Just came in from Quinchamalí, and the boat's full of provisions. There's hardly room for anyone else, and I don't want any extra weight aboard, especially since it turns stormy here quicker than a seagull can steal a fresh catch! You're just lucky you're not much bigger than a sack of spuds!"

Fergus Bacon laughs heartily at himself and starts to unfurl the sail. I still can't move. I look desperately at Cristóbal, who seems to be struggling to get something— *English maybe?*—out of his mouth.

Sir Fergus continues, taking the tone of a gallant knight, "Since your case is an urgent one . . . I'm making an exception for you, missy." His voice turns raucous again. "But I'd rather have just *one* of your young lives on my conscience!" He laughs even louder until his chuckle becomes a low growl. "Don't tell me you're scared?"

I can't tell if this crazy man is kidding or dead serious. Finally Cristóbal shouts out in English, "No! No! Stop!" and finishes his protest in Spanish, "Señor, por favor, Celeste and I can't be separated!" But no sooner does he get those words out than he turns to me and says, "Celeste, this might be your chance. Your *only* chance. You can do this, Celeste!" Cristóbal's voice is urgent. He puts his hands strongly on my shoulders and rests his forehead against my own. It's the closest I've ever been to him. He looks deep into my eyes. "You are the bravest person I know. I promise to stay here on the beach with my pendulum, charting your map in the sand. I'll be right here waiting for you."

"Cristóbal, I . . . I . . . "

"Sorry, laddie! My answer's still no," Fergus booms, jolting my limbs back to attention so I can finally lift my feet from the sand. But not before I kiss Cristóbal on the cheek.

"You'll be back soon," he tells me. His lower lip is trembling.

Unshakable Faith

Without another moment's hesitation, I wade knee-deep into the water and pull myself into the dinghy. The winds begin to blow hard, and the wooden vessel springs to life and leaps from the shore. I look at Fergus—pulling on the lines, trimming the sail—expectantly.

"Now, missy, if you want to find what you are looking for, you have to work for it. You have to lead us to your destination."

"But how can I? If you . . . *you* are the one who knows where we are going! You *do* know where we're headed, right?"

"Of course I do!" Fergus throws back his head and cackles. "But what use would that be to you? Didn't you tell the old fisherman that you feel your father is close at hand?"

I nod and look at the sailor in disbelief. He *is* crazy. I look back desperately to Cristóbal on the shore. *Oh, what have I gotten myself into?*

"Then show me, missy! I need some proof—these are dangerous times . . ."

"But—but—" I stammer in protest. "Didn't you say I look like him? That's your proof!"

"Har!" He shakes his head. "No, that's not enough for old Fergus! Show me . . . or I'll feed ya to me pet shark!"

My first instinct is to throw myself overboard and swim to shore. But when I rise to my feet, a wave rocks the dinghy and I fall down—hard—on my backside. I want to cry, but I burst into fits of laughter instead. I laugh and laugh until I hiccup. Fergus winks at me. "Now, that's more like it. Light and easy now, missy. Light and easy. You just tell me a direction to take when you feel it."

I take a deep breath and make a decision. There's nothing left to do but trust Sir Fergus. I ask for a sign like Nana Delfina taught me.

The fog is so thick that I can hardly see my own hands, let alone the red-bearded giant sitting next to me. But I hear Fergus loud and clear as he starts to sing: "*In south Australia I was born! Heave away! Haul away! South Australia 'round Cape Horn! Bound for south Australia!* That's a sea shanty for ya, lass!"

Fergus's booming voice seems to echo off the water. Or are those other sounds I hear?

Squawk! Squawk!

I close my eyes and strain to listen. *Squawk!* It sounds . . . just like . . . the pelicans! "Celeste, Celeste!" But how is it that I understand—*really* understand, not like when I was little—what they're saying? *Squawk!* Their cries are growing louder and impatient. "This way, Celeste!"

"Fergus, let's go this way." I wave toward the darkest point on the horizon.

"Downwind it is, then, missy!" With one swift motion Fergus pushes the tiller and hauls in the sail. "Jibe ho!" Fergus cries out as the wind violently catches the other side of the sail. "Watch your head, missy!" As the boom flies over my head, I duck just in time. The boat lurches to the left, and I steady myself, more thankful than ever that I learned English! Then Fergus sits down next to me and nods approvingly.

"Now I can tell you, missy. Beyond the island of Chiloé there are the tiny prison islands. You've pointed us in that direction. You've also pointed us in the direction of an ancient ship. It was a whaling ship once, but I've named her the *Pirate Queen*. She's my home, moored in the cove of an island so small that it doesn't have a name, doesn't appear on any maps. Most people think that the island is a myth, but even still, very few men dare sail there to find out because they are afraid of ghosts. Do you believe in ghosts, missy?"

"I do. But I'm not afraid of them. And I call them spirits." I think of Delfina burning cinnamon and talking with her ancestors before going to bed.

"Well, I'll be!" Fergus scratches his head in disbelief. "You are an odd one! Just like him. Not afraid of ghosts? Hmmmph! Well, me neither, missy. But you won't catch me talking to one neither!" As Fergus speaks, a sudden gust of wind dissolves a small patch of fog, leaving a window for us to peer through.

"Look lively now, missy! Do you see over there?"

"Lights?" I can barely make them out, they're so dim, and the fog is rolling back in, clouding my sight, just as quickly as it lifted.

"Those are the prison islands," he says grimly. "Not all of the prisoners have been released. They fear the temporary government in Santiago has forgotten them."

I shiver. *Could Papá be a prisoner there?* I tuck Nana Delfina's shawl close around me and urge Fergus to continue. "Go on, please."

"I don't like talking about such things to a young thing like yourself." He hesitates. "But these be odd times, that's for sure. What's wrong is right and what's right is wrong—your country's been flipped upside down, like a boat keeling over."

"It's okay, Sir Fergus." I reassure him. "I'm stronger than I look."

He looks at me with—perhaps—admiration in his eyes?

"I'd say that's another thing that's for sure, missy. Well, I don't know how long you were in the North, missy, or what you've heard since coming back, but prisoners . . . well, they were . . . thrown." Fergus inhales sharply. "Thrown. From planes. To the sea." The wind picks up with a howl. It's a sound like sorrow. A sound that should fly out of me when I open my mouth in terror. But no sound comes out. I grip the edge of the dinghy. I'm afraid I'm going to throw up.

But Fergus continues. I hang on for dear life, digging my fingernails into the wood, trying to keep hold of something, *anything*, that won't disappear. *Is that where they all went? To the bottom of the sea?*

I stare down at the ocean below, and grow dizzy. Maybe the real Celeste can spin away from here inside me? But then I hear Fergus say, ". . . Sometimes they were thrown when they were already dead. But other times . . ." Fergus's voice becomes gruff.

I let go of my grip on the boat and finish for him. "Other times they were alive." My voice sounds like it's coming from someone else. So cool, so calm. It *must* be the voice of someone else. Maybe this is all a long nightmare, about a girl searching for her father in an ocean that's become a burial ground for prisoners. And pretty soon I'll wake up in my house on Butterfly Hill, and Papá will be downstairs with Mamá, drinking café con leche before heading to the clinic. Because it couldn't—*it just couldn't*—be Celeste Marconi's Papá out there—a prisoner . . . a body . . . that's alive . . . or maybe . . . dead. No, this couldn't be

Celeste Marconi's real life! Because this couldn't be her Chile!

Fergus hasn't stopped speaking. "Now and again I would find somebody, and sometimes it was not too late. I'd take them to my ship, feed them, let them rest a few days before they went on their way. Not all of them had been thrown. Some of them foolish souls had escaped, swum for hours, been floating in the sea so long, their skin near peeled down to the bone."

I summon the courage to ask. "Sir Fergus, this man you are taking me to—did you find him in the water?"

"Ay! That I did, missy. Facedown in a bed of seaweed and only half-alive."

"Oh, poor Papá!" I gasp, unwilling to imagine it. "But then, Sir Fergus, that means . . . he's alive! That is, if this man you saved *is* my father. But he *has* to be. I just have to keep unshakable faith, like my grandmother says."

Fergus puts his finger to his lips and then peers out at the fog. I feel we're surrounded by thick gray curtains. But I watch in amazement as slowly, instinctively, Fergus pulls on the tiller and turns the dinghy into a swell. "We need to sail around the prison islands," he whispers. "Far enough away to not be spotted, but close enough that we don't drift off course."

We sail on in silence for a while. Then, still

whispering, I say, "Sir Fergus, please tell me more about the man you found."

"He had escaped from the prison, some time ago now. I had him stay on with me because he was a help taking care of the other wretches that washed up in my path."

I suck in some salty air, excited. "Why? Why was he such a help?!"

"Oh, he's a doctor. At least that's what he told me. And from what I've seen, it seems he ain't lying."

I clap my hands together, and would stand up to dance for joy if the water weren't so choppy. "Sir Fergus, this man is my father for sure!"

Fergus's voice is brusque. "I hope so, missy. For both your sakes."

The dinghy rides up and down the high, foamy waves. I hold my stomach and keep my eyes on the sky. The curtain of fog is thicker than ever. But Sir Fergus doesn't need to see far. He lifts his hand and moves it this way and that. "Feeling for the right wind, missy." He must have found it, because suddenly Fergus pulls on the lines, and the sail harnesses the wind. *Whoooosh!*

We skim along the water, and I hold on tight. "There. There she is!" Fergus points to a patch of fog in the distance. "Wait for her, missy. She'll reveal herself."

And like he promised, a sheet of clouds moves aside, and dim sunshine fills my eyes. As they adjust to the light, they focus on a massive black ship.

"There she is—the *Pirate Queen*! No woman was ever better to old Fergus." Fergus pulls me to my feet. My eyes are fixed on the *Pirate Queen*, then dart about to take in the tiny island where it is moored. "Welcome to my home, the ship the ghosts have lent me."

Fergus pulls the dinghy to the side of the old whaling boat, right next to a long rope ladder. "Go ahead, missy, climb aboard! I am just going to tie on to the side here. I'll be right behind you." I gulp and look up at the long climb and the churning seas below. I begin to pull myself up with my arms. The ladder sways in the winds, and some of the rungs are coming loose. I close my eyes and climb with all my might.

I tumble, exhausted, onto the deck. At first I cannot see a thing. The fog has descended again and completely engulfs the ship. I walk blindly, one foot in front of the other. The musty smell of rum and rotting wood fills my nostrils. I am trembling with fear, but I force my lips to form a word, any word, the only word.

"Papá! Papá! It's Celeste! Papá!"

I shout until hot tears roll down my cheeks.

"Papá! ¿Dónde estás? Where are you? Papá!"

A small, hunched figure emerges from the shadows.

Marjorie Agosín

Slowly—almost sorrowfully—he stretches out his arms. Is it really him? Could it be? After all this time?

"Papá?" My voice breaks as I call to the dark figure just a few feet in front of me. The fog blurs his face.

"Celeste, hija mía." When he answers me, his voice also breaks. But it's *his* voice! I'd know it anywhere! It's him!

"Papá!" I shout without any hesitation, running headlong into his embrace. And we stay there holding each other until every last trace of fog has lifted.

Our Country Is
Blue

Fergus takes us back to Chiloé in the early-morning hours.

I hardly believe I am sitting next to my father. I keep pressing his thin arms to see if he is real. "You're so thin!" I tell him. My father nods with tears in his eyes and wraps me in his arms, and his head with its long tangled hair and dark fuzzy beard rests heavily atop mine.

Some of his hair hangs limply in front of my eyes. Much of it has gone gray. It makes me sad . . . but . . . I am also angry. Here he is! Papá! Alive! Living, it seems, for a while with Fergus on his boat. Didn't he know the General was dead? Why didn't he go home to Butterfly Hill? Why didn't he look for Mamá? Did he wonder at all about us?

I feel so frustrated and confused. My head spins, and my heart goes from dark to light to dark again. Just like the early-morning sky with its fog and windswept clouds.

Cristóbal is waiting for us on the shore, waving a lantern back and forth. Oviedo is there too, yelling at the top of his lungs. Fergus lifts me from the boat and holds me up to his height for a moment. "Pleased to make your acquaintance, missy. Don't think I will ever forget you."

"I know I will never forget you, Fergus. Thank you for everything. Thank you for saving my father."

Then Fergus turns and embraces my father. They say nothing, but hold each other tight for a long while. Then my father climbs from the boat, and Fergus lifts his cap to us and starts rowing back home to his ghost ship, the *Pirate Queen*. We watch until he is swallowed up by the blackness between the sea and dark sky.

As tired and worn as he is, Papá carefully examines Señor Oviedo's eyes and promises that all he needs is Nana Delfina's herbal eyedrops to clear the sand and salt away. "We will send them first thing, and anything else you may need," my father tells him as he shakes his hand. "I am forever indebted to you."

I hug Oviedo tight. "I don't know how to thank you, Don Oviedo. But I promise I will write to you from Valparaíso!"

"Ay, Celeste Marconi. I am so glad your story is turning out a happy one. What you can do for me is live a long, happy life, young lady. And if you pray, please pray for my daughter-in-law Javiera, and for an abundance of fish for all the fishermen on the island of Chiloé."

* * *

"Papá, our country is blue." I lean against my father while we gaze out the window at sapphire stretches of sea and mountain and sky as the bus taking us home makes its way north. As the sun rises higher in the sky, it melts the impatience I was feeling toward my father . . . at least for the moment.

"Mmm-hmm . . ." My father kisses my forehead. It's as if he is too tired to speak. At times he looks distant and lost. In the early light of dawn I glance at my father's eyes. Once dark and brightly dancing like the night sky with stars, Papá's eyes are now dull amber, almost yellow, like a tired sun burning out so it can rest. My mother always joked that she fell in love with Papá when she saw the map of the stars in his eyes. But I see that sadness can alter even the colors we were born with. Maybe he cried so much that all the brown faded, like a poem written in ink runs on paper in the rain? Maybe the sparkling lights sunk somewhere to the bottom of my father, to a place deep inside where he hides his pain, deeper even than his heart?

Papá barely speaks for the entire fourteen-hour trip. He just gazes out the window and runs his hand down my unkempt braid. *Oh, Papá! Something so awful must have happened to you,* I think. *And I know that once you arrive at Butterfly Hill, you will come back to life.*

I have so much to ask him, so much to tell him, but I

summon my new skill—patience. But at one point I can't help laughing and asking my father, "Papá, did one of the rats aboard the *Pirate Queen* bite off your tongue?"

My father was intently watching the busy streets of Santiago flash by, almost as if he were looking for someone. Looking for my mother. But he turns his face from the window. "Celeste, brave heroine and daughter of mine, soon I will tell you all you want to know. But now let your father rest and get used to the fact that I have to only reach out my hand to touch you."

Of Ships and
Secrets

"Celeste, Celeste." I roll over onto my stomach and force one eye half-open. I see my nana's gap-toothed smile.

"Papá? He is here? It wasn't a dream?"

"No, Delfina's brave girl. You have been asleep nearly two days! Your father said to let you regain your strength. He is downstairs eating sopaipillas with your Abuela Frida."

"It *wasn't* a dream! My father is home!" A happiness runs all through my veins.

"Señor Andrés has already told Delfina and Abuela Frida all about the *Pirate Queen*. We are all so proud of our girl."

All day my father sits in his study, listening to the sounds of people going about their ways. He smiles ruefully at me. "I am not used to so much noise." At night I bring him a cup of peppermint tea and sit next to him. I want to know how he managed to survive.

"Celeste, during those weeks, months, perhaps years, I lost track of time. I was in a jail cell so small, your dolls' garden would not even fit there." Then he clears his throat and says, "It was all inexplicable, so much cruelty and so much goodness. Sometimes the guards beat us up and then, an hour later, would give us cigarettes. It was hard to remember the life we had, Celeste, and if I thought of you, I would have cried so much that the tears would have created a flood. And yet if I did not think of you, my heart would have become a desert. There was no choice but to remember you and Esmeralda, your grandmother Frida, Nana Delfina." He sips at the tea, which is now almost cold.

"Celeste, sometimes memory is dangerous, but on most occasions it can be a salvation. Sometimes remembering means to live a moment in the past again, and in that way survive the present. I will try to share my story with you little by little, as I am able. It is good to get these things out. Something I learned, Celeste, is that words can save you."

I wring my hands impatiently. "Papá, can you just tell me one more thing for now?"

My father smiles with a solemn look I recognize that means, *Patience, Celeste*. "That depends on what you want to know, hija."

I look at his tired face and can't bring myself to ask about Mamá—not yet. "I want to know how you escaped, and how you met Fergus!"

My father sighs a heavy sigh and reaches his arm out for me. I sit close to him, and he begins to recall his last days on the prison island.

"About six months ago—although I am not completely sure because there was no way but the sun to keep track of time—rumors began making their way into the prison that the Dictator was losing power, that there was dissent among his generals. The thought of losing power made the Dictator crueler than ever, and he ordered prisoners' rations to be cut in half. I had only a piece of bread and an egg delivered to me every two days. And I was given very little water. I could feel my body growing weaker, my organs failing, and I decided that the way I was living was worse than death. I felt that if I stayed there, I would surely not survive. So, I decided to take a chance and escape."

I wince, heartsick at the thought of my father so ill and mistreated, all alone with no one to help him. "How, Papá?"

"I didn't have to do much." He laughs bitterly. "I just pretended I was dead when the guard came to check on me one morning. I was thrown onto a small boat piled with bodies. The stench was horrible. I kept my eyes closed but could hear a motor running and the breeze blowing for a short while. I guess when they figured we were far enough out so that anyone who was faking would surely drown, the bodies were dumped into the sea. I held my breath and let my body sink. And then when I felt I was deep enough, I swam and swam until finally I had to come up for air. When I came up, thankfully, I could see a small island in the distance. I don't know how I did it, but I managed to swim to shore. I must have collapsed, because when I opened my eyes, Fergus was leaning over me, trying to pour water through my lips. I was half-dead and covered with blisters from lying in the sun for God knows how long."

He rubs his hand over his now clean-shaven face, as though feeling for those blisters.

"We couldn't speak much to each other, but there was not much I was able to say to any man at that point, even if he did speak Spanish. Fergus stayed by my side for about a week, fed me potatoes, eggs, and fish. He built a fire in the nighttime so I wouldn't be cold and covered me with his coat. Finally I had enough strength to walk, and Fergus took me to the other side of the island, where the immense ship was."

"So, you hid there on board with him, Papá?"

"Yes. I stayed belowdecks most of the time."

"But . . . but . . . why didn't you try to come back to Valparaíso?"

"It was still much too dangerous, Querida. Remember, the Dictator had supporters, and the entire military behind him. I can only imagine how angry some became when he died and they lost their power. As painful as it was, I decided to bide my time."

"Fergus told me you treated other prisoners he found in the water."

Papá nods. "It's true. Once in a while Fergus would find someone for me to care for. So I consoled myself by making myself useful—at least there were people who needed my help."

Papá's answer frustrates me. What about me? What about Mamá? Didn't we need him? But I don't know how to tell him that. He looks so frail—I'm afraid to hurt his feelings. So I look down at my hands.

After an uncomfortable silence he clears his throat and continues: "Fergus made me a hammock out of a fishing net, and I would spend the daylight hours there, resting, or in the galley peeling potatoes. Sometimes, when the thickest fogs rolled in, Fergus would leave for a few days. He would always come back with fish and eggs, and one time he came back with fresh clothes for me. Fergus and I spoke little. But sometimes we played cards. Poker, mostly. We didn't seem to have to speak each other's language for that. We gambled with seashells." My father chuckles. "Boy, did Fergus have a temper! He did not like to lose at cards!"

"Thank goodness you were only playing for shells!"

I exclaim, and reach over to hug him, my frustration calmed for the time being. I'm once again just happy to have him home again.

"And thank goodness you learned to speak English so well on Juliette Cove, my smart girl!" *Why doesn't he tell me about the prisoners he helped? He probably doesn't want to scare me. As if you could protect me now?* My father turns serious once more. "Celeste, never forget this: I was able to survive by having faith in this one old man. I think it was his craziness that made me believe in him. That and the fact that we didn't know each other's words. Everyone else had told me too many lies." He grows quiet, but I have to ask him one more thing.

"And, Papá, what about Mamá? Can we go look for her? I am sure we will find her if we just ask Cristóbal to bring his pendul—"

"Shhhhh. Patience, Celeste Marconi." Papá kisses my forehead. "I believe that your mother is also alive, and I also believe that to keep her alive, we need to bide our time. It is still very dangerous out there, Celeste. There are soldiers angry that their general's government has crumbled, and they have our pictures, just waiting to take their shame out on somebody before peace is fully restored. I wish more than anything that I was by your mother's side right now, that I had been there through it all. But we decided it was best not to stay together . . . because if something happened to one of us . . ." His voice trails off, and he looks away from me.

"I know, Papá," I say gently. "If one of you didn't make it, you hoped the other would for my sake."

Papá turns to meet my gaze. He is crying. "My brave girl," he whispers, his voice raspy.

"I'm not a baby anymore, Papá. And nobody is after *me*! Why can't I go look for her and bring her home like I did with you?"

My father shakes his head. This time his voice is firm. "No!" He wipes his eyes with hands that look like nothing but bones wrapped up in old wax paper. "No, Celeste. And that's final. Esmeralda and I couldn't live with ourselves if . . ." His voice trails off again, and he clears his throat, changing the subject.

"I wrote a letter last night, and Delfina posted it for me this morning. I know that letter will reach your mother somehow."

"Papá, do you know where she is? Why can't we—" I cry out, but Papá squeezes my hand.

"I don't know exactly—this letter will go from friend to friend to friend—someone will know. And I know she will be home soon. Trust me, my girl."

"I do, Papá."

"Now, my turn to ask a question! I want to know

how you gathered enough courage to search for me."

"I don't know, Papá. I just had to do something! I waited two years to find you. I couldn't just not do anything when we were so close once again."

But doesn't Papá feel the same way about Mamá . . . and what if it isn't as dangerous out there as he imagines? As if listening to my thoughts, my father sighs. "Celeste, there is nothing I want more in this world than to have your mother home, and nothing I wouldn't do for her, or for you for that matter. So, trust. Trust and help me have faith."

The Alphabet in
My Hands

On Sunday night, after a week of sitting in his study, my father climbs out to the roof, where I am sitting with my mother's big book of maps of the stars. "Delta Crucis. Gamma Crucis." I am naming the stars in the Southern Cross, my mother's favorite constellation, saying them aloud, hoping she is looking at the stars too, and that she is comfortable and has enough to eat, and a soft pillow for her head because she is such a light sleeper. I remember how Mamá made my father sleep with a clothespin on his nose so he wouldn't snore and wake her up. The family joke is that he has been doing this since their honeymoon, and that he was born with a small nose that swoops a bit to the sky like mine, but night after night with the clothespin made his nose grow long and narrow with a bump below the brow, like a condor's beak.

My father sits next to me and looks up at the sky. "I am sure she is sitting beneath the Southern Cross too, Celeste, and thinking of you."

I lean against my father's arm. "Thank you, Papá. Are you feeling bad tonight? You didn't eat much at dinner."

"I am well, hija. Don't worry about me. I am concerned about you, though. I think it is too gloomy for you to be stuck in the house here with us somber old folks. Don't you think it is time for you to go back to school?"

I shake my head stubbornly. "Not until Mamá returns, Papá. I know you sent a letter, but we need to do more! Why can't we go look for her?"

"It is still dangerous out there, Celeste. Looking for her, asking around for her, would put her in more danger. It would let others—those who mean harm—know that she *is* out there. And revenge—well, it's an ugly thing. Trust me, there are some things you are still too young to understand."

I cross my arms and glower. My father rarely says things like that—too young to understand—and I hate hearing it. But then I inhale quickly. My arms drop to my sides as I take in the full meaning of his words. Had I put Papá's life in danger by looking for him? I feel the anger dissolve from my face as I reach my arms around him and hug him tight. How lucky I was! How lucky we both were!

"She is on her way, Celeste. I feel it. You must too, deep inside."

"Sí, Papá . . ."

"I know waiting is almost unbearable . . . but I think it will help if you're more productive. I want you doing something that makes you happy. I will allow you to wait until your mother returns to go to school. But that doesn't mean your talent is going to waste. I had Delfina go down to the market today." My father puts his hand under my chin and looks into my eyes. "Celeste, it is time for you to write again."

Papá pulls a little blue notebook from his pocket, places it beside me, and climbs back down into our house.

I have been too afraid, ever since returning from Juliette Cove. The thought of burned books, of smoke rising from the hills, of the ash remains of ink and paper and dreams and thoughts and lifetimes of hard work scattering to the winds is too awful. I know that the Dictator is dead, but fear remains with me. How could it not, when even Papá is afraid—afraid to search for Mamá? Afraid to tell me about everything he's been through? And what if what I write gets my family in trouble? That is what happened to the families of so many writers. Like Lucila's. It was most likely her father's weekly opinion column that got them in trouble. He was always praising Alarcón's policies. I shiver when I think that writing—simply putting an idea into words on a piece of paper—caused Señor López to be taken away in the middle of the night and made an entire family disappear.

Slowly, reluctantly, I open the notebook and stare at its first blank page. "What do I dare write about?" I ask it.

The distant cry of a seagull is the only incoherent reply. How I wish my pelicans would return!

I set the notebook down and watch the harbor. The different-colored sails float here and there in the wind. I especially love the little white sails of the dinghies the fishermen take out into the ocean every day. Maybe the best thing I can do for Ana in México, for Tía Graciela in Maine, for Lucila somewhere in this wide world, for Gloria now a stranger to me in Valparaíso, for Cristóbal who no longer sleeps, for Abuela Frida gazing out the window waiting for her daughter, is to write what we all know and love, write what I see coming back to life before my eyes.

I begin:

Night falls over the harbor. In the distance I can see the first boats light up as though they're sleeping angels. Every day the fishermen of Valparaíso risk their lives by going out to sea, and every night their women wait up for them. Many of the vessels are named for wives, mothers, daughters—Marisol, Azucena, Eugenia. Tonight the boats sleep side by side along the docks of Valparaíso Harbor.

Her Bare Feet Make **No Sound**

Writing must be magic. It summons the spirits. That night I dream about Mamá. That is, I *think* it is a dream, but it seems so real that I almost feel her arms wrapping around me as we curl up to sleep together on my bed. She sings me a lullaby about sailing to the stars on firefly wings.

I wake up happy, and with more of an appetite than I remember having in years! The coffee brewing downstairs smells delicious, and I run downstairs to make myself a cup. "Hola!" I smile at Abuela Frida and my father, already helping themselves to breakfast.

"Delfina, you made eggs!" I clap my hands excitedly. "And it's not even the weekend or a special occasion! It's like you knew how hungry I was . . ." I ramble on, distracted by my growling stomach, not noticing how one by one the gazes in the kitchen turn away from me and toward the hallway.

She must have come in without knocking at the door, her bare feet making no sound at all. I don't know how long she stood at the entrance to the kitchen, listening to me chatter on, her wide green eyes filling with tears of joy.

Then all of a sudden Abuela Frida stands up, her chair clattering to the floor! She lets out a cry. "Esmeralda! Daughter! ¡Hija mía!"

Mamá. Mamá! Can it be? And we erupt into cries, practically scrambling over one another to reach her, my mamá who looks so frail, with her long hair that's been dyed black, and large, sad eyes.

Papá—trembling, laughing, and crying all at once—catches her in his arms and leads her to the empty chair—Mamá's chair!—next to Abuela Frida. I run to throw my arms around her. I can't say a word, but Mamá holds me on her lap, buries her face in my hair. Everyone gathers around us—overjoyed, tongue-tied, incredulous, and grateful. After a long silence, the most beautiful silence I have ever heard, she says, "Celeste, can you still hide under tables?"

"Yes, I can!" And I show her how.

Above, I hear everyone erupt into peals of laughter. Then Delfina pulls me to my feet, wipes her face and mine with her apron, and starts to prepare boiled eggs and toast for my thin and weary mother.

And I am with my entire family sitting around the table!

I am with my mother!

I feel happier than I ever have.

But I also sense how much she has suffered. Her fingers intertwine with my father's as if making a knot so that she will not blow away in the wind.

All I Wanted
Was to **Talk** to
Her

Mamá tucks me into bed that night. For so long all I wanted was to talk to her, to hold her hand, and now that I can, I feel so strange. Almost shy. How do you tell someone every thought and feeling and experience that makes up two years? Two years that were so dark and sometimes so light? How do I tell my mother all these things? I realize there is nothing to do but plunge in.

"I missed you so much. And sometimes I was happy. And I know you and Papá sent me away to protect me so I wouldn't have to suffer in hiding like you did. But it was so hard for me, too!"

I am taken aback by the words rushing from my mouth. Mamá gets under the covers and wraps her arms around me. We lie there cheek to cheek, tears flooding both our faces. And all of it—two years of loneliness and fear, and two years of happiness, too, comes out in a jumble: the Juliette Cove school, being laughed at, feeling so different, not understanding anything, the silence of Tía Graciela's house, Miss Rose teaching me English,

Sal's Pizza, watching soap operas, playing in the fog on the beach, the lighthouse, the trailer park, Kim and her paper birds, Tía Graciela's conch shells, Mr. Carter and his letters, the lonely darkness of winter nights, the deer that danced over the lawn, how hard I laughed the first time I saw wild turkeys fly into the trees to sleep, and despite my constant worry about people and places so far away, the peace I found the day I lay in the fresh spring grass to look at the clouds with a boy named Tom.

". . . and one day, Mamá, he reached out and held my hand. Right there in the grass. My whole body shook from head to toe. I felt so nervous and shy, but I didn't want him to ever let go. And then . . . one day . . . Tom and Kim were gone. Just like that. Gone without saying a word." I begin to sob.

"Shhhh, shhhhh! My baby girl. It's all right. Everything will be all right." Mamá pulls me to her chest, softly rocking me back and forth.

So **Strange**
Here Sometimes

Dear Tía Graciela,

I know that Mamá has written you, but I wanted
to tell you too. There is still some fear that
phones may be tapped, but Papá promises that
we will be able to call you soon and hear your
voice. Yes, we are all together again! I found
Papá! And Mamá returned soon after! Now
the only one I am waiting for is you, Tía. But
I know you have to take your time, and thank
goodness whoever made the world made plenty
of time in it.

It is so strange here sometimes, Tía. My parents
hardly talk about what has happened. They hold
hands often, like they are afraid they will fall from
each other's fingers. Their clinic was looted and
vandalized, but they haven't said a word about
putting it back together. . . . They haven't gone
back to work.

I also have to tell you about Tío Bernardo. You
remember how he used to make costumes for the

community theater you acted in when you, he, and Papá were at the university together? Well, Mamá and Papá said Tío Bernardo fled across the mountains dressed as a nun! They think he is in Argentina, and they are hoping to get word to him so that they can help him return home.

How is the mailman Mr. Carter? In your last letter you said he came over unexpectedly on Sunday—even though there's no mail on Sundays—and convinced you to go see a movie with him. When I told that to Mamá, her eyes lit up and for a moment she seemed like her old self again—not so anxious and unsettled. She got a mischievous grin on her face, and told me to ask if he has come to visit again, and reminds you to always make sure your hair and makeup are done, just in case. She promises to write you again soon, and explains that her silence is only because her head aches too much to concentrate on letters these days.

As for me, I am just glad you have found such a good friend in Mr. Carter, Tía.

Nana Delfina sends her love, and I do too.

Your niece,
Celeste Marconi

There Will Always Be a Young Person Who **Remembers** a Poem

I ask my mother the questions I've kept inside for so long. "Will you tell me what happened to you while we were apart?"

We are on the roof, sitting side by side. My mother puts her willowy arm around me and pulls me close.

"Celeste, so many times I was more like a small boat than a person. My heart was beating as fast as the rhythm of the waves. I had peaks and valleys as the waves carried me from one shore to another, from one cove to a different one. I moved from place to place, always lived on the kindness of friends and strangers. But I want to tell you about the last place, the months I stayed in Isla Negra, where Pablo Neruda used to live." She smiles at me but then rubs her temples and squints in the sunlight. She seems to have a constant headache, and the shadows under her eyes look like bruises.

"Like so many things in Chile, things there are not as they seem. Isla Negra is not an island. It's a peninsula. And it is not black! It is a fishermen's cove. Abuela Frida and Abuelo José used to take me and Graciela there on vacation. On one trip I saw the poet. He walked slowly out of the forest toward the ocean, like a fish on land.

"On my first night in Isla Negra I slept in one of those friendly trees from my childhood. I was so hungry and so, so cold. But I wanted to live to tell you that each tree of this universe is like a loving arm. I hid in the forest all the next day, and then the next night I started hunting for the poet's house.

"When I finally found my way there, some fishermen saw me. I told them that I was going to seek shelter at the poet's house. They said it had been abandoned for nearly a year, and all offered me their homes, but I thanked them and said that if I needed them, I would knock at their doors.

"On my way there all I could think of was you. I had heard that Neruda's home was a child's house, full of bells and canaries flying free, telescopes and kaleidoscopes, colorful wine goblets, huge blue glass bottles, and even a purple locomotive that wound its way throughout the house and let out real smoke! When I arrived, I felt my heart break as I saw the broken bottles, the canaries dead at the bottoms of their cages, the smashed glass goblets, and the train broken into a thousand pieces."

"What happened?"

"The same thing that was happening everywhere— the soldiers. Because Neruda had supported Presidente

Alarcón. But Celeste, Celeste! There was one thing the soldiers couldn't destroy—his poetry! Every day young people would come to carve his poems into the wood beams of the house. Sometimes one of them would recite a poem out loud. You should know, Celeste, that they can destroy the furniture, burn the books, but there will always be a young person who remembers a poem and will share it with others.

"I can't remember how long I stayed there, but I was still there when spring came and there were tiny yellow flowers everywhere. At times I had to talk to myself or sing out loud just to hear a voice. But other times I discovered the enormous generosity of the people of Isla Negra.

"The fishermen would come to bring me firewood. And their wives would come when they could to bring me bread and honey and a cup of hot tea. They told me not to worry, that things would turn out fine. And when I was sitting by the fire, I could see your face, or your father's face, emerge from the flames.

"An old fisherwoman let me know that it was safe to come home. I saw her approaching the house with a dirty envelope in her hand, and I knew immediately it was from your father. Her face, usually lined with wrinkles, became as smooth as a wild peach when she smiled and handed it to me. I cried and cried when I saw your father's handwriting. And even more when I saw that

it had become a bit wobbly. Probably like mine. Like all of me, it feels at times, Querida."

Although she remembers these details so well, Mamá is forgetful when it comes to everyday things. And she always seems scared. But right now a smile is coming to her face.

I look up. Her smile is so like Tía Graciela's, like Abuela Frida's, and so—I realize—like my own! "But now"—her voice brightens—"I want to hear more about your time on Juliette Cove! You have grown up so much, my beautiful girl!"

I lean my head on her shoulder as I tell her about Miss Rose's class, and John Carter the mailman, and my second blue room at Tía Graciela's house. We talk until way past midnight.

And when she finally tucks me into bed, like when I was a little girl, I whisper, "Mamá, I want to tell you more about Kim's brother, Tom. But I don't really know what to say . . ."

"You liked him a lot, didn't you, Querida?"

"Sí." I nod and feel so relieved to see the understanding in my mother's green eyes.

"We'll have to have café con leche, Chantilly cream pastries, and a long talk at Café Iris this Sunday. Just us girls. How does that sound?"

"Muy bien, Mamá."

I Knew There
Would Be
Changes

Another week passes, and I start to believe that I am at home with my parents. They are still quieter than I remember, but other things are as they always were: drinking café con leche in the morning, reading books in the afternoon. And at night—the thing I missed most when we were apart—Mamá comes to the roof to help me name the stars.

"There, Mamá." My finger outlines two shimmering strands in the sky above us. "There's the Southern Cross."

Mamá leans close to me and says, "And so it is. How I love that cross of light." She waits a moment, and then puts her lips to my hair and murmurs, "I don't see a shooting star tonight, but I am going to make a wish. It's a wish for you, Querida." I glance up at her serious face and suddenly dread what she is about to say.

"Celeste, tomorrow's Monday. A new week. A fresh start. It's time for you to return to school."

I shake my head and look down. A cold knot of fear pulls tighter and tighter across the soft hollow below my heart. "Celeste, you always loved your school. Are you afraid, hija?"

I choke back tears. "Sí, Mamá. I am. I don't know why, but my stomach gets julepe whenever I think of it!"

My mother reaches for my hand. "I understand. Believe it or not, as much as I wanted to see you all, I was scared when it was finally safe for me to return home to Butterfly Hill. Because I knew there would be changes. That life would never be precisely the same as it was before."

I nod. That's exactly what I'm feeling about school.

"I will never lie to you. When you return to school, you will see that so much has changed. There will be empty seats and distant gazes. But at the same time I can also promise that you will find that many people you love survived the dictatorship and will still be there, trying to make the Juana Ross School the wonderful place it once was. Don't you think you should be there to help them? You have spoken to me so much of the lighthouse on Juliette Cove. Well, at school you will be like a lighthouse for everyone there who has missed you so much."

I think for a while. Slowly I feel a new energy replace the fear. The julepe shrinks and hides in a little corner of my heart.

"Mamá, if I go back to school, will you reopen the clinic?"

"My smart girl!" Mamá smiles her firefly smile. "That's an offer I can't refuse. Yes, we'll reopen the clinic. I promise."

Julepe at
Juana Ross

Today is my first day back to school. Nana Delfina worked late into the evening to let out my old school uniform so that it fits. I remember it used to swallow me whole like a brown paper bag. Now I have to tug at the skirt so it fits over my hips and the hem doesn't ride up above my knees. I glance at myself in the mirror, and then I quickly look away. Then, almost shyly, I face myself.

Mamá says I am still too young to wear lipstick to school like I see some girls my age wear on the street. "You look prettiest with your face fresh as a daisy," she promises. But as I glance at myself again in the mirror, I put my hand over my mouth and begin to laugh. Partly in happiness, partly in surprise, and a little bit in fear. My legs have grown stronger, and my waist is becoming a guitar like my mother's. My face is serious, but when I smile, I like what I see. It seems what everyone has been telling me is true! I am not such a little girl anymore. I decide not to put my hair in braids and leave it flowing down my back like a waterfall.

"Niña Celeste, come eat your breakfast! You'll be

late!" Nana's school-day morning voice is as loud as ever!

"Coming, Delfina!" I am halfway down the stairs when I remember Tía Graciela's conch shell. I quickly grab it from my nightstand, wrap it in one of Abuela Frida's blue scarves to keep it from breaking, and put it in my backpack for good luck.

The *zuzu, zuzu* sound of the cable car sends shivers up my spine. It speaks to me in a funny voice like Abuela Frida's bumblebee accent. *Zzzzz, zzzzz, zzzzz!* Back to zzzzzschool!

The first thing I see when I approach the courtyard of the Juana Ross School are the bright colors of the Chilean flag. I remember learning a song that taught us the meaning of the national colors on my first day as a student here. I was five years old and also had julepe in my stomach. I hum softly to myself and remember: "White snow of the Andes, red blood of our heroes, blue skies with a single brave star."

As I move closer toward the tall metal fence separating the courtyard from the street, I see many young children running around whom I don't recognize at all. That used to be us: me, Cristóbal, Ana, Gloria, Marisol, Lucila. Now I am one of the "big kids" in the eighth grade at the high school. The julepe churns like a storm inside me—there's no more Ana, no more Lucila. As I pass through the front doors, I notice there are small holes and jagged cracks in some of the windows. *Earthquakes or gunfire?* I shiver.

The hallways have their same familiar musty smell. The paint on the walls—as white as a winter day on Juliette Cove—has begun to crack. Beneath I see the colors of the murals we painted years ago to celebrate the election of Presidente Alarcón. Those memories guide me back to Marta Alvarado.

She is there, sitting at her desk, wearing her long red coat. Her head is turned down toward a pile of maps. "Señorita?" my voice barely comes out in a whisper.

"Celeste? Is it you? Celeste Marconi!" Señorita Alvarado springs from her chair and nearly knocks it to the ground as she runs to catch me in a tight hug. "Oh, what a sight you are! How beautiful! What a miracle you are back!"

Marta Alvarado gives me the traditional Chilean greeting I missed so much: a kiss on both cheeks. Her dark hair is thinner, and like Papá's, streaked with strands of gray. "Celeste, welcome back!"

"Gracias, Señorita Alvarado. I am so happy to see you!"

"Celeste, you look lovely and, I must say, a bit taller . . . though not too much!" Señorita Alvarado stands on her tiptoes, and we laugh and embrace again.

"Come, I will take you to your classroom." She guides me by the elbow. "Did you know that Principal

Castellanos has returned from exile in Spain?"

"No, I didn't!" My heart takes a happy leap.

"Yes, but instead of being principal, he has returned to teaching Spanish literature at the high school. He told me that reading the classics gave him hope during the years of worry for all his friends here, and so he wants to pass that on to you young people."

"That's wonderful!" I exclaim. "Then he will be my literature teacher?"

"Sí! And knowing you, I am sure you will be his prize pupil!"

Suddenly so much in my world seems right.

"Here we are, Celeste, classroom 14." Señorita Alvarado peeks around the doorway. "I see someone who will be very happy to see you. Go ahead, Celeste, but don't forget to visit at the end of the day to tell me how everything went."

I step through the doorway. Julepe. Then I spot a girl in the back. Her head is down, and she is scribbling furiously in a notebook, but I would know that glossy black hair anywhere. "¡Hola, amiga bonita!"

Marisol slams her book shut and looks up with a start. "Celeste! You scared me half to death!" She gets up to kiss me on both cheeks. "I'm doing last night's homework, and I thought you were the teacher! Oh! I am so glad you are back in school!"

"I am so glad you are here." I confide in my old friend, "I feel nervous, Mari."

She nods understandingly. "A lot has changed, amiga . . ."

My heart aches. I've reminded her of Lucila. But I know what might cheer us both up. "Mari, before the bell rings, let's go play hopscotch with the little girls for old time's sake!"

Marisol grins. How I have missed that grin! "Well, I was trying to finish my algebra . . . but . . ."

"But that is what lunchtime is for, right?" I tease her. "Isn't that what you always say?"

"All right, all right! For you—hopscotch, kickball, jump rope, whatever!" Marisol gives in. "I just hope the senior boys don't see us!" She smoothes some flyaway strands of hair back into her red barrettes.

"C'mon. You look gorgeous!" I urge her out the classroom door. We link arms and walk down the corridor. Marisol begins to skip, then tips her head back and shouts, "Guess what, everybody?! Celeste Marconi is back!" The echo of our laughter and footsteps fills that whole long, empty space.

Tremors

When we walk outside, I forget I ever wanted to play hopscotch. My mood changes almost instantly from light to dark. Why pretend things are back to normal? My eyes drift over the school yard. I don't know half of the kids here, and so many who I expect to see are missing! Marisol must read my thoughts. "I know," she says with a squeeze of my hand. "I can't say you'll ever get used to it, amiga. But it will start to feel more normal. Not that it's a good thing . . ." Her voice trails off.

"Look! There's Cristóbal waving us over!" Marisol sounds relieved. I am too. Cristóbal is sitting at our old bench. I am so happy to see him, especially with his pendulum—once so dangerous to take to school—swinging from his left hand! Marisol and I sit next to him. Nobody says much. Maybe, like me, they are missing Lucila . . . and Gloria, too. We sit like that—close together but in our own worlds—until the first bell rings.

The rest of the day passes by in a blur. In high school, our classes, as Marisol put it, "are more sophisticated now, like us!" It's true, and that's the best part about being back in school. There are so many new things to explore—philosophy, psychology, physiology—and best of all, languages. I am grateful that either Marisol or Cristóbal is in all of my classes . . . except for English. Marisol decided it would be more romantic to learn Italian, and Cristóbal is taking the beginning English class. When I walk into the classroom for Advanced English, I find there are only five other students. They are all seniors, except for a junior boy who speaks English with his Canadian father at home. Once I would have been so afraid to be in a new class with older kids, all of them strangers. It would have felt like such a big deal. How much the past two years have changed me!

The final class of the day is Spanish Literature. I rush down the hallway to make sure I arrive early. For the first time since seeing Marisol this morning, I feel actually happy. My old principal is back!

I rush through the door, and there he is, scrawling "metaphor" on the blackboard. "Señor Castellanos!"

He turns around and smiles. "I'd know those eyes anywhere! Celeste Marconi?"

"Sí, señor. Welcome home!"

He nods his head somberly. "Gracias. And the same to you. I hear you also went away. Where did you go?"

"The United States. And you, señor?"

voice floats over me from the front of the class. I raise my head, confused.

"I feel dizzy. Can I go to the bathroom?"

"Why don't you go to the nurse's office instead," Señor Castellanos says. "Marisol will take you."

The nurse is not the same nurse as before. But she is kind. Marisol gives my arm a squeeze. "I'll come by for you later," she says. I nod. All I want to do is close my eyes and forget.

How strange that not long ago I was on Juliette Cove, closing my eyes to remember!

"To the place I was born, Celeste. Granada, Spain. My parents brought me to Chile when I was a baby. To me, Valparaíso was always home. But I am glad I had a second motherland to flee to when our own became so troubled."

I look at Señor Castellanos. I have so many thoughts in my head, so many questions to ask, but I can't seem to get any words out! He smiles understandingly. "Why don't you take a seat, Celeste. We have a whole school year ahead of us to talk about many things."

"Sí, señor." I turn from him and see Marisol waving excitedly from the second row. She is sitting at a desk and has put all her books at the one right next to it.

"Saved you a seat!" She grins. And suddenly for a moment it feels like old times. Just when I thought things would never be the same.

Too many tremors. Too much shaken up inside me. They settle into place only to be shaken up once more! I hold on to the edges of my desk. Will things ever just stay put?

What is happening to me?

I look down at my white knuckles. I didn't realize how hard I was holding on. "¡Amiga! ¡Amiga!" Marisol whispers. "There isn't an earthquake! Celeste, let go!"

I take a deep breath and put my head down on my desk. "Celeste, is something wrong?" Señor Castellanos's

Love Among Empty Spaces

When the dismissal bell rings, I am tired, but I feel better. Marisol is waiting for me at the door of the nurse's office. "Come on, I'll walk you home." She threads her arm through mine.

"I promised Señorita Alvarado I would come by," I say. "And I think I just want to be alone."

Marisol looks a bit hurt, even though she is smiling. "Okay, feel better."

"Gracias, Mari." I hug her tight, and she hugs me back even tighter. In that hug I know she understands.

I knock on the door of Señorita Alvarado's office. "Come in!" she calls. I open the door and see her sitting beside Señor Castellanos.

"¡Hola, Celeste!" they speak in unison, and then smile at each other.

"Hola, Señorita Alvarado, Señor Castellanos."

"Are you feeling better, Celeste?" Señor Castellanos asks. "I know that the first day back can be full of so many emotions—"

Suddenly the question I have to ask can't wait. I do something I have never done and interrupt my teacher: "Please tell me! Where are all my old classmates? It seems that half of them aren't here!"

Señor Castellanos, grim-faced, looks to Señorita Alvarado, then back to me. "We don't know, Celeste."

"Things have gotten so much better," Señorita Alvarado adds, "but we are still afraid to ask for their whereabouts. Hopefully, day by day, more familiar faces will arrive back at our school, just like today. Such a happy day for us, Celeste!"

Señor Castellanos looks again at Marta Alvarado. He shrugs his shoulders and puts out his hands as if asking for help, as if he is carrying a great weight and doesn't know how to put it down.

Señorita Alvarado moves closer to him and speaks. "It is such a blessing for Marisol López especially to have you back. She always tries to put on a brave face, but the disappearance of her cousin has been very difficult for her. Those girls are like sisters."

Marta Alvarado looks down, and I watch in disbelief as Señor Castellanos puts his arm around her. He clears his throat and adds gruffly, "You have heard, Celeste, that Gloria was sent to a private school?"

"Sí, Cristóbal Williams told me."

I am afraid to ask them another horrible question

they can't answer, but it burns in my throat and I feel like I might choke on it. "Celeste, what is it?" Señor Castellanos's face is concerned.

Then he looks at Marta Alvarado yet again. I sense them casting question marks over my head. They are fishing for some sort of answer from me. Señorita Alvarado's soft voice carries her own sorrow to my ears.

"Celeste, we miss . . . everyone . . . so much . . ." Señorita Alvarado speaks to me like I am still eleven years old. "We just have to wait and be patient. . . ."

"But that's what I did for two years on Juliette Cove!" I am surprised by the anger in my voice. Why is it so hard for adults to tell the truth?!

I wave my hands in frustration. I think of Mamá. How she always did the same thing. "She's so like you, Esmeralda . . ." I remember Papá's words. I suddenly need my mother so badly.

Mamá . . . please be safe at home! Please don't ever go away!

"I went and found my father! Why can't we go look for Lucila?! Why do we all just sit here waiting?"

Señor Castellanos holds me firmly by both shoulders. "Celeste, try to understand. Right now no one can—or will—say where they went. Just like no one could, or would, say where you had gone."

I look down, feeling the familiar weight of having

to accept unknowing. It may be worse than loss. Loss is a heavy stone that sinks to the bottom of the heart, but then the sands of time bury the pain so I feel it less. Not knowing is a smaller stone, but it's sharper, constantly churning back and forth inside me.

There is a long silence. The kind I used to try to break, but now I am too tired, too frustrated. "We are going to have coffee at Café Iris," Marta Alvarado begins. "Will you join us, Celeste?" they say in unison. I now realize how familiar they seem with each other.

"Thank you, but Abuela Frida is waiting for me. I don't want to worry her."

I close the office door behind me and blink. My eyes must be wide with wonder. Señorita Alvarado and Señor Castellanos! Could it be? Who would have thought?

The
Elections

Dear Miss Rose,
All week Chile has been celebrating our first
presidential elections after the fall of the
General. The port is full of sailboats with Chilean
flags, and ladies are selling carnations and
parsley just like for New Year's. Colorful buses
come to Valparaíso from the smallest towns
surrounding the city. Papá tells me that people
walk in from the countryside for miles on foot
just to cast their vote. Politicians walk up and
down the hills asking for votes and passing out
chocolates.

When I asked my mother how she decided
who to vote for, she said: "It is good to listen
to what they say, Celeste, but even better to
observe their actions." The candidate that Mamá
chose is Mónica Espinoza. She was imprisoned
by the General and suffered for years. She talks
a lot about helping Chile heal her wounds, and

*especially is concerned with the poor and the sick,
which is maybe why Mamá likes her so much. If
Señora Espinoza wins, she will be Chile's first
woman president.*

*The voting took place on Sunday. Men and
women vote separately in Chile, and everyone
dresses up like it is an elegant occasion. Even
my Abuela Frida—who has grown very frail
and doesn't leave the house much anymore—
powdered her face and went down the hills,
propped up by my mamá on one side and Nana
Delfina on the other! She insisted on walking the
whole way. "I want to be a part of everything!"
she told me.*

*And something else: Do you remember I told
you about the pelicans who would fly by my
window every morning? And how they stopped
coming regularly when troubles came to my
country? Well, they're back! All eight of them!
Even my favorite, who's older and slower than
ever. I think they're back because they know
democracy's been restored. Call me crazy, but
these pelicans have shown me just how smart they
are more than once. I'd say they might be wiser
than owls.*

Miss Rose, tonight the whole family is waiting

*for the results to be announced on the radio
from Santiago. Papá is pacing back and forth,
and Nana Delfina can't stop peeling potatoes—
she says it calms her nerves. All of Valparaíso
is holding its breath! I will write to tell you how
everything turns out.*

> *Your student,*
> *Celeste Marconi*

*P.S. I have been trying to keep up my English.
I hope that I wrote well enough for you to
understand!*

I lick and seal the envelope just as my father calls
my name, "Celeste! Come! The radio just announced it!
Mónica Espinoza has won!" I run to the balcony, where
my entire family has gathered. We wave to our neighbors
as people flow into the streets.

"Come!" Papá takes Mamá's hand and mine. He
clears his throat, and I can see his eyes are wet. "Let's
go down to the harbor!"

The streets move slowly as a sea of people come
down the hills to celebrate. Cristóbal is waiting for me at
the bottom of Butterfly Hill. He is smiling, awake, and
excited! I jump up and down, and Cristóbal grabs me

by the waist and we dance until we are dizzy. Joy fills
my body and shakes out all the heaviness of hard times
and leaves it on the side of the road with old carnations,
candy wrappers, and signs that say VOTE! I know the next
rains will wash that old heaviness into the gutters along
with the dust.

"I Should Still Continue to Be"

This week Mamá and Papá reopened their clinic, the repairs all completed, just as my mother promised. Many people from all over Valparaíso come to see them. Not only do my parents listen to their heartbeats, but they also listen to their stories. They sit down and let their patients talk to them because, Papá says, speech cures pain. When the patients depart, they give my parents fresh eggs, bread, or sweets, like they always have, because they don't have any money to pay.

Tonight my parents return before dinner, and Papá hands a burlap bag to a scowling Delfina, who frets about "Delfina's Esmeralda working long hours for peanuts, and with her feeble health!"

But Papá tells her, "Delfina, queen of the kitchen! We have delicious eggs to eat for breakfast. Smile."

As if she is reminding him who really runs our house, Delfina makes scrambled eggs for dinner. "We'll have them now, since they are freshest!" She places a plate heaped high with what look like fluffy yellow clouds in front of my father and, with eyes full of mischief, hands him a fork.

Mamá winks at Delfina and then turns her attention toward me. "How was school, Celeste?"

School never stops being strange. Seeing the empty spaces. What happened in the past hardly mentioned at all. But instead I say, "We are reading *Wuthering Heights* in my Advanced English class!"

"Oh!" Abuela Frida exclaims as she slowly walks toward the dinner table. "Emily Brontë. How she knew love!" she speaks to us in German. Her voice is as animated as a young girl's. "Chapter nine gave me goose bumps! I would read it over and over again when I was your age, Celeste." Abuela Frida closes her eyes. Then as if she is reading from a page in her mind, she begins:

"If all else perished, and he remained, I should still continue to be; and if all else remained, and he were annihilated, the universe would turn to a mighty stranger: I should not seem a part of it."

How like my grandmother I am, I think, as I begin to translate the words from German to Spanish for Nana Delfina. My own copy of the book opens to that passage every time I lay it down on its spine—that's how many times I have turned to it!

We all bask in the rays of Abuela Frida's smile. But

then the light in her eyes begins to dim again. She falls quiet. Is she missing my Abuelo José? I think of Lucila. I know that the passage talks about the love between Catherine and Heathcliff, but somehow it always reminds me of Lucila. She must be alive somewhere! So we all— me, Cristóbal, Marisol, especially Marisol—"should still continue to be . . ."

After dinner I sit on the purple swing under the eucalyptus tree. I feel impatient . . . for what? For my friend to return, yes. But for something else, too. For something to happen? But what?

I see Nana walking through the garden toward me. She begins to speak in that stern, listen-to-Delfina tone I have known since I was little.

"Niña Celeste. Your Nana Delfina knows you very well. You are full of worry. Delfina understands. But Delfina thinks what Nana's girl needs to do is to find a purpose. Too often my Celeste wants to be alone. Nana Delfina has noticed this. And Nana Delfina has a project for her girl."

Delfina pauses and looks down to the ground. "If you accept." Her voice sounds nervous. Nana has never been shy about asking me—or any of the family—to do anything! In fact, she usually *tells* us!

"Go on, Delfina," I coax her, patting the pink swing beside me. Nana looks back and forth to make sure the neighbors aren't watching, and then she tosses her apron over her shoulder and hops onto the swing.

Her face as serious as ever, even with her legs dangling in the air, Delfina continues: "Niña Celeste, even though the family never talks about it—probably not to embarrass Delfina—you know that it is hard for Delfina to read and write."

I look down at my own feet hanging idly above the grass. Suddenly I feel ashamed for all I have, when my nana has so little and asks for even less. "Sí, Nana, I know."

"Delfina only went to school for about two years. Delfina had to walk almost an hour. You know Delfina didn't get her first pair of shoes until arriving in Valparaíso. So, on days when the ground froze, we stayed home. And bit by bit it seemed more important to stay home, and to help Delfina's parents with the work there. Delfina began to weave shawls with Mamá to sell in the markets. And to cook and take care of her baby sister."

I kick my legs forward and jump from the swing to land right beside Delfina. I am astonished to find that I have grown taller than her, and hadn't even noticed. "Then I am going to teach you to read! Wait right there!" I run into the house and upstairs to my bedroom. I pull every box out of my closet and search through them—old finger paintings, photo albums, and dolls scattering to the floor around me. It has to be here somewhere! Finally, at the bottom of a box of old dresses, I find my old phonics book from second grade!

I run back outside to the swings. "Let's start right now, Nana!" I say as I open to page one and motion for her to sit on the ground beside me. And we sit there, under the eucalyptus tree, and talk about the sounds every letter in the alphabet makes. Then we blend letters to make simple words. We begin with three, and then four, and then five letters.

I remember that this is how I learned to read, sitting on Papá's lap. We would make up sentences that rhymed so I could learn letters and combinations and the sounds they make. "The cat sat on the mat. The hen is in a pen."

Delfina smiles impishly. "How about, Celeste is small, but her brain makes her tall?"

I laugh until my side aches. "Nana! You are a poet!"

¿Dónde
Están?

Sunday is overcast. I sit at the kitchen table reading *Wuthering Heights*. Delfina sits next to me, practicing writing by copying down a page from my old "notebook of words." Every so often she tugs on my sleeve so I can help her sound one out. "Ser . . . en . . . dip . . . ity."

"Oh, like Delfina's magic!" she exclaims, her eyes lighting up.

"Kind of," I say, thinking how teaching something you know is just as hard as learning something new. "It's magic that people call good timing."

Nana turns her head back to the page and writes the word down. I watch her shaky *S* rise and fall on the page. "How mysterious it is to learn to read, Celeste," Nana Delfina tells me as she slowly forms the *Y*. "All these words speaking to Delfina but in silence."

The telephone interrupts us. Delfina springs up and runs to the hall. A few minutes later she comes back. "Your friend Marisol," she tells me, her pencil already back on the paper.

"¡Hola, amiga!" I say into the phone. "I'm glad you called! Guess what? I am teaching Nana Delfina to—"

Marisol speaks over me in a rush. "Cristóbal just called! We are going to Plaza Aníbal Pinto!"

"Why are you going all the way down there?" I ask, slightly annoyed that Cristóbal called Mari first, and then annoyed at myself for being annoyed in the first place! *Why do I care? It's not like I like Cristó—*

"To join in the demonstration."

"What demonstration?"

Marisol lowers her voice. "My parents don't want me to go. People who want to know what happened to family and friends who were disappeared during the dictatorship are gathering outside the government buildings. They are demanding information. If those who disappeared are alive still or, if not, what the government has done with their bodies. . . ." She pauses. My heart beats fast. "I heard a man talking on the cable car. He said many people who lost loved ones during the dictatorship gather in one of Valparaíso's main plazas every Sunday."

"I am coming with you," I say decidedly.

"Let's meet in front of Café Iris in one hour," she says. "And bring an umbrella!"

I open the coat closet and pull out my raincoat. "Nana!" I poke my head into the kitchen. "I am going out with Marisol." I wince. It's not a lie. But it's not the whole truth, either. "We can go over the list of words when I get back."

Delfina looks up. "Be back in time for dinner, Querida. I don't want your parents to worry."

I quickly run to Abuela Frida's room, where she is napping, her plate of half-sucked lemons on her night table. I kiss her forehead. *She* would understand why I have to go to this rally.

I meet Marisol and Cristóbal outside the café. The first thing I see is the sign in Marisol's hands. Lucila's picture, larger than life. Her eyes like almonds. The dimple in her chin. And below, the words. LUCILA LÓPEZ. 14 YEARS OLD.

Plaza Aníbal Pinto, one of the largest squares in the city, is crowded with people holding large signs like Marisol's above their heads. So many photographs of missing people! Most of them look so young!

Other signs have giant letters in red paint asking, ¿DÓNDE ESTÁN? WHERE ARE THEY?

Or black paint demanding, ¡JUSTICIA! JUSTICE!

I am stunned at the number of faces of missing people waving in the air. And the number of heartbroken faces below them. Waves and waves of the heartbroken yet hopeful. Some angry. Some sad. Some whose mouths are shouting, "¡Justicia!"

Marisol presses Lucila's photograph to her chest and elbows her way through the throng. Cristóbal and I follow her into the middle of the plaza. Hundreds of people are marching in a circle.

They chant: "They were taken away alive! We want them back alive! Tell us where they are! Tell us where they are!"

All around us, protesters bang on pots and pans. Pang, pang, pang! Spoons are being whacked against metal saucepans, and pot covers clapped together like defiant cymbals.

Students from the university pour into the streets, playing trumpets, flutes, and drums. Taruntun tun. Tarun tun tun. "¿Dónde están? Where are they? ¿Dónde están?"

Echoes of voices and clangs vibrate inside me. Then the rain begins to fall. Harder and harder, the rain beats the ground as if it is marching with us. It shouts like a dented saucepan.

"Look!" Cristóbal points. "There are Marta Alvarado and Señor Castellanos!"

"Where?"

"There! By the fountain! See her red coat?"

Cristóbal takes us each by the hand and pulls us toward our teachers. They look surprised to see us. It is hard to hear one another over the chanting crowd, but Marta Alvarado motions for me to come close and whispers into my ear, "You are participating in the history of your country!" Our eyes meet. Her smile is fearless.

She Used to Have All the **Answers**

Sunday evening, when everyone seeks a quiet place to digest their empanadas, I look for my mother and find her sitting on the green couch next to Abuela Frida, who has fallen asleep in her rocking chair. Neruda's "Tonight I Can Write the Saddest Lines" lies open on Mamá's lap, and she is gazing out the window with her chin resting on her hand.

"¡Hola, Mamá!" I whisper as I wrap one of Abuela Frida's blue scarves, this one half-finished but long enough for my mother's slender shoulders, around her.

"Hola, Querida." Mamá's face looks tired.

My mother pushes the book aside and reaches out her arms. "Come here, my little girl. You are still small enough to sit on my lap, and I can tell you have something serious on your mind." Abuela Frida stirs a bit but doesn't wake up. She spends so much time in sleep lately. "It's most comfortable there," she tells us.

How good it is to still be able to sit on Mamá's lap, even though I am thirteen years old. "Mamá, I get to have you and Papá back with me, but Lucila is missing . . . so many are. . . . Sometimes I feel embarrassed about how lucky I am—I have you, and Papá . . ."

"All we can do is be grateful, Celeste."

"I know, Mamá! But I want to do something!"

Mamá puts her finger to her lips. "Hush! Don't wake your grandmother." I didn't realize my voice had grown so loud.

"And it's not just that, Mamá," I whisper. "Why isn't *anyone* doing anything?! Why can't Presidente Espinoza send out search parties? And why can't she jail all those military people who did such awful things? It wasn't just the General who was evil. . . . We can't all pretend nothing ever happened!"

Mamá is quiet. She used to have all the answers, but even she can't know why there are so many unfair things in this world.

"Maybe, Celeste, you will explain all of this to me someday. I still don't know. . . ." She rests her chin on my head and sighs. "Maybe you will be one of the people who make a difference."

The
Assignment

At the end of Spanish Literature class on Monday, Marisol and I huddle close to talk about the rally. "Did your parents find out? Do you think it could actually help find Lucila?"

"Maybe if someone had seen her—"

Señor Castellanos's booming voice interrupts us.

"Señorita López. Will you excuse us? I want to talk with Señorita Marconi for a moment."

"Sí, señor!" Marisol throws me a question mark with her eyes and scuttles out of the classroom. I gulp. Does he want to talk about the protests? Is he going to tell me it's too dangerous, maybe ask if my parents know? Which they don't . . . yet.

"Celeste, sit down." He gestures to a seat in the front row. "I have great news for you!" I breathe an audible sigh of relief.

"Today the Juana Ross School received a letter from the Ministry of Education, signed by our new Presidente Espinoza. She wants the young people of

Chile to write about what they want for this country we are reconstructing. It is a contest called 'My Dream for My Homeland,' and the prize is a scholarship for college, and the most important newspaper in the country, *El Mercurio*, will publish it." He pauses, holding up the letter. "I want you to write a letter, Celeste. Use your gift of words and all the experiences you have gained in the past few years, to show Chile how resilient we are, and what wondrous possibilities await in our future."

My heart starts its all-too-familiar butterfly beating. Me? Me?! I hardly know what to say, so I stammer, "Maybe—I will—write it, Señor—Castellanos."

He shakes his head with stern eyes but a slight smile. "No, Celeste Marconi. I know you, and I know you *will* write that letter. They gave us an official envelope so that the school can mail it for you. I expect it on my desk in no more than a week." Then he grins. "Consider it the most important homework I'll ever assign to you."

I nod and instantly feel the weight of responsibility— that word my father always says with a long roll of the *Rrrrr*s for emphasis—on my shoulders. But—oddly!—it doesn't make me stoop forward or sink into the floor. Somehow—oddly!—that weight makes me stand taller.

I decide to walk all the way home instead of taking the cable cars. The afternoon sun casts beautiful shadows on the cobblestone streets. I wave to the chess players in the square, and as usual, Don Gregorio takes off his fisherman's cap and nods his head to me. Sometimes I stop to chat with him, but today I just want to be alone to think. Is it finally time for me to let others read my words? The whole country? In a newspaper? You haven't won it yet, Celeste! You have to write something first!

I think of Kim, of Tom, of Charlie and Valerie, of Miss Rose, of Lucila and Ana, of Abuela Frida, of all the people I have promised I would one day become a writer. I have never felt so excited or so terrified.

My Dream for
Chile

On Saturday the letter is on my mind all day, but I seem to find many excuses not to do it. Studying for my biology test, trying Mamá's silver hoop earrings on in the mirror, reading some more of *Wuthering Heights*, napping on the green sofa in Abuela Frida's parlor while she snoozes in her rocking chair.

All but a crescent of the bright orange sun has been swallowed by Valparaíso Harbor by the time I crawl onto my favorite perch on the roof with my notebook and pen, and a pillow.

"Celeste!" my father calls up. "Do you want me to bring you a candle so that you can see what you are writing?"

How do they know I am writing? It's so hard to have *any* privacy around here! "¡Estoy bien! I'm fine, Papá!" I try to shrug off my annoyance, but my voice is somewhere between a shout and a sigh. "The stars are my candle; just ask Mamá how she did it when she was a girl!" I hear my father chuckle and his footsteps descending the creaky wooden stairs.

I carried Tía Graciela's conch shell up with me. I take a deep breath, put it to my ear, and listen. The sound of the sea, its wordless language of constant rhythms, soothes me. I listen to the tides, my body slowly rocking back and forth, back and forth, until—finally—I am ready to write.

Gracias, Presidente Espinoza, for calling on the young people of Chile to share with you our dreams for our homeland. I take this opportunity to write to you with humility and gratitude. My Abuela Frida, who came to Valparaíso as a Jewish refugee from Nazi-occupied Austria, taught me that placing these two words—"humility" and "gratitude"—side by side makes the most generous offering in any language.

I am from the port city of Valparaíso. My city reminds me of a balcony because of the way it is always teetering farther toward the ocean. From this balcony, and from the roof of my own house atop Butterfly Hill, I think and write about what my country could be.

Soon after the Dictator came to power, my parents went into hiding. I was an exile in the state of Maine in the northernmost United States, about as far from Chile as you

Marjorie Agosín

*can imagine, for nearly two years. Now I am
home, but at night when I look at the lights
over Valparaíso Harbor, I am also seeing the
Juliette Cove Harbor in Maine. I have learned
that although the planet Earth is immense
and diverse, our world is truly one. The swells
of the same ocean move all of us in these
interconnected lands that we only imagine as
separate from one another. People like to think
of themselves as individuals. But I believe that in
our hearts, Chileans know differently. We know
the meaning of solidarity. We understand that
what happens to a neighbor also happens to us.*

*I love my country. It is full of generous and
courageous people. So many times our cities and
towns have been in ruins, and so many times
we have risen up again. And in our most recent
history, thousands of people, some only a little
older than me, were disappeared. And though we
have yet to see so many of their faces, I believe
it is contests like this one that will inspire my
generation to make sure we lift one another
to a place from which Chile cannot fall again.
Earthquakes do not shatter our dreams.*

*Honorable Presidente Espinoza, I want to work
to end illiteracy in our country. My dream for the*

new Chile is that all Chileans learn to read and write. I have always loved to read, and I dream of being a writer someday.

It also is my dream that every resident of Valparaíso, and eventually every town and village in Chile, have access to free literacy classes. I dream that they are able to take these classes without spending money on transportation, or losing wages. I believe this is the key to our freedom. Reading and writing, which mean the ability to learn and express oneself freely, will help Chile heal from our past and create a happy future.

Respectfully,
Celeste Marconi
Cerro Mariposa

Fireworks
over the Harbor

New Year's Eve has arrived! It's a hot summer night, and although I brushed and brushed to make my hair smooth, I can feel little curls starting to spring at the back of my neck.

"Who is this elegant young woman?" Mamá laughs as she watches me model my New Year's outfit. I am wearing her silver hoop earrings and her blue sundress with yellow flowers that used to belong to her when she was my age. Nana Delfina hemmed it to fit me, and I love how the skirt has a bit of crinoline beneath it so the skirt flounces out below the yellow ribbon at my waist. I have always loved this dress. When I was little, I called it the buttercup dress. "Now just dab on a bit of the red lipstick Abuela Frida gave you—but not enough to make your father frown and pull you back through the door by your skirt." Mamá, my co-conspirator, grins at me.

I smile at myself in the mirror. I give a final twirl for my mother and tell her, "Mamá, I am so glad you never throw anything out! I love old-fashioned clothes." She groans and throws a pillow at my backside.

"Well, I am so glad you have an antique mother to borrow dresses from," she teases me with a rueful laugh.

"You are still known on Butterfly Hill as the beautiful Esmeralda with the firefly smile, and always will be, Mamá." She squeezes me tight, and I smell her rose-water fragrance. "Mamá, can I wear a bit of your perfume?" I am already dashing down the hall to her bedroom.

"Just a bit," she calls out. "It's on my dresser. Now, remind me of your plan for tonight so I don't worry about you!" I return smelling like a rose garden.

"I am going to meet Marisol and Cristóbal at Vergara Pier at eleven. I told Papá I would meet you both back at the statue around three to go home together."

I give her a good-bye kiss on both cheeks.

"I guess that sounds like as challenging a place as any to find you among thousands and thousands of people," my mother says with a yawn. "Your old-fashioned mamá may need a nap before she goes down to the harbor— either that or the fireworks will wake me up!" Little by little my mother's fun-loving spirit is returning.

"Unless you've gotten too deaf to hear them, Mamá!" I call up to her.

"What's that you said, Querida?"

I giggle at her silliness. "Welcome back, Mamá," I whisper.

* * *

I make my way down the hills in a cable car filled with people dressed in bright clothes, holding parsley and carnations for good fortune, as well as bunches of grapes for making twelve wishes at midnight.

I squeeze through throngs of people in the plaza to make it out to Vergara Pier. Maybe it is because I remembered the snowy, quiet New Year's Eve I spent with Tía Graciela in Maine, or maybe it is because Chile is coming to life again, but the streets seem louder and more raucous than I ever remembered them. People wearing masks, carrying sparklers, candles, and streamers. Women dressed in samba outfits. Men smoking two cigars at a time. Old couples and young couples dancing the cueca with white handkerchiefs in their hands. And children holding so many balloons, you'd think they'd fly away. Along with the aroma of empanadas and humitas, music wafts from every corner of the plaza: tango, rock and roll, African drumming, disco fever, traditional Chilean folk songs.

I can barely see over the mass of heads, so I climb up on the low roof of Don Jose's sweet shop. Suddenly I spot Marisol—she is turning heads and causing men's cigars to drop to the ground, sauntering down the pier in a new red dress. Her arm is entwined with Cristóbal's. He seems to be propping her up. I can't see, but I am sure there are red high heels teetering beneath her feet. And someone is behind them. I forgot that Cristóbal had told me he might bring an old friend. As they approach me, I see a girl in a sea-green skirt with her head tilted down, her hair shining gold in the moonlight.

Cristóbal spots me. "¡Hola, Celeste!"

Marisol cries out, "It's time for a new beginning, amiga!" and nearly falls down. She grabs on to Cristóbal, and they almost topple over in laughter. The girl behind them lifts her head and meets my eyes.

Gloria!

We stare at each other for a moment. I don't know what to do or say. Half of me wants to run to her with my arms open wide, and half of me wants to shout at her, "Why didn't you stand by me? Why did you pretend not to know me? What happened to you?"

She looks back at me with her bright hazel eyes. Is she thinking the same thoughts about me? Slowly she walks my way and pulls a red carnation from the braided chignon at the nape of her neck. She reaches her hand up, and I reach mine down to take the flower from her. Then I reach my other hand out to her, and she clasps both her hands around it, and I pull to help her climb atop Don Jose's tin roof.

"Ay! Celeste! Help!" We both nearly fall as I hear her making a soft sound between laughter and sobbing. I pull her into a hug, a hug that I hope tells her everything I don't know how to say. That despite our parents' differences, despite everything that happened, she is still my friend.

"Amiga, what happened to you?" I whisper.

"I should be asking that of you," she replies. Suddenly two more pairs of arms wrap around us. "Can we join you?" Marisol laughs. And the four of us sit on the sloping roof of Don José's shop on Vergara Pier with our arms around one another's shoulders. We share a bag of fried sunflower seeds and see who can spit the shells farthest into the water below, and wait for the clock to strike midnight.

"Cristóbal, don't fall asleep now!" Gloria jabs him in the ribs.

"Have you noticed he only falls asleep once or twice a day now?!" Marisol comes to his defense. "Unless that older girl María Carlota Fuentes is anywhere nearby, then he's wide-awake!"

Cristóbal is blushing beet red. Marisol and Gloria are rocking back and forth with laughter. I think of Lucila. Right now she would be saying, "Oh, leave poor Cristóbal alone! He can't help it that that girl is so flirty and wears black mascara that makes her eyes trap him like a fly in a spiderweb!" So I say it for her. I feel her near us. A soft breeze rises from over the harbor. Marisol reaches over and squeezes my hand. She must feel her cousin too. It sends shivers through my body.

"Chicas!" Cristóbal takes his father's watch from his jacket pocket. "It's one minute to midnight!" He quickly hands us the bunches of grapes his mother packed so that we could put one in our mouth as the clock strikes midnight. Each grape represents a wish for the new year. And suddenly all of Valparaíso rings out as a single voice. "¡Feliz Año Nuevo! Happy New Year in the city and the sea!"

Bong. Bong. Bong! As the clock counts out each hour, I bite a juicy grape and make a wish: truth for all those who seek it, light like that found in agates by the shore for those who are sad, courage to write with an open heart . . .

"Come on, Celeste!" My friends pull me down from the roof to join the masses of revelers dancing on the pier. Someone hands me a cup of lemonade that tastes more like champagne, and I gulp it down, thirsty and elated. *Boom! Boom!* The fireworks burst in the sky—turquoise, violets, golds—to cheers and waving hands below. Voices begin to call out, "Long live Valparaíso! Long live Chile!" Cristóbal shouts, "¡Que viva Chile! ¡Viva la libertad! ¡Y que viva la Presidente Espinoza!"

And I hear Gloria softly murmur, "¡Que viva!"

The Secret
Library

"Check on your abuela, please, Celeste. And then can you come help Delfina peel potatoes?"

"Sí, Delfina."

I walk slowly into the parlor. "Abuela, would you like some lemons?" I ask to tempt her. Her appetite is poor lately.

But Abuela Frida shakes her head. "I can't taste their tartness anymore," she tells me.

Mamá and Papá moved Abuela Frida's bed, with its bedposts carved into vines and roses, into the parlor so she could watch the harbor from the window. During the days she lies beneath her blue bedspread, propped up with as many pillows as Delfina can fit behind her without them falling off the bed. The sunlight streams through the open window like a blossom blooming before her face. And she watches.

She is so small and narrow in her wide bed. I sit next to her and sometimes we talk, but most of the time we just look out the window at our garden and the path that leads down Butterfly Hill from our doorway, and in the distance the harbor with its billowing sails. "Abuela, your hair grows more and more by the minute," I tell her as I softly brush her curls with the small ivory comb she brought here from Austria when she was just a year older than I am now.

I wind her hair into a bun at the nape of her neck, the elegant way she has worn it every day I have known her. Then I help her powder her cheeks and nose with the fine rice powder she loves. She blinks her eyes and says, "Celeste of my soul, give me your hands." I hold them out to her, covered with rice powder. She takes them in her own frail hands and gives mine a squeeze. Her sudden burst of strength surprises me.

"These hands are so small, yet they do so much good. Use them to write, always. And . . ." Her eyes sparkle with girlish excitement. "I have another job for them."

"What is it, Abuela?"

"An important task. One I started, and which you will finish."

I'm so curious, and impatient for her to tell me, that I shift back and forth, jiggling the mattress a bit. "Ay, Celeste, I'm too old to have you bouncing on the bed like when you were a little girl!" Abuela Frida laughs at her own joke. "Bring me my shawl from the rocking chair,

Querida, the one that looks like an onion skin, and I'll tell you all you need to know."

I drape the gauzy peach-colored shawl over my grandmother's shoulders, then gently sit down on the bed by her side.

"Now then, where was I?" Abuela Frida clears her throat and begins, "During the years you lived on Juliette Cove, many people knocked on our door with their arms full of books, asking me to hide the books and keep them safe. As you know, the Dictator had ordered soldiers to raid all the homes on all the hills and to burn any books he called 'dangerous.' That meant books with ideas he didn't like—ideas about individual freedom and expression, especially. These people asked me to save these books so that no matter what happened in the present, future generations could read them. I hid all sorts of books—old and new, poetry and astronomy, history and psychology . . ."

"Abuela Frida!" I exclaim. "What a dangerous— what a brave—thing to do! Banned books hidden *here*? How could you have kept this a secret all this time? Who else knows about this?"

I have so many questions, but Abuela Frida calmly tells me, "Celeste of my soul, listen and all will be revealed in its time."

"Sí, Abuela." I sit, alert, my back straight against the

headboard of her bed. "Go ahead. I'm listening."

"Ahem!" Abuela Frida continues her story in German. "Celeste, I never had the heart to tell you this until today, but soldiers invaded our house too while you were on Juliette Cove. They turned everything helter-skelter with their snapping dogs and dirty boots. But they never found anything but two old women, one sitting in her rocker knitting a blue scarf, and the other in the kitchen shucking corn. I know I always tell you to be ladylike, but I confess that I spit lemon seeds at them, and I am proud of it. For Delfina and me, a Mapuche peasant and an Austrian Jewess, the time to fear ignorance dressed up in a uniform already passed long ago."

"Soldiers? Here? Oh, Abuela, no!" I shake my head, unwilling to think of soldiers storming in on Nana Delfina and my grandmother! Unwilling to think of what could have happened to them.

Abuela Frida pats my hand. "There, there, Celeste. You already know that I am an old lady, with too much experience with these sorts of things."

"Si, Abuela. I know." I rub my eyes and sniffle.

"Now save your tears for happy times, and listen: When I was your age, the Nazis burned books, and I learned to hide them. I never thought I would have to rely on this skill again. But, Celeste, I hid all the books given to me by the people of Valparaíso, along with our own, in a part of the house you don't even know exists. Yes, even you—who hid under tables to eavesdrop as a child—don't know of a small hiding place beneath the stairs. Your parents didn't either, until I told them last night—I told them the story I'm telling you now, and about the important task I am giving you. Your Abuelo José and I had the house built this way, with a secret place only we two knew, because the fear from the Shoah was still fresh within us."

I shake my head some more. "I can't believe that in all these years of hiding all over this house I never saw a thing! And Mamá, too? After all her years living here?"

"Well." Abuela Frida wears the smile of a mischievous girl. "It was expertly built, as a secret that was meant to be kept. The door is small. You have to crouch down to find it, and it's hidden by the wallpaper. There is no knob. You just carefully peel back a small flap of wallpaper, insert a key in the keyhole, and push the door open."

Abuela Frida points to the drawer in the nightstand beside the bed. I open it and pull out a large, old-fashioned copper key. I stare from the key to my grandmother, speechless with wonder.

She beams proudly and continues, "Every day while you were gone we would have to rip down the wallpaper and put it back up. Cristóbal would come with paste and plaster and help us with that often. Ask him about it. I am sure he hasn't told you yet because I asked him not to. Cristóbal will grow up to be a fine man someday, Celeste."

"Cristóbal? Really?" The story that Abuela Frida is telling me is just so unexpected, and even more wonderful.

"Really!" She laughs. "Now listen closely, Celeste. The hiding place is filled with what I hope will become a library. The books are in fruit boxes from Cristóbal's mother, and wrapped in blankets and my blue scarves. Celeste, I want you to organize them into a traveling library for the people of Valparaíso."

"Abuela, they built their library themselves, without even knowing it!"

"Exactly." Abuela Frida winks at me. "And now I want these little hands"—she reaches out and gives them a squeeze—"to tackle a big job."

Treasures

It's like entering a labyrinth. The hideaway beneath the stairs is full to the brim with overstuffed boxes. Old blankets and cloaks are haphazardly strewn over the various shapes. I recognize a crimson blanket that Delfina brought with her from her home in the south. It smells like smoke and cinnamon, and when I lift it up, I see beneath a collection of books written by a British scientist named Charles Darwin. I kneel down and flip through the pages excitedly. Señorita Alvarado taught us about Darwin and his voyage on the *Beagle* to the Galápagos Islands of Ecuador, and how he developed his theory of evolution when he noticed differences among the finches on each island.

Over one box I recognize the calico dress Abuela Frida wears in the photograph where she is holding Tía Graciela days after she was born. Wrapped inside are books of poetry by the Indian Rabindranath Tagore and Chile's beloved Gabriela Mistral. There is also a novel for young adults called *Heart* by an Italian named Edmondo

De Amicis. And at the very back of the hideaway, wrapped in silk shawls like those of a Hindu princess, I find *One Thousand and One Nights*, a collection of Middle Eastern and South Asian folktales.

How many times must Abuela Frida have climbed in here to hide these books? I stay there in the hideaway for a long time, lifting one book and then another into my hands and turning through the pages. Abuela Frida left me the history of the world in these boxes! I decide to start with one and pull a box covered in blue scarves out into the hallway. I look through the various titles. *Mapuche Medicine*, *Mysticism*, the cello music to Beethoven's Ninth Symphony with the famous "Ode to Joy."

I really should unpack the books in Abuela Frida's parlor so she can watch. She'd want to see all the treasures she saved. Besides, I want to hear the story behind each one.

I heave the heavy box into my arms, letting loose the thin layer of dust that had settled upon it. My nose twitches as I struggle to carry the box down the hallway. Finally I reach the entrance to the parlor, and I lean in the doorway to catch my breath. The lights are dim—Abuela Frida always lowers them this time of the day so she can see the sunset in the harbor from her window.

"Abuela Frida, these are amazing," I tell my grandmother, huddled under her shawl in her rocking chair. "I promise they will fall into the hands of people who will treat them like treasures . . .

"Abuela Frida?"

"Zzzzzzzzz."

I take a few steps closer, my eyes adjusting to the dark, and stifle a giggle. Abuela Frida has fallen asleep in her rocking chair, snoring softly, as always, like the letter Z.

I put the box of treasures down quietly at her feet.

"Gute nacht," I whisper. "Good night, Abuela. Thank you for this gift."

The last tendrils of sunlight shimmer on the window. And I watch as the colors of dusk rise to dance upon her face.

The Skin of an Onion

I like to borrow Abuela Frida's shawl—the one that's like the skin of an onion—when I am sorting the books. It reminds me of what she always says about people being like onions: When you begin peeling away the layers, you discover who they really are. Some have long roots, and others are only empty skin, without history or flavor. *And maybe a person can be like a cardboard box?* I wonder as I pry open a particularly well-sealed one. Who knows what words, what wisdom, might fill it?

Thinking of onions makes me think of the boy with the big appetite, who helped my grandmother with the books. I leave her room and walk to the telephone in the hallway. It is late, but I call Cristóbal anyway. He answers with a sleepy voice. "Cristóbal? I know what you did to help my Abuela Frida. Amigo, what would we all do without you?"

"Celeste, it was nothing." Cristóbal's voice is shy.

"Cristóbal, tomorrow will you help me carry books to Café Iris? I can already imagine el mago reading poems out loud. And I will take some to the community center."

"And maybe we could find a way to make my mother's fruit crates waterproof so that we could leave books at the cable car stops and on the stairs that go up and down the hills?" Cristóbal suggests.

"That would be amazing, Cristóbal. And maybe we can put books by the harbor for the fishermen and travelers? And maybe your mother could have some at her stand in the market? There's so much we can do!"

"All right." Cristóbal yawns.

"Call me when you wake up, sleepyhead. And rest up tonight. No using the books as a pillow tomorrow, like you did in class when we were little!"

Cristóbal laughs. "Buenas noches, amiga."

"Buenas noches, amigo."

My mother's voice floats down from my parents' bedroom upstairs. "Celeste, it's late. The boxes will be there in the morning."

"I'm heading to bed, Mamá. Soon."

I yawn. It *is* late, but maybe . . . maybe . . . I'll open just one more box.

I head back to the hideaway, holding the onion shawl against my nose and mouth—ready for the dust, eager to unbury treasure.

When I finally do sneak up to bed, it's past two o'clock, but sleep seems impossible. I toss and turn for what feels like hours. Delfina is restless too. I hear her praying in Mapudungún and I smell burning cinnamon leaves. That's the sacred tree of her people. She performs ceremonies with the leaves only when something important is about to happen. I feel myself drifting off on a cloud of toasty cinnamon. "I wonder," I say to myself, yawning, "if something will happen tomorrow."

The next morning I open my eyes just as the sun is stretching its first rays over the top of Butterfly Hill. Usually I don't wake up until the tenth blast of a car horn or Nana Delfina's shouts wake me up. She is in the kitchen already. I hear the sweep of her purple broom and the grinding of coffee beans.

"¡Buenos días, Nana!"

"Celeste, you are up early!" Delfina says. I smile. "Delfina heard you up late last night too! Did you smell your nana burning cinnamon leaves?"

"Yes. Do you have any predictions, Nana?" I ask as I sit down.

Now it is Delfina's turn to smile. "It is good you are

up early, Querida. Meant to be." I cast her a quizzical look and open my mouth to ask why, but Delfina turns to the stove and begins to hum one of my favorite old Mapuche songs. I shrug. Then the telephone rings.

"At this hour? That's so strange, Nana!" I don't move from my chair, though, and I take a bite of warm bread just pulled out of the oven. Delfina always answers the phone—she considers it one of her duties, and she takes all her duties seriously. So I almost choke when she says, "Celeste, go answer the phone, please. Delfina is busy."

I run out to the hallway, where the phone sits on the antique chest my Abuelo José bought as a young man from a Bolivian horse breeder. "Hello? . . . Yes, this is Celeste Marconi. How can I help you?" I see Nana's head peeking around the corner, a broad smile on her wrinkled brown face.

A serious, high-pitched voice tells me: "On behalf of the Office of the President, I congratulate you. Señorita Marconi, you have won the prize for your letter, 'My Dream for Chile.' By next Friday your college scholarship check will arrive, and on that same day your letter will appear in every Chilean newspaper."

I can say only one word. The word that my Abuela Frida says one should say frequently: "Gracias." Delfina's arms wrap around my waist. I lean against her so I don't fall down.

Most of All,
Be Happy

Later that morning Cristóbal and I decide to stop at my parents' clinic during our rounds to distribute books. "You should tell them the good news!" he says excitedly.

When I tell them about the letter I wrote, and the prize I won, my mother's happy tears are gleaming pearls on her pale face. "Celeste, it is you and Cristóbal and your entire generation who will be the New Chile. The dark times are truly over."

That night Mamá cuts my hair on the roof under the light of the full moon. "This is what Delfina taught me when I was your age," Mamá murmurs as the scissors fly snip snip snip around my shoulders. "A woman should always cut her hair beneath a full moon to ensure beauty and abundance of all kinds. You are a young woman now, Celeste, and I couldn't be prouder of the person you are."

When Mamá is done cutting my hair, I tell her, "I am just going to stay out a bit longer to think."

"And let me guess—to write, perhaps?" she teases me.

The hills of Valparaíso spread below me like a garland of flowers. The lighthouse and the white sails in the blue harbor melt into one gleaming light, like great bunches of grapes or swarms of fireflies. My heart hears the whistle of the Ship Called Hope, whose sails are made from the feathers of seagulls, from moths and from angel wings.

I think of what Abuela Frida said when I told her about my scholarship. "I am so proud, Celeste of my soul. Education is such a wonderful—*the most wonderful*—gift."

"Sí, Abuela," I said. And now she is snoring like the letter *Z* downstairs, and I speak to the stars. "Education *is* a wonderful gift. So wonderful that I want to share it."

I begin to write another letter:

Dear Señora Presidente,
I am honored to have been awarded the prize
for my essay, "My Dream for Chile." I am
also so grateful for the generous scholarship.
It is true that one of my own dreams is to go
to college to study literature, but I have three
more years to make that dream a reality. But I
also have a dream that is not only for me but
for Chile. And I would like to start by making
it come true in my city. I wrote to you about

how everyone should have the chance to read. Now my grandmother has left me with many books that she rescued from burning during the dictatorship. Respectfully, I ask your permission to use the scholarship money to begin a free traveling library, which will bring these books as well as literacy classes to people living high in the hills on the outskirts of Valparaíso. These are the poorest people who work all day for very little money. They can't even imagine being able to visit the center of town to buy a book or to learn to read and write . . .

My pen sails until the waking moon spreads a soft light over the page.

A **Great** Thing

A week passes with no word from Presidente Espinoza. I check the mail frantically every day, hoping to get my hands on the letter with the presidential seal first so that no one asks me a million questions about it. But on Saturday morning, as I sit drinking café con leche and reviewing a literacy lesson for Delfina the next day, Delfina sits down next to me and quietly slides a letter beneath my book. "This came yesterday. Nana was curious, but the spirits told her to ask you about it alone." I look at her nervously. Everyone was so happy to not have to worry about the money to send me to college. I fear her disapproval. And I fear the president's answer. Even though my family might be disappointed, I still hope she has said yes. Nana pulls a small knife from her apron pocket and uses it to unseal the envelope. Then she hands it to me.

"No, Nana. Why don't you read it to me?"

"Delfina read it, Niña Celeste?"

"*You*, Nana. I know that you can!"

Dear Señorita Marconi,

It is an even greater honor to be writing you this second letter. My answer is yes . . .

"Whoopee!" I jump up, knocking my chair to the floor. The clatter drowns Nana's voice out, but she has not moved her eyes from the page. She keeps on reading. "'. . . traveling library . . . money for books . . . classes in the hills . . .'" Then she looks at me, her mouth a copper smile like the sun. I right the chair and clasp my hands behind my back. I feel like a little girl. Will Nana scold me for making such a decision without talking to my parents first?

"Niña Celeste, you have done a great thing."

All the commotion has stirred Abuela Frida from her parlor. She appears in the kitchen doorway in her nightgown with her cane in one hand, an unfinished blue scarf in the other. Her eyes are full moons of surprise as she looks from Delfina to me and then back to Delfina. "You are reading so well!" she exclaims. "Querida Delfina, read me some more."

Nana Delfina's dark cheeks bloom like ripe cherries. She continues, "'The generosity that has inspired you to donate your scholarship money . . .'"

Abuela Frida hobbles to my side, kisses my cheek, and whispers, "Now, why don't you go to the clinic and tell your parents?"

"Right now, Abuela? They might be busy with patients—"

"Sí. Right now," Nana interjects with her no-nonsense voice.

As I look through the coat closet for my rain jacket, Nana says in a casual voice, "Oh, Delfina will not take her lesson tomorrow. She might be getting a flu."

"You *might* be?" I walk over to feel her forehead. "That's the first I've heard of it . . ."

Delfina takes a few steps back and retreats to the stove. "No, no. Nana doesn't want you to catch it. Delfina will be fine. Now run along, Celeste. Go tell Esmeralda and Andrés."

I walk out the door and think, *Nana sure is acting odd.* I know it has to do with the letter. But then again, everything feels strange right now. The green and gray of the eucalyptus trees are brighter, and their fragrance envelops me in a cloud that carries me all the way down the hills. I stand at the entrance to the clinic without knowing how I arrived there.

The door opens, and my father and mother come out and embrace me. "Celeste, we are so proud," my father says, and clears his throat.

"So proud!" Mamá echoes him, her eyes like two great lakes.

"But how did you know . . . ?" My voice trails off as I take a deep breath of relief. They aren't angry with me!

"Oh, Celeste," my mother says, laughing, "Mamá told us last week all about the letter you were busy writing up on the roof. And when I saw your face glowing like it is now, I knew a response arrived this morning."

"Abuela Frida?! But how did she *know*? I swear I didn't say a word to anyone."

"You know your grandmother." My father smiles as if such things are commonplace, which—I am beginning to believe more and more—they are. "She's a wise old girl."

Serendipity

On Sunday, Papá asks me to go to the bakery for empanadas. Which is strange, because Mamá and he have done that together every day since I can remember! "Take your time. Buy something pretty in that shop you like, or stop for a coffee at Café Iris," he says, putting a few extra pesos in my hand. Another strange thing! Papá still hasn't lost all his fear and doesn't like me to "wander around the city alone," as he puts it. But I shrug my shoulders and go, enjoying the walk down Butterfly Hill in the late-morning sunshine.

A few hours later I emerge from the bakery, my arms wrapped around a warm paper bag. I close my eyes and inhale the yummy fragrance. The smell of Sundays in Valparaíso. I smile, remembering those dark Sundays just before I left for—

"Niña Celeste, over here!" I turn around with a start and spot Alejandro and his old brown taxi parked across the street.

"¡Hola, Don Alejandro!" I call.

"Come, Niña Celeste, let me take you home." I run across the street and hop into the backseat. "What a serendipitous occasion, to find you here today!" he says. "Serendipity." I remember that word, hearing two ladies on the street use it so long ago, when—I now realize—I was such a little girl, and writing it in my blue notebook.

"Sí, Don Alejandro. It is nice to see you! I was thinking of buying some suspiro de monja—a light, sweet pastry that looks like snow—on my way home. Could we stop at Café Iris? They have the best ones. But I came here first because Panaderia Estrella has the best empanadas in Valparaíso, of course! My parents won't buy them anywhere else."

"Well now, Señorita Celeste." Alejandro fumbles over his words. "I am quite busy today, so I can only take you directly to Butterfly Hill."

How odd! Then why was Alejandro sitting there across the street, seemingly idling about, in the first place? And why offer to drive me home if he is so short on time? I am about to protest that Café Iris is on our way up Butterfly Hill and will only take a minute, but decide against it. I can hear Abuela Frida telling me a lady always accepts favors graciously, and treats her elders with respect. I remember how Abuela Frida said Don Alejandro treated her "as good as gold, like a queen, from my first years in Valparaíso when I dressed in rags, to today when I am an eccentric old woman who won't go out without red lipstick and a ring on every finger."

I gaze out the window. Every child in Valparaíso must be flying a kite today. The scent of bougainvilleas in bloom tickles my nose. "Ahhhh chooo!"

"¡Salud! God bless you, Niña Celeste. God bless you." Once again, Alejandro sounds so solemn. I catch his brown eyes in the rearview mirror. They sparkle with tears. How strange he is acting today! Maybe the scent of bougainvilleas is making his eyes water, like it is making my nose run.

I sit up as the old car uses all its will to climb Butterfly Hill. "Oh!" I catch my breath. Our blue-and-yellow house is decorated with bunches of balloons, tied to every possible place: to the front door, the terrace, streaming through the windows, even blowing in the breeze from atop the roof! I stick my head out the window to get a better view. For once, Alejandro doesn't tell me to be careful and sit back down. He just laughs and honks the horn. I see the front door open, and long streamers of silk in blues of every shade wave in the wind. Mamá and Papá are waving. Then Abuela Frida opens her parlor window and calls to me.

"Celeste! Come!"

"Abuela, what on earth is going on?"

She shrugs her shoulders and ducks her head back into the house. "Come and see!"

La Gran
Fiesta

I run into the house, and nearly run back outside from the surprise of it all! It is like entering a beehive of the sweetest honey. So many people I know and love fill our house on Butterfly Hill! Everyone calls out, "Congratulations! Three cheers for Celeste!" They gather around me and clap. I look around to see Marisol and Gloria, Cristóbal and his mother, Soledad, and Señor Castellanos and Marta Alvarado! "I thought you might be up to something, but I never imagined . . . ," I say, losing my breath from the surprise of it all. Then a smiling Señora Atkinson emerges from the kitchen holding a tray heaped with cups of tea. Neighbors have come holding baskets of flowers, stewed tomatoes, and fried fish.

"Delfina came to each of our homes to invite us to the party. She told us of your prize, and the gift you are giving to Valparaíso," Señora Atkinson whispers to me excitedly. Nana!

"She wasn't sick with a cold today at all!" I say.

Señora Atkinson shakes her head and laughs.

"Rumor has it Delfina has been making her famous sopaipillas with chimichurri all afternoon!"

Hearing her name, Nana Delfina emerges from the kitchen with a plate of steaming pumpkin cakes and her eyes filled with pride. I am speechless and trembling with happiness. Suddenly two large hands cover my eyes, and a gruff voice says, "Guess who?" Before I can say a word, Tío Bernardo grabs me in one of his famous bear hugs and spins me around the room, which has started to buzz with music. He introduces me to his beautiful Argentine wife, Ingrid.

"We met traveling over the Andes!" Tío Bernardo laughs. "We were both trying to escape our countries and bumped into each other on the way! She was going west, and I was going east, but we stopped in the same spot off a narrow pass near the summit of Mount Aconcagua. The highest peak in the entire Western Hemisphere—the air sure was thin up there. We were both tired, trying hard to catch our breaths. She offered me some water, and I gave her some dried fruits. Then and there we decided to travel and hide together. We turned south, and the rest—as they say—is history. You must have heard I was dressed like a nun? Well, can you guess what Ingrid was dressed as?"

I put my hands over my mouth. "Don't tell me! A priest?"

Tío Bernardo twirls his wife in a circle. "If that's not destiny and opposites attracting and whatever else they say about love, then what is?"

"I'd say you are right, Tío! Congratulations! And I am so glad you are home safe!"

Abuela Frida begins to tap Mamá's tambourine. With her long white braids down her back and her beaming smile, today she looks like a young girl. Papá takes up her rhythm on the piano. Delfina and I hold hands and spin in a circle. "Ay, Celeste. Nana's never been so dizzy," Delfina says, laughing, "or so proud of her girl!" And there smiling behind Delfina is the magician from Café Iris!

"Look, Delfina!" El mago pulls a canary from his waistcoat and lets it fly around the room. "A gift for you, Celeste!" He bows to me like an old-fashioned gentleman.

Delfina grins and says to me, "Delfina remembers that trick. He used it to impress your Tía Graciela. They went to school together and were kind of boyfriend and girlfriend, but not quite. You know, just like you and Cristóbal . . ."

I toss my hair and go back to the dancing, determined to ignore her sly comment. "Just wait and see, Celeste. When has Nana been wrong?" Then she shouts across the room, "Oye! Hey! Cristóbal! Why don't you dance with Celeste?"

Epilogue:
The Ship Called
Hope

"Celeste! Come down from the roof this instant! You'll be late for school!"

"Coming, Delfina!"

I give one more glance to the morning sky. There they are! My old friends pass by our house on Butterfly Hill and nod their long beaks in my direction.

Good morning, pelicans! ¡Buenos días, Valparaíso!

I scamper down the stairs, which are creakier than ever, plant a kiss on Delfina's leathery cheek, and fly out the door.

"Celeste, you almost blew me off the hill!" Señora Atkinson is strolling beneath a violet parasol. She pats her chignon as I whoosh past her to catch the cable car to school. She speaks to me in English, and proudly I call back to her, "Sorry, Mrs. Atkinson! And good morning, Mrs. Atkinson!"

"Good morning, dear!" Ever prim and proper, she somehow manages to shout in a demure voice. "Slow down and enjoy how October has arrived all dressed up in yellow!" She is right. The mimosas spread their petals into golden crowns, and as I jump aboard the Cerro Barón cable car, I breathe in their aroma mixed with the salt of the sea.

I sit and catch my breath. "How is it March already?!" Almost an entire month has passed since my surprise party. My life has settled into a routine and would be rather normal if it weren't for my imagination and all the colors and sounds of Butterfly Hill.

Of course, I have school during the day and homework that gets more and more demanding at night. Señor Castellanos grades my literature papers especially hard because he says I am a writer in the making, and as my teacher he has a responsibility to my readers.

My time after school is filled with long chats with Cristóbal at Café Iris and walks through the market with Marisol. Occasionally the three of us still play on the swings, or in the rain, or even both.

There is still no word about Lucila and her parents. Marisol talks about her cousin less and less. I tried to write about Lucila once, but I felt too afraid of what words might appear on the page. Maybe someday. Or maybe someday she will come back and help me with the traveling library! I like to imagine her teaching with me, with all of her kindness and patience.

Once in a while I run into Gloria. We always hug each other, and then we go our separate ways.

I am making new friends too—sophomores, juniors, even some seniors!—all students from the Juana Ross High School who volunteered to help organize the traveling library. Presidente Espinoza also had my second letter published in all the newspapers, and I have begun to receive book donations from all over Chile. Last week a chemist in Santiago sent me an entire set of encyclopedias!

And now it is night. Another night in my house on Butterfly Hill. The lights from the harbor shine around the city like a halo. "Buenas noches, Nana Delfina." I close the door of the little room filled with cinnamon smoke that wafts into the hallway from below the door. I know the light below the door glows into the wee hours of the night—slowly, patiently, Delfina is reading Pablo Neruda.

Every night when I'm supposed to be asleep, I write in my notebook and practice using the typewriter that our neighbors on Butterfly Hill gave me at my surprise party. At first I was using only two fingers, one from each hand. But now I am up to three, and Papá promises that if I keep typing away, I soon will make it to five. The first letter I typed out, I sent to Kim and Tom. I still don't know where they are, so I typed it out two times—in English!—and put two envelopes in the mailbox. One addressed to Kim and Tom Ahn, North Korea. And the other addressed in care of Mr. John Carter, postman, Juliette Cove, Maine. If they ever receive my letter, this is what they will read:

Dear Kim and Tom,

It has been so long, but I haven't forgotten you.
Neither have I forgotten my promise to send you
something I have written. So I have included a
poem along with this letter. The poem is called
"The Ship Called Hope." I wrote it one night as
I sat on my roof and looked at the stars, when I
remembered asking my Abuela Frida if she was
a refugee. I was five years old and didn't know
what the word meant. And her eyes became very
big as if they were filled with seawater and she
looked at me for a long time. Then she said,
"Yes, I am a refugee. And it is a beautiful word, a
beautiful thing. I am an exile. That means I am a
traveler of the world, and I belong to nothing but
the things I love."

We haven't seen each other since that day long
ago when we lay in the grass on Juliette Cove,
but I still hope to see you soon. Until then, may
you both belong to the things you love. And I will
belong to the things I love too.

Your forever friend,
Celeste Marconi